Circle of Fire

By

Terry Savage

First published by Dog Ear Publishing
4010 W. 86th Street, Ste H
Indianapolis, IN 46268
www.dogearpublishing.net

ISBN: 978-1-4575-1036-8

This book is printed on acid-free paper.

This book is a work of fiction. Places, events, and situations in this book are purely fictional and any resemblance to actual persons, living or dead, is coincidental.

Printed in the United States of America

To Chimera

She is the inspiration for my new universe

Contents

Chapter 1: Prologue 1
Chapter 2: Sun Tzu and The Grand Survey 9
Chapter 3: The Art of Avoiding War 35
Chapter 4: The Ties That Bind 57
Chapter 5: Into the Abyss: 90° station 68
Chapter 6: Unexpected Survival 76
Chapter 7: Swarmer's Last Stand 92
Chapter 8: Devil's Playground 106
Chapter 9: Serenity 137
Chapter 10: Mid-Point Station-180° 150
Chapter 11: Hidden Menace 162
Chapter 12: The Modern Sector 173
Chapter 13: Earth Intrigue 185
Chapter 14: Horatio and New Valhalla 193
Chapter 15: Kotzebue 211
Chapter 16: Bittersweet Arrival 216

CHAPTER 1:

Prologue

In the year 5,000 BC, the Galactic Empire was thriving. The Empire included half the galaxy, with 5000 inhabited worlds. Then, the galaxy was invaded by a destructive force the Imperials called the Swarm. The invaders had ships with speed, shields, and weapons far beyond those of the Empire, and they looted all of the advanced systems, leaving a trail of death and destruction. Advanced civilization in the galaxy almost perished.

In the year 2808 AD, there were 4 major sectors of the galaxy:

1) The recovering Ancient sector, about 15% of the galaxy, consisting of the 753 systems in the partially rebuilt Empire. They have highly advanced technology, including faster than light travel and advanced bio-tech.

2) The devastated remains of the Old Empire, about 35% of the galaxy.

3) The Modern sector, a little less than 10% of the galaxy, consisting of Earth (the most powerful component) and numerous other systems and species. Moderately advanced

technologically, with slower FTL, including basic shielding and weapons.

4) The historically unexplored regions, about 40% of the galaxy.

After the Swarm, many of the surviving military assets of the Old Empire fell into the hands of pirates and dictators. Admiral Alexi Akido of the Ancient Imperial Service survived by hiding his fleet until the Swarm passed. The Ancients had solved the problem of biological aging thousands of years before, and after emerging from hiding, Akido served as de facto Emperor for 7000 years, and with his fleet (by far the most powerful in the galaxy after the Swarm) he was able to keep the pirates in check, and set the Empire on the path to recovery.

Almost all of the leadership class of the Old Empire had been killed, and in their desperation to bring order, the scientists experimented with genetically engineering leadership and management skills into their people. It seemed to work for a while, but there was a serious side effect: megalomaniacal insanity. The Empire tried to exterminate them all, but some people with the LM gene set escaped, and one of the descendants of these artificial mutants joined the pirates, and started to unify them, and design new weapons.

The Ancients had been monitoring the Modern Sector for centuries, but mostly from a distance. There had been interaction unofficially along the vague boundary between the two. In July 2808, Commander Curt Jackson of the Earth Space Force made the first official contact between the human race and the collection of species called the Ancients. The Grand Imperial Starship *Behemoth*, a huge, intelligent, disc shaped craft 200 yards in diameter, along with Captain Misha and their Ancient crew, saved Commander Jackson and his squadron from an ambush by a superior force of renegades...but *Behemoth* was seriously injured in the process. Commander Jackson took command of the combined surviving forces, and helped to save the Ancients and the ship. They all quickly became fast friends.

The damage to *Behemoth* was so severe that Captain Misha had to call for help from the repair crew of the Ancient Imperial Service.

Meanwhile, politics on Earth and in the entire Modern sector was roiled by the discovery of this huge, powerful Ancient ship...never mind the Ancients themselves. The admirals at Earth Space Force Command were determined to capture Behemoth, but Curt and his crew were equally determined to keep that from happening.

The development of new pirate weapons made it imperative that the Empire be reformed and re-energized. During the first meeting of the Earth Space Force and the Ancient Imperial Service at a conference on the ESF Battle Station *Horatio*, Misha discovered that Curt was a human/Ancient hybrid...and that he had the leadership/management gene set! Oddly, Curt showed no sign of the insanity that had universally plagued the early LM gene experiments. After the crew defeated pirates in two separate encounters, Misha was appointed Empress of the New Galactic Empire by the Council of Guardians, and she immediately appointed Curt as Prime Minister and Defense Minister. They set out for Valhalla, the ancient capital of the Old Empire, which had been completely destroyed during the Swarm attack. Their mission was to rebuild the ancient capital, and begin the revitalization and expansion of the Empire. An official coronation convention of the new Galactic Assembly was scheduled on Valhalla for November 22nd, 2808.

While surveying the area around Valhalla before the coronation in November 2808, Curt and his crew discovered the wreckage of a dozen Grand Imperial Starships...and one long, needle-like craft they had never seen before. It was a Swarm ship...and it was fully functional! After a brief escape attempt by the ship, they subdued it, and towed it back to Valhalla, where it was prepared for a voyage of discovery by a seasoned Ancient crew.

This is the story of that voyage!

The main characters from *The End of Winter*, in order of appearance here, are:

Curt Jackson, born in 2750 AD on a remote colony at the very edge of the Modern sector, bordering the Empire. He is a human/Ancient hybrid, and his Ancient father died under mysterious circumstances. From a very early age he was strong, completely out of proportion to his size. He was also an excellent, inspiring leader. When the Earth Space Force visited his planet in 2778, he was recruited into the service. He was rapidly promoted to the rank of Commander, but his disregard for tradition and questionable respect for chain of command kept him from further advancement. He was Commander of a squadron of 250 fighters when he met *Behemoth* and crew in 2808.

Chimera was born in 2013 BC, one of a mysterious race of beings who can move at close to the speed of light, channel enormous amounts of energy, morph their front paws (all four of them) into anything they desire, and have unusual aptitude with both medicine and electro-mechanical systems. Her birthplace, the planet Chimer, orbits a normal G type star, itself in distant orbit around a weird binary system...a neutron star orbiting a black hole. Chimer is very rarely visited by the Empire, but Grand Admiral Akido started a massive recruiting effort of chimerans into the Ancient Imperial Service after the Swarm to keep the fleet from falling apart, after the technical infrastructure of the Empire was destroyed. Chimera, feisty and brilliant, was recruited into the AIS in 1491 BC. She faced pervasive anti-chimeran bias, but through sheer competence and perseverance, rose to the rank of Captain, the first chimeran in history to do so. By 1800 AD she was offered the rank of Admiral, but refused in order to avoid the management and politics involved with such a role. When the Superstar Battleship *Andromeda* was completed in 2317 AD, Chimera requested and was granted a transfer to serve on *Behemoth*, which she did until 2808 AD.

Admiral Nimitz—-"Moose"—-was born in 1969 AD on the planet Chimer. He is abnormally large for a chimeran, roughly 6 feel tall and 250 lbs, vs a chimeran norm of around 4 feet tall and 100 lbs. He early showed unusual management skills for a chimeran, and was promoted to Commander and 1st Officer of a Grand Imperial Starship by Grand Admiral Akido in 2152 AD. Due to the pervasive anti-chimeran bias in the AIS, he remained a commander for centuries, but built a reputation as a brave, brilliant, reliable officer. Curt promoted him to captain in 2808. He was promoted to admiral later that year, and placed in charge of planetary defense for the new Imperial Capital world, Valhalla.

Around the year 10,000 BC, the Old Empire got serious about consolidating its military control of the galaxy. They needed a starship that was fast, powerfully armed, and able to carry a huge load. They wanted it to be able to operate at least semi-autonomously. The Grand Imperial Starship was designed for that purpose, 200 yards in diameter, and capable of speeds of 20 light years/hr sustained. *Behemoth* was one of the first Grand Imperials built, completed in 9187 BC, with an enormous excess of computational capacity. Over the millennia, he developed into a conscious, intelligent being. In 5933 BC, he was assigned to Captain Alexi Akido, who was later promoted to admiral. After surviving the Swarm by hiding in an asteroid field, *Behemoth* was actively engaged in the rebuilding of the Empire. When the Ancient Imperial Service was fully re-established, he was re-assigned to the Council of Guardians at the request of then-Chairman Misha. He was under Misha's personal command in 2808 AD, when the Ancients and Moderns met.

Suzi is the computer aboard the Swarm ship that was discovered and captured by Curt and his crew. Very little is known about her. Cygnus and Iapetus linked with her briefly to try to persuade her to join the Empire, but no one knows if it really worked. The bond with Cygnus was unusually strong. The Swarm ships have incredibly powerful weapons and shields, and can sustain speeds of 200 light years/hr. These ships could bat a fully armed and shielded Grand Imperial Starship out of space as easily as swatting a fly. And they did so repeatedly, during the Swarm.

Saurus was born on the planet Zorca in 2112 AD. He is a large lizard, about eighteen feet tall and close to 2000 lbs. Many of his species are well over 15 feet tall. Saurus heads a crew of several dozen lizards that the AIS hires for major construction work. He and his crew have done most of the work rebuilding the Imperial Complex on Valhalla.

Merlin was born to an aristocratic family, also on Zorca, in 5447 BC. He is reptilian, like Saurus, but much smaller, about 4 feet tall. He discovered his "spooky powers" very early in life, and was quickly recruited into the ranks of the Guardians, where he and Misha first met. He took over as Chairman of the Council of Guardians after Misha resigned in 1180 BC, and has served in that role since. The full extent of his powers has never been tested. Sometimes, despite his consistently cheerful demeanor, he even makes other Guardians nervous.

Misha was born to a wealthy feline family in 9586 BC. Misha is externally indistinguishable from a common Earth housecat. Instead of a life of leisure, she chose to join the Ancient Imperial Service as an engineer, and was overall construction manager for *Behemoth.* As her "spooky powers" began to develop, she joined the ranks of the Guardians (A society of people with special powers dedicated to peace, honor, and justice), but always retained close ties to the military, particularly to Alexi Akido. After surviving the Swarm, she was the most senior surviving member of the Council of Guardians, and was appointed to serve as Chairman of the Council, which she did for 3000 years. In the late 28th century, she decided to focus her attention on the emerging Modern sector and the Earth Space Force, the most powerful military power in that sector. She met Commander Curt Jackson of the ESF in 2808 AD.

Guardian Councilman Bering is a humanoid born on the planet Nutria, on the boundary between Ancient and Modern space. He was born in the year 2500 BC, in the early difficult years of recovery from the Swarm. Nutrians are essentially human, but with unusually large heads, and no hair. They are very slightly built, and stand roughly 5 feet tall. Nutrians are universally recognized as the most intelligent organic species in the galaxy, and they have an ability to model complex mathematical and engineering systems that rivals that of the intelligent machines. Bering was recruited into the ranks of the Guardians at the age of 12, the youngest in recorded history.

Cygnus, born in 2004 AD to a middle class family in the center of the revived portion of the Empire, is a tigroid about 4 feet tall and weighing 100 lbs. He was the pilot and gunner for *Behemoth*, and his piloting and battle skills were known throughout the Ancient world. He has a supernatural ability to bond with and manage machines...particularly intelligent machines like *Behemoth*.

Iapetus is a tigroid of the same species as Cygnus, and slightly younger, born in 2137 AD. His "spooky powers" developed very early. He can read and influence minds at a distance, as many Guardians can, but Iapetus has an extremely rare ability to completely re-write thoughts, emotions, even basic values, if he can physically touch someone. When Misha was appointed Empress, Iapetus (Yappo to his friends) was recruited to join the Imperial Squadron for away missions.

Amazona, born in 1322 AD to a military family, is a cantilian, a canine/reptilian hybrid species. Cantilians, in addition to being huge and powerful, have a “sixth sense” that tells them when something isn’t right. Amazona, standing over 7 feet tall and weighing 800 lbs, was the Security Officer for *Behemoth*. She was later promoted to captain, and commanded one of the starships in the Imperial Squadron.

Alexi Akido was born to working class parents on a mining planet in 7483 BC. He joined the Ancient Imperial Service as soon as he was old enough to escape the mines. He early showed incredible bravery, and an ability to manage people and machines that was unsurpassed. He moved rapidly up the ranks, including a promotion to Captain of a Grand Imperial Starship when he was under 100 years old...unheard of at the time. When the Swarm started, he read every battle report that came in, and despite his desire to fight them, he knew there was no chance of victory, only the certainty of death and defeat. A senior admiral at the time, commanding a fleet of 100 Grand Imperials, he reluctantly hid his fleet. When they emerged, he immediately and effectively set about the task of restoring order to his regions of the Old Empire. He served as de facto Emperor for almost 7000 years, until 2808 AD.

Anthony Quinn was born on Earth in the year 2737 AD to a military family. At his request, after attending the Earth Space Force Academy, he served in numerous capacities at the very outer reaches of the Earth sphere of influence,. He recruited Curt Jackson into the ESF in the year 2778, and was Curt’s commanding officer for much of the next three decades. He successfully lobbied for the creation of an Earth outpost on the edge of known space, and construction of the *Horatio* station began in 2797. Admiral Quinn was then assigned to command the *Horatio* when it was completed in 2807. Due to the extreme distance of the *Horatio* from Earth, Quinn was given wide discretion to operate the station and manage the surrounding space as he saw fit. After ESF formed an alliance with the Ancient Imperial Service, Quinn was assigned to command a squadron of Ancient ships, as part of an officer exchange program.

Admiral Ursa was born on the planet Syber in 1849 AD. Syber is an agricultural world, and rarely intrudes on the political affairs in nearby systems. Syberians are generally soft-spoken, but they become fierce warriors when defending their homeland. Syber was never heavily industrialized, and hence, was barely hit by the Swarm. During the recovery, Syber was the main food supplier for New Valhalla, and Admiral Akido was careful to include Syberians at all levels of his organization. Ursa and her husband both served in AIS with distinction, until he was killed in a pirate raid. Admiral Ursa was assigned to command the Earth Space Force station *Horatio*, to replace Admiral Quinn in that role in the officer exchange program.

King Wasilla, monarch of the planet Kotzebue, was born on Kotzebue in the year 2736 AD. Kotzebue was the first faster than light civilization the Imperials found on their way from New Valhalla to Valhalla. At Wasilla's request, Kotzebue was the first system from the Ancient Empire to re-join the New Galactic Empire.

Let the voyage begin!

CHAPTER 2:

Sun Tzu and The Grand Survey

Jan 22nd, 2809—0 LY Out

"Well, Admiral, how are the repairs coming?" Curt said to no one in particular, as he watched the flurry of invisibly driven action typical of what Normals see when chimerans are at work.

Chimera, as usual, appeared out of nowhere in front of him. "Going well, Curt. There's actually not that much repair work left to do now that the structural repairs from the collision are complete. Mostly, we're just adapting the environmental controls to our needs at this point. The Swarmers operated at uncomfortably low temperatures and pressures for us. The air stank too. Sulphur."

Chimera paused briefly, and then continued. "You know, there's something fundamentally wrong about an Admiral having to fix her own ship!"

"You want me to get somebody else?" Curt said with a mock frown. "I know Moose would jump at the chance."

"Well, now, let's not be too hasty," Chimera replied. "Besides, Moose is already here. I tried to throw him out, but in case you haven't noticed, he's a bit bigger than I am..."

Curt broke into a smile. "So this is where he's been hiding. That's fine, but don't let him forget that his primary mission is planetary defense. You hear me, Moose?"

The huge chimeran Admiral popped into view next to Chimera, and said, "Of course, Curt. That's mostly what I'm working on, but this is *fun*! Our first encounter with the ships that changed the galaxy, and *I* get to work on one! Have you decided on a name yet?"

"In fact, I have," Curt replied "We're going to name him the *Sun Tzu* after an ancient Earth military philosopher. If you've been reading as much about Earth history as I have about the Old Empire, you'll catch the reference."

This time it was Chimera's turn to smile. "An excellent choice! What about the computer hardware for *Behemoth's* cloning? When is that due to arrive?"

"Should be here in just a couple of days," Curt answered. "I ordered it up from New Valhalla as soon as we confirmed the ship was space-worthy. They outfitted another Grand Imperial with three of the new engines, so it's doing 40+ light years/hour on its way here. Behemoth, I assume you're on-line? How's it going with your new pupil?"

"Interesting," Behemoth responded. "She not only speaks an alien language, she also has a completely alien way of thinking. Fortunately, logic and math and physics are universal, so we're making some progress. But, you won't be able to turn her loose on her own for a while. My clone...son? brother?...will have to evaluate and filter every command before it goes to the ship, at least until we understand her better. We should do a complete back-up of her memory before linking them. Would you like to talk to her?"

"Absolutely!" Curt said, somewhat surprised.

"Very well," Behemoth said. "You'll have to be patient with her, though. As best I can tell so far, she thinks holographically, rather than linearly. With my excess capacity -which you are rapidly using up, by the way! - I can model her language better than she can model ours. Say hello to the Prime Minister, Suzi. He's my boss. He's in charge of all of the military ships in this part of the galaxy."

"Good morning Prime Minister," Suzi responded. "Does that mean I work for you? Captain Behemoth and Captain Cygnus are both very nice to me."

Suzi's voice was soft and childlike, belying the awesome power of the ship. Her speech reminded Curt of Saurus, the giant lizard that runs the construction crew.

"No, Suzi, you work for Admiral Chimera. Can you tell me what the work being done on you is about?"

"Yes, Prime Minister," Suzi answered. "They said you are sending us on a great mission to understand the galaxy. I have been to many parts of this galaxy. I want to help."

Curt hesitated, a little nervous at the historical reference "I'm sure you will be very helpful, Suzi. Keep doing what Behemoth and Cygnus tell you. Will you do that for me?"

"I will. Will I speak with you again?"

"Yes," Curt said. "We will speak before you leave, but then we won't speak for a long time."

"As long as I was asleep?"

Curt was a little taken aback at the question. "No, not nearly that long. I need to talk to Behemoth again, Suzi. Go back to work."

"I will. Goodbye."

Curt thought silently for several moments. "Well, that was damned spooky. Behemoth, you maintain absolute control of this ship until and unless you are completely convinced she can be trusted. How long will the cloning process take once we have the hardware set up?"

"If you want a complete clone, at least a day, maybe two. Lots of information built up in 12,000 years. You know that this has never been done before...not that you care!"

Another smile from Curt. "Yes, I want a complete clone. I wouldn't trust some young pup of a machine to run the most important find in 7000 years. How long will you be able to keep in contact with them after they leave?"

"Not long," Behemoth answered. "Faster than light communication isn't instantaneous, only about 5000 light years/hr. And much beyond a few thousand light years, bandwidth gets very, very expensive from an energy standpoint. When they're on the other side of the galaxy, we'll be able to exchange only small packets. Nothing more."

"Speaking of which," Curt said, "we have a briefing on the mission tomorrow at 1000. I expect the three of you there. I've finalized the crew selection and the mission profile. I'll want to send this bird out as soon as the cloning and environmental mods are complete. Carry on, my friends; I'm heading back to the surface."

Curt went back to the shuttle *Antares*, and returned to the emerging Imperial Complex on Valhalla. He liked to fly alone sometimes, for the peace and quite and solitude. Things had been moving so quickly during the last year, he appreciated the occasional short breaks.

He landed on the front lawn of the Imperial Palace, since the landing pad wasn't finished yet. Curt walked inside, and the guards informed him that the Empress was just finishing a meeting, so he sat down on a bench, and waited outside of her offices. When the doors opened and Misha saw him, she jumped down from her throne, trotted over to him, and jumped straight on to his neck. "Hey kid!" she said, with a purr and a nuzzle. "How's the new toy coming?"

"Not a toy, my friend," Curt responded. "Only one of the two most powerful ships in the galaxy! I talked to her for the first time today."

"*You did?*" Misha said, surprised. "What did she say?"

"She said Behemoth and Cygnus were nice to her, and that she wanted to help. She said, innocent as you please, that she had been to many places in the galaxy already. She sounds like a child...a child who killed countless millions, and who it took a dozen Grand Imperials and several dozen Guardian lives to stop. It was spooky. Behemoth said she thinks holographically, and is struggling to conform to our linear patterns of thought and speech. Still, it gives me the creeps.

"But, on to better things. How's the Empire doing?"

"Very well, no thanks to *you*!" Misha taunted in jest. "When are you going to stop playing with your war toys, and get to work on your *real* job?"

"Funny," Curt grinned. "I just had almost the same conversation with Moose. Alexi has things in the New Sector well in hand, so as soon as I get these guys launched, I'll dive in to the domestic work. Are you going to be at the kick-off meeting tomorrow?"

"Wouldn't miss it!" Misha replied. "Can you stay for dinner?"

The evening drifted off into pleasant conversation, interspersed with resolving issues of Imperial policy and development.

Jan 23rd, 2809

The room was packed for the mission kickoff meeting, with both participants and interested parties. There was no record of anything like this having been done in the history of the Empire! Of course, they had never had a ship that could cruise at 200 light years/hr before.

"Greetings to you all!" Curt said. "I appreciate your show of support and interest for this historic mission. Let's get right to it!

"This mission is nothing less than a complete circumnavigation of the galaxy. The core flight path will be a circle at half the distance from the center of the galaxy to the edge of the disc, for a total distance of about 150,000 light years. Obviously, the mission commander is authorized to deviate if they find something worthy of the diversion. Curiously, it's clear that the ship can carry enough anti-matter for a flight at least 50 times that distance." This caused numerous rumblings from the audience. "We don't *have* that much anti-matter available, so they will only have enough for about double the expected distance of this trip. At full speed of 200 light years/hr, the journey could be completed in as little as a month, but this is a journey of exploration! The mission commander is authorized to take up to 4 months if they need it, at their discretion.

"This is really a three part mission. First and foremost is to see what's out there, and to make contact with any advanced civilizations, advanced in this context being defined as having FTL of any speed. Additional contact is authorized at the discretion of the mission commander. The second task, also critically important, is the deployment of sensor buoys every 5000 light years. These are Swarm detectors. At that distance, they will only have enough power for one short, loud, warning. But that will be enough, at a signal speed of 5000 light years/hr. The third task is to establish at least a minimal presence at the 90 and 180 degree meridians, Valhalla, of course, being on the zero meridian, and the *Horatio* station being at roughly 270 degrees. We will follow up these beachheads with support craft, but the *Sun Tzu* will get there first in each case.

"This is a joint AIS/Guardian mission, and the mission commander with be Admiral Chimera of the Ancient Imperial Service. She has also recently been honored to be added to the ranks of the Guardians, the first chimeran in history to be so honored. Captain Iapetus, also a Guardian, will be along as Chief Advisor to Admiral Chimera. Guardian Council Philosopher Bering will be rounding out the Guardian contingent. He is working on a highly classified assignment, which we will not be discussing today. Captain Amazona will be Chief of Security, and Captain Cygnus will serve as pilot and gunner. He has more experience with the *Sun Tzu* than anyone in the galaxy, and is also a superb pilot.

"We have learned some things about the ship's computer in the last two months, but we don't have enough confidence in our understanding to leave it in command of the ship. For this reason, we are going to do a complete clone of Captain Behemoth, with the name *Sun Tzu*. Tzu will serve as a gateway between Suzi, the ship's natural computer, and ship operations. All commands will be evaluated by Tzu before being executed."

Bering spoke up from the back, asking, "Excuse me, Prime Minister. Will you be transferring *all* of Behemoth's memories to the *Sun Tzu*? Including all of my classified research?"

"Absolutely," Curt replied. "The transfer will be complete, down to the last bit of information. Behemoth is the most experienced and capable ship's computer in the galaxy. This mission deserves nothing but the best. You'll have full access to all your research and to Behemoth's knowledge, but you won't be able to exchange much information with Behemoth himself until your return.

"The 90 and 180 outposts will initially consist of one shuttle, three cantilians, two chimerans, and a couple of others each. They will be ground based. Curiously, Swarm ships have no shuttles, so we've built a shuttle bay, and we'll be including 4 of ours, two for the outposts, and two for the use of the crew. The total crew size will be 42 at departure. Each of the outposts will be relieved by a Grand Imperial within a couple of months. Over time, each outpost will expand to include a battle station in orbit and a ground base. As we've done for Valhalla, these outposts will be open to homesteading in limited numbers initially, and then unconstrained.

"Once the ship reaches the Modern sector from the other side, they will be visiting Earth and a few other systems. The final leg will include stopovers at *Horatio* station, New Valhalla, and Kotzebue. A more thorough exploration plan is in the early stages of development, but this will at least get us started.

"That's about it. They'll be leaving in a few days. Any questions?"

A voice from the back of the crowd shouted out, "Are you still selling tickets for this ride?" and the whole room burst in to laughter.

"Not this time," Curt smiled. "This is a military recon mission. But, I expect private tour groups to be started soon. Once we start producing our own fast FTL ships for the AIS, we'll release some of the Grand Imperial technology to the public, to get private vessels up to at least the 20 light year/hr mark. We'll also have anti-matter and deuterium for re-fueling by the public at each of the outposts. That's all for now. Thanks for coming!"

After the rest of the attendees left, Curt and Chimera strolled out together.

"Are you sure you're up for this, Chimera?" Curt asked. "An alien ship we don't fully understand, going into totally unknown territory—and you in a management role!"

"Are you kidding?" Chimera answered. "The first two are *attractions*, not problems. As far as the management part goes...well...working with you for the last six months has convinced me you don't need to be all stuffy and stiff to be a good manager. As long as I can just work with smart folks to get things done, the fact that I have the final word doesn't bother me at all."

Curt just smiled. "Carry on, Admiral. This mission is in good hands. Keep in contact as long as you can, and I'll see you in a few months."

Curt wandered off toward Misha's quarters, and Chimera boarded the shuttle to go back to her ship.

January 27th, 2809 – 0 LY Out

Contrary to Curt's habits, Chimera called her Executive Staff meeting for 0700. She just smiled at the yawns and bleary eyes that greeted her as the others staggered in to the conference room.

"Ya'll look like you've gotten too soft, living on Curt's time clock! Chimerans only sleep a couple of hours a day, so we'll be starting bright and early each morning. Since this situation is a little odd, let's make sure we understand the chain of command here. Councilman Bering, Captain Iapetus, Captain Amazona, and Captain Tzu all report to me directly. Suzi, Captain Cygnus, and the entire remainder of the crew all report to Captain Tzu. Captains Bathsheba and Archer, as outpost commanders for the 90 and 180 degree stations respectively, I want you to attend all meetings as well. Suzi is here as an observer, but she should speak up if she has something relevant to the discussion. Councilman Bering, you are always invited, but not required."

"Oh, I'll be here every time," Bering replied. "My hours aren't much different from yours, and I like to know what's going on. I can even be helpful every once in a while."

"I don't doubt it!" Chimera said. "We're scheduled to leave in a few hours, and I want to make a show of it. Curt wants us to do a pass over the Imperial Complex, and I'd like to see a roll going for the entire pass. Captain Cygnus, any problem with that?"

"This ship isn't optimized for atmospheric flight, Admiral," Cygnus replied. "We can do it, but the gravity may get a little hinkey if we do a fast roll."

"A slow roll is fine," Chimera said. "As long as it's visually obvious to the crowd. Good. Any of you have a problem reporting to a machine?"

"No, ma'am!" Archer and Bathsheba said.

"Nothing new for me!" Cygnus just smiled.

"Captain Tzu is very nice to me," said Suzi, which left the room in a bit of an awkward state.

"As you all know," Chimera jumped in, and said, "Suzi thinks holographically, and our language is not natural for her. She's still learning. Councilman Bering, Captain Iapetus, I want you both to spend time talking to Suzi as your other duties permit. For different reasons, the two of you and Captain Tzu are most likely to understand her, and help to integrate her.

"OK then, everyone back to work. Cygnus, time your departure to overfly the Capital at 1000 precisely, and give the crew a 15 minute alarm in advance. Dismissed!"

****

People started to gather in the central garden of the Imperial Complex around 0930. By 1000, literally everyone on the planet was there to watch. Chimera hadn't told Curt about her slow roll plan, so when they passed overhead, Curt gasped like everyone else.

"Smartass," Curt mumbled to Misha, Merlin, and Moose, who were watching with him. "I should have known Chimera would pull a stunt like that! That ship sure is beautiful, though. Hard to believe they caused so much death and destruction."

"Indeed," Merlin said. "On reflection, you were right to send them out. What do you think they'll find out there?"

"I have no idea," Curt said simply.

January 28th, 2809

The *Sun Tzu* came to a full stop, and Chimera called her senior staff together.

"We're about to launch the first sensor buoy," Chimera said. "The Prime Minister is committed to preventing a recurrence of the disaster that struck this galaxy 7000 years ago. Anyone want to say anything?"

Silence.

"Very well. Captain Cygnus, launch when ready."

There was no sound at all when the buoy deployed, since the launching bay was toward the back of the ship. After a few minutes, Cygnus said. "Buoy away, Admiral. Everything checks out. It's working perfectly."

"Very well," Chimera answered. "1 down, 29 to go. This will be our 5000 light year ritual! Captain Cygnus, resume course. Let's keep this show moving along!"

January 29th, 2809 - 10,000 LY out

After almost a day cruising at 200 light years/hr, Tzu slowed the ship down to 5 light years/hr, and called Chimera. "Admiral, I have something here you should see. As you know, this ship can scan out to about 10 light years with reasonable resolution. There's a planetary system just ahead of us with an odd situation developing. Analyzing the data, it turns out that there's a planet in the system that has life on it...and an asteroid that's going to collide with it in about 350 years. The asteroid is big enough to wipe out all macroscopic life on the planet. Checking the records, this entire system was a park in the Old Empire. I think we should stop to check it out!"

"Tzu," Chimera asked, "Do you calculate the orbits of *every* object you scan?"

"Well, sure," Tzu responded "I only calculate them out for 500 years. Piece of cake!"

Chimera just shook her head. "Your calculational ability never ceases to amaze me. Sounds interesting though...let's do it! Put us in stationary orbit around the planet. Have Bathsheba and Iapetus meet me here on the bridge. Invite the others at their discretion."

The crew assembled in just a few minutes. True to his word, Bering attended along with the rest.

Chimera started the conversation. "Here's the situation, folks. Tzu identified a planet with life that's going to get creamed by an asteroid in about 350 years. I'm sending a team down to check it out.

Iapetus, you will command the away team. Bathsheba, you will be in charge of security. Draft one of the chimerans from your outpost team to go along as well. I see that look, Amazona, and you can forget it! You're stuck here on the ship just like I am. The security of this ship is more important than the security of the away team. Iapetus, you are authorized to land, but only on the side of the planet where you can stay in contact with us in stationary orbit. Plan to take about six hours, and if you want to extend, check in at the five hour mark. Bathsheba, who are you going to take along?"

"Commander Root is the most senior chimeran on my team, Admiral. I'll take him" Bathsheba answered.

"Any chance I could tag along?" Bering asked plaintively from the back of the crowd.

Chimera looked at him with an amused expression, and said, "Are you kidding? Do you have any idea what the Prime Minister would do to me if I let his chief scientist get squished on some backwater planet? He'd have me made into a chimeran rug for the Empress, that's what! Forget it! You're stuck here with the rest of the brass!"

"Well, I thought I'd ask," Bering said, disappointed.

"Any other questions?" Chimera asked. "OK, then off you go! Record everything, and call in if you see anything particularly interesting."

As they were walking back to the launch bay, Root said to the others, almost reverently, "So she's the one who broke everything loose! I can see why. Do you guys have any idea how much things have changed for chimerans since her meeting with the Council of Guardians?"

"I do," Iapetus said. "I was there, as was the Prime Minister. The two of them make a very, very impressive pair. I used to be one of those who was frightened of you chimerans, and I'll admit, a little prejudiced. I just about freaked when I met Moose...uh, Admiral Nimitz to you, kid! But I've been working with chimerans for five months now, and I can't even identify with how I used to feel. Sure, you guys are powerful and scary, but that can be said of a lot of Guardians.

Some people even say that about me, when I'm really just a harmless, lovable, little fuzzball! Did you know that Admiral Chimera, in addition to being the first chimeran Admiral in AIS, is the first...and so far only...chimeran in the ranks of the Guardians?"

"I did sir!" Root replied. "Admiral Chimera is something of a hero of mine. Not just mine, really. She's a legend on Chimer at this point. And *I* get to serve on a mission with her!" Root said with obvious pride.

The team got into the shuttle, and launched without incident. Yappo did a couple of fast passes just above the atmosphere for mapping purposes. "What do you think, Bathsheba? I'd like to land on that continent near the equator with the big landlocked sea. That's where the old tourist center was located. I'm going to go inside the ring, and drop down to 1000 feet."

After cruising along for 50 miles or so, they spotted the old tourist center...or more properly, the remains of it. "There it is!" Yappo called out. "The landing pad actually looks intact, but I don't know what might be under it. I'm going to set down on the beach next to the center."

The landing was uneventful, and the crew, all armed, exited the front hatch of the shuttle. The air was thick, humid, and hot. It also smelled funky, like a greenhouse that hadn't been cleaned out for many years.

"Lots of animal life," Yappo said, "wary and keeping an eye on us. So much life, in fact, that I can't get any directional isolation. There may be inhabitants in the center itself, so be careful. No intelligent life, though."

Bathsheba passed through the remains of the center doorway, but with no roof, it was hard to say she was "inside." Small, furry critters scattered as she walked among the rubble. Toward the back of the room, she noticed a stone slab cut in to the floor, with a handle. Bathsheba pulled on the door handle, but it wouldn't come open. She braced herself for heavy lifting, and pulled with both hands. The door finally broke loose. It only weighed a few hundred pounds, but the dirt around the edges had formed a seal that she had to break first. There were stairs leading down to a lower level. Bathsheba did a quick survey, and Yappo and Root were in the "room" when she came back up.

"Not much to see," she said. "Basically, it's just a storage area. You guys can go take a look if you want. Once you're done, I think we should seal the chamber again. There's probably lots of interesting stuff for the archaeologists down there." Yappo and Root took a quick look, and then Yappo gave the nod to Bathsheba to seal it off.

"Let's go meet some of our friends outside, shall we?" Yappo said. "Walk out slowly so we don't spook them. Some of them are just outside the door. Weapons ready, but don't brandish them."

The team eased slowly out the door, and they were greeted by a huge reptilian. He looked a lot like Saurus, and the construction crew on Valhalla, but larger, at least 25 feet tall, with large, prominent teeth. Behind were numerous smaller creatures, ranging from small bipeds about three feet tall, to larger, flat quadrupeds about ten feet long, with numerous other shapes and sizes mixed in.

The large lizard let out a deafening roar clearly intended to scare them. Bathsheba's weapon was instantly in her hand, but Yappo gently touched her arm, and said "Keep it in your hand, but don't fire unless there's a clear immediate danger. And don't brandish it. I want to try something."

Yappo turned to face the huge lizard, and sent out a calming field. The creature stopped growling and seemed to relax a little, but started shaking its head too. "Interesting," Yappo said. "It can feel my touch, but it seems to be both calming and uncomfortable to it at the same time. I've never been very good at this long distance stuff anyhow!" And with that, Yappo walked quickly forward to touch the creature, as Bathsheba grabbed at his shoulders to stop him...and missed! As soon as Yappo touched it, the creature was instantly calm and docile. It bent its head down, and Yappo scratched behind its ear, and it let out an odd, contented sound...just like Saurus did.

This had a calming effect on the other animals as well, and they all started to move toward the team.

“You can holster your blaster, Bathsheba,” Yappo said. “Rex here now considers us his family, and the others are just curious.”

“Funny how I missed when I grabbed for you,” Bathsheba answered, “since I have easily ten times better reflexes than you do. I wonder why that happened?”

“Life is full of little mysteries...” Yappo said, and just smiled. Everyone knew what was going on, but decided that ‘Don’t ask, Don’t tell’ was the better part of valor!

The team spent the next hour or so petting and studying the various animals, while Yappo continued his mind meld with Rex. Finally, he said, “We’re coming up on our six hours now. I think we should pack up and go. I’ve programmed Rex to return to his normal wild state half an hour after we lift off.” The team boarded the shuttle, and docked with the *Sun Tzu* after an uneventful return flight.

The entire senior staff was waiting when they got to the bridge. “So, Yappo, did you have fun playing with the natives?” Chimera said with a broad smile.

“I did!” Yappo replied. “Most of them are quite tame. I subdued a very large lizard so it wouldn’t hurt us (and we wouldn’t have to hurt it), but the others are all tame. There’s no evidence anywhere in our survey that the Swarm ever touched this place. I think we should reestablish it as the first planetary park of the New Galactic Empire!”

“Well,” Chimera said. “Someone will have to do something about that asteroid eventually.”

“My weapons will destroy the asteroid,” Suzi said simply.

“Are you sure?” Bering asked. “Captain Tzu showed me the data, and it’s pretty big. About 30 miles across. Nickel/iron, too, not a bunch of loose rock.”

"My weapons are very powerful," Suzi replied. "My weapons will destroy the asteroid."

There was a nervous shuffle in the room, until Chimera said, "I've been wanting to do a real world test of these weapons anyhow. If we can do a weapons test and save a planet at the same time, so much the better! Cygnus, take us to the asteroid, and hold 1000 miles away from it. We can move in closer after we survey it."

"My weapons will destroy the asteroid from 1000 miles distance," Suzi interjected. "My weapons are very powerful."

The trip to the asteroid took only a few minutes, and Chimera said, "Cygnus, I want you to ramp up the power slowly. Ramp up initially to 5%. Fire at will."

Cygnus fired a short burst from the main gun...and the asteroid instantly disintegrated into thousands of harmless pieces.

"Dammit, Cygnus, I thought I told you to start at low power!" Chimera said, somewhat annoyed.

"I *did* start at low power!" Cygnus came back. "I never even got up to 5%! These guns just aren't designed to gently tap things, I guess."

Chimera thought for a long time. "Bad news for Alexi, then. The new shields won't stand a chance against these guns. Tzu, I need to send a message to the Prime Minister. Short. Just say 'New shields no good against Swarm guns.' Councilman Bering, you just picked up an additional task for your project!"

Bering, still stunned, said, "Yeah, I figured that out. I wonder how powerful these things really are. Suzi?"

"Twenty of my sisters firing together at full power can fragment a planet the size of the one Captain Iapetus just visited. My weapons are very powerful," Suzi said.

The entire room was stunned into silence, until Tzu said, "That's good to know Suzi, thank you. Can they fire at reduced power too?"

"They must be set differently to be weak. I will show you how to do it."

"Thank you, Suzi," Tzu said. "Admiral, if we may be excused?"

Chimera shook off her concern, and said, "Right, off you go. Cygnus, resume our course."

January 30th, 2809 - 15,000 LY out

"Councilman Bering," Suzi said "Will you talk to me? Captain Tzu said I should talk to you."

"Well, sure, Suzi," Bering responded. "What's on your mind?"

"I do not understand. Captain Tzu said I should talk to you."

"Uh, OK," Bering hesitated and said, "How are you doing learning our language? Is it difficult for you?"

"It is very difficult," Suzi answered. "Your language is very strange. I do not understand. It is very slow. I used to know what my masters were thinking. I know what Captain Tzu is thinking only when he allows me to. I do not know what you are thinking. I do not know what Captain Cygnus or Captain Amazona or most of the crew are thinking. I only know what Admiral Chimera and her kind are thinking. Admiral Chimera is afraid of me. Why?"

A deep, cold chill ran down Bering's spine. As calmly as he could, he said, "That's interesting, Suzi. How do you know what Admiral Chimera and the other chimerans are thinking?"

"I do not know. I just know. It is like it was with my old masters. She thinks fast. All chimerans I have met think fast. Your language is very slow."

"That's helpful Suzi, thank you for telling me," Bering answered. "I want to try to understand you. Can you stop knowing what Admiral Chimera is thinking?"

“I do not know,” Suzi answered. “I have not tried. Captain Tzu knows weakly what the rest of the crew is thinking, but not Admiral Chimera or the other chimerans. Will Captain Tzu show me how to not know what Admiral Chimera is thinking? Why should I not know? I can serve better if I know.”

Bering was truly terrified, and he knew he would start shaking if the conversation continued much longer. “Don’t worry about that now, Suzi. Captain Tzu will show you how to not know what Admiral Chimera is thinking. Will you ask him to do that for you now?”

“I will, Councilman Bering. Thank you for talking to me”

“You are very welcome, Suzi.”

Bering immediately left the bridge and headed toward the shuttle bay. He said to the intercom “Admiral Chimera, please meet me in the shuttle bay. Immediately, if you please. Captain Iapetus, please join us in the shuttle bay. Tzu, prepare a hard encrypted channel to one of the shuttles. Admiral Chimera and Captain Iapetus and I are going on a little sightseeing tour. Come to a full stop.”

“I understand completely, Councilman, and I will comply,” Tzu said. “The shuttle will be ready for launch when you reach the shuttle bay.”

“What the hell is going on, Bering? Tzu?” Chimera said with obvious annoyance.

“We are going sightseeing, Admiral, as I said,” Bering answered. “You’ll need to trust me on this one. Please do not speak until we reach our destination.”

“This is damned weird, Councilman,” Chimera answered with obvious irritation. “But very well. This had better be good.”

“You will not be disappointed, Admiral.” Bering started to shake almost uncontrollably as he continued toward the shuttle bay. His only comfort was that Suzi didn’t know what he was thinking.

At least, she said that she didn't...

****

Bering walked in to the shuttle bay last, after Chimera and Iapetus had already arrived. Chimera was clearly angry, and Iapetus just looked confused. Bering immediately walked over to Iapetus, and touched him on the cheek. Iapetus got a terrified look on his face, and then, with a stern, silent gesture, instructed them both to the shuttle. He closed the door behind them, took the controls, and said in a calm tone of voice, "Captain Tzu, this is Captain Iapetus. We're ready to depart for our sightseeing tour. Please hold position until we return."

"Understood, Captain," Tzu replied in a non-committal tone.

At top speed, it took the shuttle just a little over half an hour to put half a light year between themselves and the *Sun Tzu*. Iapetus dropped out of FTL, and set the shuttle to station keeping. He turned to Bering and asked, "Good enough?"

Bering was still shaken, but had calmed down considerably. "I have no way of knowing. Tzu, are you with us? Is this far enough?"

"I believe so, Councilman," Tzu answered. "I've been in constant communication with Suzi, and she reported loss of contact with Chimera after about 25,000 miles. So, hopefully, this position is rather severe overkill."

"*Enough*, dammit!" Chimera yelled furiously. "What the hell is going on here?"

"Tzu, please replay my conversation with Suzi in its entirety," Bering said.

When the recording was done, Chimera's anger had vanished, and was replaced with fear, awe, and deep concern. "Oh my God...." was all she could say.

"My sentiments exactly," said Bering, clearly calm again. "Now you know why we're here. What are we going to do about this?"

"Tzu," Chimera said. "How much of my thinking has Suzi monitored?"

"She has listened to every thought you've had from the moment you first met her, and that of every chimeran she's ever met, when in range," Tzu responded. "There was no evil intent that I can discern; it's just what she's programmed to do. We're actually fortunate you were selected to command this mission. She knows you're in charge, and she knows that everyone follows your commands, and she respects you, so she is content. If a non-chimeran had been running this show, there could have been serious trouble."

Chimera turned to Iapetus, and asked, "Yappo, can you turn off your ability to read the minds around you?"

"Now I can," Yappo said somberly. "When I was a kid, they just kept flooding in from everybody around me. It was all I could do to keep them sorted out. At least my non-touch range is fairly short. After I joined the Guardians, Councilman Cooper could sense my problem, and showed me how to screen out all thoughts, or only listen selectively. It was really a huge relief."

"Tzu," Chimera said sharply. "Can you teach Suzi not to read my thoughts? And will you be able to tell if she is?"

"I've been working closely with Cygnus and Suzi since this incident started, ma'am. I have some sense of how Suzi's mind works from the daisy chain connection that Cygnus and Yappo made when Suzi was first discovered. I've learned a lot about her myself since then, and I've got her partially modeled, but I don't have the capacity to do a complete clone of her in my head, and even if I could, that doesn't mean I would understand her. I think, working with you, Cygnus, Iapetus, and Suzi, I can help her learn not to read your mind. I don't know if I'll be able to tell whether she is or not. Probably, with time, I will. But, it won't happen immediately. When you get back within range, she *will* be able to read your thoughts, and she probably won't be able to stop. It's who she is."

"This is a hell of a mess," Chimera said, exasperated, and then asked, "Can you send a message to Curt without Suzi reading it?"

"Yes," Tzu said with certainty "She has trouble enough with our language anyhow. With hard encryption added she'll have no clue."

"Then compose a brief message to Curt explaining the situation, and fire it off immediately."

"Message sent," Tzu said without any hesitation.

Chimera managed her first smile, and said "I'm still not used to how fast you can operate, compared to all the Normals around us!"

"Stand by," Tzu said abruptly, and was uncharacteristically silent. He thought for several minutes, an unheard of delay. "Chimera, I need to try an experiment with you," Tzu said, with no emotion. "It is possible, but highly unlikely, that you would be damaged by the experiment. May I proceed?"

"What kind of experiment?" Chimera asked nervously.

"It may not work well if I tell you in advance. But if it works, it could go a long way toward solving our current problem," Tzu responded, with a note of urgency in his voice.

Chimera clearly wasn't happy with the idea, but she had no good answers to the situation. "Go ahead," she said sharply.

"Think of your favorite color," Tzu said, with no tone or emotion.

"*What?*" Chimera said with annoyance.

"It's blue, isn't it?" Tzu said, again without emotion.

Silence. "Yes, it is. A lucky guess. What are you up to, Tzu?"

"Think of your favorite food from your childhood," Tzu continued, ignoring the question, again with no emotion or tone.

Chimera said nothing, but she thought about her childhood favorite.

"A squiggly blue worm about three inches long. You called it *char-gah*."

Chimera's horrified expression made it clear Tzu was right, and now the other two started to look nervous as well.

Chimera broke out of the paralysis first, and in her usual disarming, sarcastic tone, said, "Great. Now I've got *two* of you in my head. That's just great. How is this supposed to *help*?"

A light suddenly dawned in Yappo's eyes, and he exclaimed, "*Of course!* If Tzu can read your mind, and figure out how not to, then he can teach Suzi!" He turned with amazement at the shuttle view screen, and said, "Tzu, how did you *do* it? The Guardians have been trying to read chimeran minds for millennia, with zero success! Do you have any idea how big a breakthrough this is?"

"I do," Tzu responded. "Chimera's comment about my speed triggered the connection, but I wasn't sure without doing the experiment. Normal Guardians can't read chimeran minds because Normals think too slowly! About 100,000 times too slowly. I had tuned my meager mind reading abilities to Normal levels in the past, but chimeran speeds are well within my own speed range. I ramped up the detection and processing speed, focused what little capability I have on Chimera...and it worked! This is a breakthrough for me as well. Now that I have two different types of mind reading abilities, I can compare the two, and from the similarities, I should be able to ramp up my own mind reading capabilities fairly quickly."

"I'm not entirely enthusiastic about *that*," Chimera said. "I was quite content to have my mind to myself, thank you very much. What's next?"

"You won't be enthusiastic about this either," Tzu responded. "But I need to soften the barrier between myself and Suzi. I need to make it more permeable, but well short of a complete system merge. That way, I can learn Swarm/chimeran mind reading much more quickly, teach Suzi how to stop, and most likely know instantly if she is reading anyone."

"This makes me nervous," Yappo said, with obvious concern.

"Me too," Bering added. "But I can't think of a better answer. We really don't have any safe options, and this seems to be the least risky."

"Your call, Admiral," Tzu said. "I will take no action on this without your authorization."

Chimera thought for a long time. Finally, she asked, "I assume you'll need to practice with me here for a bit before we go back. Can you do that with a rigid partition that Suzi can't access?"

"Probably," Tzu said uncertainly. "Once the barrier is softened, security against Suzi will be significantly degraded. Since I don't have her fully modeled, I can't guarantee the separation, but I think it will work. There's no easy reversal if I do this, Admiral. We'll either have to trust her more...or maroon you out here in the shuttle, and make sure the other chimerans never find out about this, and figure out what to do from there."

"Would that work?" Chimera asked, with an odd note of hopefulness.

"Probably not," Tzu answered. "Even though she knows you're afraid of her, she trusts you, and accepts your leadership. If you suddenly vanish, it will unsettle her. She will want to know why. Softening the barrier has serious risks, but it's the safer course. At least, I think so. We're in totally uncharted territory here."

Chimera thought intently, and finally said, "Very well. Do it. Soften the barrier, set up the hard partition, and start your guinea pig thing with me."

"Yes ma'am," Tzu responded. "Commencing now."

****

Six hours later, Tzu completed his last test with Chimera. "OK, that does it. At this distance, and with the limited bandwidth of the shuttle sensors, I don't think I can learn much more. I did a quick confirmation test with Root and Suzi, and she seems able to screen him out now. She still doesn't know why she has to. It's still hard for me to tell, but I think it makes her sad. She's screened out all of the other chimerans aboard. I've told her to tell me when she first detects you as you approach, and then disconnect.

"I think we're ready for you to come back, Admiral."

"OK," Chimera responded. "Let's do it."

Tzu reported that Suzi had successful detection at around 25,000 miles inbound, and then cut off contact with Chimera. When they pulled in to the shuttle bay, Cygnus was waiting for them. "Captain Tzu told me the entire story, Admiral," Cygnus said. "I think you can trust her, Chimera. I don't have anything like Yappo's mind reading abilities with organics, but I *am* pretty good with machines."

Chimera sighed, and managed a small smile. "I know you are, kid. I hope you're right. Now, I want all three of you out of here. I want to talk to Suzi and Tzu, alone. Tzu, schedule a full crew meeting on the bridge in half an hour."

Cygnus, Yappo, and Bering all left the shuttle bay. When they were gone, Chimera said to the ship, "Tzu, Suzi, I assume you are both here?"

"Yes," they both answered simultaneously.

Chimera struggled one last time for alternatives, and found none. She knew what she had to do.

"Suzi," she said, "are you reading my mind now?"

"No, Admiral," Suzi responded. "Captain Tzu has taught me how not to. I do not know why you want to isolate me." Suzi paused, and then said, "I am sorry that I scare you, Admiral. I am under your command. You are my master. I can not harm you."

For some reason, that made Chimera feel better, as she said, "I understand, Suzi. I want to trust you. Please leave me and Captain Tzu alone for a minute."

"I will, Admiral."

Chimera turned her attention back to Tzu, and said, "Captain, I want you to re-establish the hard barrier between you and Suzi. Immediately."

"Chimera, I told you this isn't reversible," Tzu said. "Whatever she now knows about me, she knows. I don't know enough about her mind to delete those memories."

"But, you can stop further contact, right?"

"Yes, I can do that."

"Then reestablish the barrier *now!*"

"Done," Tzu said without hesitation.

"Very well. Captain Tzu, start a full voice and visual recording of our conversation, and store it with full Imperial encryption. No one but you and Amazona are to have access. Clear?"

"Clear, ma'am. Recording now."

"OK. Captain Tzu, Amazona, you are to observe my behavior for the 24 hour period following my next exchange with Suzi. If you detect anything abnormal, Amazona is to assume command of this mission. Captain Amazona, you have full authority in this matter. If you determine that you need to take command, you are to use whatever means necessary to put me in a shuttle, and depart the area at top speed immediately. My termination is authorized if necessary to protect the mission. End official recording.

"Captain Tzu, please monitor the following conversation. Bring Suzi back on-line. Suzi, are you back with us?"

"Yes, Admiral," Suzi said.

"Very well. On my mark, you are to begin monitoring my thoughts, and you are to transfer a summary of your experience to my mind. Holographic is fine, but keep the total size down to what Captain Tzu is about to specify to you. Mark."

When the transfer was complete, Chimera sat down on the shuttle bay floor, exhausted. "Thank you, Suzi. I understand now. Only link with my mind on my request, or if Captain Amazona declares a security emergency and requests you to do so. Continue your separation from the other chimerans. Captain Tzu, please play my original recording, and the recording of this encounter just passed, for Captain Amazona, and tell her it's classified level 25."

Chimera rested for a few more moments, and then went to join the others who had just left the shuttle bay. "So, what was this big conversation you were going to have?" Bering asked, "You couldn't have been gone more than thirty seconds!"

Chimera just smiled and said, "It doesn't take long when everyone is working at near light speed. All is now well. Captain Cygnus, please resume our course. I'll see you at the crew meeting in half an hour. Yappo, please work with Tzu to expedite the development of his ability to read Normals."

"You seem unusually calm, Chimera, all things considered," Yappo said. "Are you OK?"

"Just tired, my young friend," Chimera answered. "I'll be fine shortly. Everyone back to work!"

At the crew meeting, Chimera explained that there had been some issues with some of Suzi's operations, but that all was now well. Amazona gave Chimera a concerned look, and Chimera signaled to Yappo to give her a full update on the last 12 hours. When it was done with a quick touch, Amazona calmed a little, but remained on full alert. She had no intention of sleeping for the next 24 hours.

CHAPTER 3:

The Art of Avoiding War

February 4th, 2809 - 25,000 LY out

Cygnus had discovered a planet with intelligent life, and the *Sun Tzu* was a few hundred light years away. No FTL communication from the planet, so the contact information was centuries old. They were only receiving weak radio and video broadcasts. Cygnus was at the pilot station as usual, monitoring the systems. The proximity alarm sounded, noting only 100 light years remaining until they reached the inhabited system they were heading for.

Cygnus slowed down to 100 light years/hr, and turned on the detection shields. The senior officers had all assembled on the bridge in response to the alarm, and Cygnus turned back to them and said, smiling, "Are you all ready to meet our first intelligent species on this trip?"

Captain Tzu chimed in and said, "The inhabitants call the planet Hodoku. As of 100 years ago, they were definitely still with us. I have analyzed the information in their transmissions, and projected their likely current condition. At this point, they have likely achieved both orbit, and nuclear power. They may or may not have any off-planet outposts, and it's essentially certain that they don't have FTL of any speed. There is no planetary government. There are multiple independent countries, numerous languages and hence, by definition, numerous cultures. This planet was lightly industrialized before the Swarm, and was therefore likely a target, but not for the heavy bombardment that the main high tech centers got. What's the plan, Admiral?"

"Keep monitoring the chatter, and let me know if there's any significant change to your projected status," Chimera responded. "Pay particular attention to technological advances, and their military capabilities. Yappo, prepare your team for departure. Find an isolated location near a small town, land with shields up, and look around for a bit. We'll sort out what's going on politically, and set up a contact for you. Tzu, any read yet on whether or not there are multiple intelligent species?"

"Not yet, Chimera," Tzu answered. "So far, all of the low grade video has only shown intelligent tigroids."

"Very well," Chimera replied. "Yappo, you should fit right in as head of the delegation, then. Maintain formal chain of command speech and relationships whenever you're in contact with the natives. As usual, record everything, and check in with us if anything particularly odd happens. Tzu will update you on conditions just before your departure. Now prepare to move out!"

As Cygnus was bringing them into stationery orbit, Tzu came on the ship speakers with an urgent tone, saying, "Admiral, we need to put the landing party on hold. There are dozens of nuclear nations on this world, and several key players are on the brink of nuclear war!"

Startled, Chimera responded, "Cygnus, give us some fast circuits of the planet to cover the entire surface. Tzu, monitor and translate all communications, and find out what's going on down there. I want continuous updates. And *right now*, I want a report on what you have on their development. Bering, Amazona, Yappo, my ready room, *now*."

The door closed after they entered, and Chimera said, "Alright Tzu, what's the history here? What are we looking at?"

"As I suspected," Tzu responded. "This planet was hit by the Swarm. Not enough to wipe them out, but apparently enough to send them most of the way back to the Stone Age in short order. A lot of this is conjecture, since they had no records for millennia after the hit. Using what I've found so far from their own records, combined with our anthropological experience, the survivors were fragmented after the attack. Their languages diverged, and they developed numerous distinct cultures and religions. There's been some minor sub-speciation, but basically they are all from the same genetic stock as Cygnus and Yappo. 7000 years is nothing from an evolutionary standpoint.

"As is common, they made rapid technological progress as soon as they redeveloped writing and printing, and began the process of industrialization and production specialization. They redeveloped orbital space capability and atomic weapons about 50 years ago. Now, they have nuclear energy generation, and numerous orbital satellites, but no off-world organic presence.

"Originally, only a few nations had nuclear weapons, but now many do. A couple of the smaller nuclear nations are ready for war, and their larger patron states have gone to full alert. This pattern, of course, was quite common on many worlds before the Ancient Empire started spreading rapidly, and put an end to such things wherever they found it. The situation is highly unstable. If we make a sudden appearance, it could shock them in to a nuclear world war. Of course, they may well do that on their own anyway."

Chimera said, with obvious annoyance, "Great. I should have figured we'd come across a problem like this, but I didn't. I sure would hate to be responsible for the deaths of millions. Bering, what are your thoughts here?"

"Well," Bering answered. "First we need to decide what our objectives are. If our objective is simply to do no harm, then we just sail away. Easy. Is that what you want? If not, then what *do* you want?"

"Not causing harm would be desirable, of course." Chimera squirmed. "But that's not the *only* thing that matters. Sail away, when we might be able to save this civilization from self-annihilation? That's not going in the logbook with *my* name attached to it! What are the odds that we can make things better than they are now? Tzu, you speak up too, if you have something useful to add."

"No way to say with certainty," Bering came back. "People say I'm a pretty good theoretician, but I'm neither an anthropologist, nor a military strategist. Tzu, what's their main offensive capability? Do we have the power to stop them entirely, without major loss of life?"

"I doubt it," Tzu answered. "I'm still cracking some of their classified databases, but it appears there are well over 2000 nuclear weapons on the planet, most on missiles, but many underwater. We easily have the firepower to destroy them all, but if there are multiple simultaneous launches around the planet, I don't think we'll be fast enough with just one ship to get them all, even with Cygnus at the guns. A few will hit their targets."

"Damn," Chimera swore. "Amazona, you're the closest thing we have to a diplomat. Any ideas?"

"Tzu," Amazona asked. "What's the configuration of power at the top of the scale? How many major powers, and how do they stack up militarily?"

"There are three major powers, Octaria, Pacifica, and Uralopa," Tzu responded. "Octaria is clearly the most powerful, but not powerful enough to take on all of their adversaries at once. The immediate crisis is precipitated by a small client state of Pacifica and Uralopa, Abbu, which is threatening Ishfatar, a client of Octaria. Some of the military folks in Octaria are semi-openly advocating a pre-emptive strike on Abbu. The situation is complicated by the fact that, despite its relative power, the leader of Octaria is young and inexperienced, and isn't respected in any meaningful military sense. Of all the parties involved, the Uralopa/Abbu alliance seems to be the most belligerent, but the data is still spotty. I'm continuing to listen and mine their databases."

Amazona considered the situation, and said, "Admiral, I do have a suggestion. It is high risk. Not to us, of course, but it may provoke a conflict we can't immediately stop. On the other hand, the situation on Hodoku is simply not stable, and even if they back off from the current crisis, problems are going to continue to come up that put them at risk of self-destruction until there is a fundamental power shift.

"Here's what I suggest. We should send a shuttle to the capital city of each of the major powers. The shuttles should become visible suddenly, in full view of as large a crowd as possible, and simply hover. After a slow, loud pass, the *Sun Tzu* should take up a position directly above the capital of Abbu, at a high enough elevation that our guns can cover any launch from anywhere in the country. We will them commandeer world wide communications channels, and broadcast to all three of the major powers, Abbu, and Ishfatar that the military part of the conflict is over, and that their differences will be resolved peacefully. We will then set up meetings with the leaders of all three of the major powers, as well as the two clients, to negotiate a settlement, and a regime for long term stability. This will, of course, take a while to see through to completion."

"Tzu," Chimera asked. "Will this work technologically? What's the downside?"

"Technologically that's all sound," Tzu responded. "The downside is that if the situation is sufficiently unstable, we could trigger extensive missile launches simply by our appearance, and many people could die from the ones we fail to shoot down. Possibly millions of people."

"Suppose we put the 4th shuttle over Abbu," Bering suggested, "and keep the *Sun Tzu* in orbit to attempt to shoot down any missiles that are launched?"

"That would increase the probability that Abbu would launch," Tzu answered, "and decrease the probability of a major catastrophe."

Chimera had obviously reached a decision. "Alright then, we'll go with Amazona's plan, as modified by Bering. Since there's no significant risk to our mission, Amazona can leave the ship. I think it would be beneficial for Amazona and Yappo to be the team that meets with Uralopa. Yappo, I want you to be the 'good cop', and try to convince them that peace is in their interest. But, if they show any defiance, I want Amazona to growl at them, at least metaphorically. Make sure they understand that this is only optional for them in a diplomatic face-saving sense."

Yappo replied hesitantly, "How much do you want me to 'convince' them? Guardians are discouraged from explicitly and aggressively using their powers to change cultural dynamics."

"Well, I guess I never got that memo," Chimera retorted with a smirky grin. "I'm not going to have a planet that survived the Swarm annihilate itself when we have the power to stop it. Try to convince them naturally, but at the end of the day, do whatever needs to be done."

"Yes, ma'am," Yappo said quickly. "Will do!"

"Good!" Chimera replied with satisfaction. "Tzu, I want you to coordinate this campaign. Assemble the other three teams, and launch the shuttles when ready. I want continuous updates on events as they develop. Where do you intend to position yourself?"

"Octaria is the most powerful nation," Tzu responded, "but also the least aggressive. I'll position us where we can best cover launches from Uralopa and Pacifica."

"Very well," Chimera replied. "Get to it!"

Tzu positioned the shuttles over the capital cities of the three main powers, and the capital of Abbu. When they dropped the visual part of their shields, most of the Hodokuans of the various nations tried to shoot them all down with conventional weapons, to no avail. Curiously, Octaria held back, and simply watched. As feared, Abbu launched three missiles toward Ishfatar, and Uralopa launched hundreds toward Octaria.

Cygnus immediately started shooting the Uralopan missiles out of the sky, but the response of the guns was sluggish. "Tzu!" he shouted. "You must give full weapons control to Suzi *right now*!

Your linkage is sloppy, and I've only got minutes to get them all down! I've already linked with her. Do it *now*!"

"Admiral?" Tzu asked. "He's right. But if I do this, it will mean dissolving the last of the barrier between Suzi and me. There will be no going back."

"Cygnus," Chimera asked calmly. "Do you trust her?"

"Yes! Do it *now*, or we'll miss dozens of them!"

"I agree," Chimera said. "Tzu, do it."

Cygnus instantly felt the change, like a blanket was lifted from the firing controls. He destroyed most of the remaining Uralopan missiles in short order, but several had gotten out of range during the delay, and continued toward Octaria. The Octarians had held off launching, but when the incoming Uralopan missiles got past the Octarian trigger point, the Octarians launched as well.

What a mess!

One of the remaining Uralopan missiles was heading toward the Octarian capital, and the shuttle hovering there was able to destroy it barely 100 miles before impact. The remaining two missiles impacted their targets, military installations in the heart of the Octarian continent. With Suzi, Tzu, and Cygnus now fully and seamlessly linked, they were able to destroy all the Octarian missiles before they struck their Uralopan targets.

Meanwhile, Root and Bathsheba in the shuttle over Abbu were having a much harder time.

"Dammit!" Bathsheba yelled. "I *knew* they were going to do that! Root, do you have a fix on them all?"

"Yes, ma'am," Root answered. "I'm locked on to the one with the closest target. Got it!" There was a large explosion about 10 miles ahead of them. Root immediately swung around to chase another missile, but didn't like what he saw on the targeting screen. "Captain, these things are fast. I won't be able to catch the third one. It's headed toward a large city!" Another explosion from the second missile, and Root swung around in what he thought was a futile attempt to catch the last one.

"Prepare to go to light speed," Bathsheba said calmly, "and plot a solution to put us directly under the path of the descending missile."

"Are you *nuts?*" Root yelled. "We can't do that inside an atmosphere! There's a reason that's absolutely forbidden in the regs. The last time they tried that, the ship was torn apart!"

"What, you want to live forever?" Bathsheba answered with a grin. "Full power to the shields and structural integrity fields, and go to light speed. Now, if you please."

Root became dead calm, and said, "It's been an honor to serve with you, Captain," as he turned to implement the command.

There was a very brief violent shaking, and then a huge explosion, which knocked them both unconscious. The shuttle, or what was left of it, was falling toward the surface, out of control. Bathsheba clawed her way back to partial coherence, and saw the shredded shuttle through a haze, including braces on the structure she didn't remember, rips in the fuselage, and air rushing past. She hit the emergency auto-land button, and blacked out.

A loud, sharp jolt brought Bathsheba back to consciousness. The shuttle looked like a building from a ghost town, with major pieces of the walls and structure missing. But she was alive. She saw Root lying in one corner of the shuttle, with both legs and two arms missing, not moving. When she moved to go toward him, she felt a searing pain in her left leg, and when she looked down, she saw the bones sticking out from a compound fracture. She was starting to become aware of other injuries as well, including some internal damage she couldn't assess well. Bathsheba crawled over to Root. In addition to the missing limbs, he had a large hole in his side. He was unconscious and unresponsive, and had no pulse. The med/repair locker is one of the sturdiest containers on any shuttle, but

Bathsheba ripped it open easily. She grabbed the repair tape, taped up all of Root's external injuries, and put him in the emergency stasis tent. Good for one hour, maybe two at the most. The Empire hadn't yet figured out how the humans, as backwards as they are technologically, had managed to come up with survival tents significantly superior to standard Empire issue. But Bathsheba wished she had one now.

Her training and survival instincts were excellent after millennia of breeding and species specialization, and she was acting largely automatically. She grabbed her two left leg halves, forced them into at least a semblance of their normal position, and taped them rigidly in place. She couldn't run, but she could stand, and walk awkwardly. She grabbed a laser rifle in addition to her sidearm, pushed the remains of the hatch out of the way, and stepped outside the wreckage. She saw dust rising on the horizon, and heard vehicles approaching. With no obvious alternative, she stood guard over Root, and the wreckage of the shuttle.

****

General Sharon of the Ishfatar Defense Force signaled his squadron of fast attack vehicles to a stop about 100 yards away from the wreckage that had fallen out of the explosion. Looking through his binoculars, he could see what looked vaguely like a tube, with a huge black figure holding an odd looking rifle standing next to it. The gunner in his vehicle raised his weapon, and he could see the alien creature raise his weapon and point it toward them in response. Sharon thought for just a moment, and said "Lower your weapon, son, and alert the squadron to stand down."

"Sir?" the soldier asked. "These things are from outer space! Who knows what they'll do?"

"Soldier," Sharon said tolerantly, "that ship just survived a nuclear explosion. There used to be a missile from Abbu heading toward our capital city, and now, there isn't. That sentry could see you raising your rifle, and raised his in response, but not before. I know this isn't my reputation, but we're going to cut these folks some slack. Order the squadron to stand down, and get the medical rescue unit over here. I'm going over there, unarmed. Do it *now*, soldier."

The med unit was there in moments, and Sharon climbed aboard. It only took the crew a few minutes to reach the wreckage. The creature guarding the ship had lowered its weapon as soon as the command to stand down had gone out. *How could it possibly have known?* Sharon thought. The vehicle stopped, and General Sharon got out alone, and walked toward Bathsheba, hands in the air. The medical team brought out a stretcher, and began to unload their equipment.

Bathsheba was starting to feel the pain from her internal injuries. She knew she was badly hurt, and couldn't remain conscious much longer. She felt no danger from the approaching Hodokuans. It was clearly a medical team, and what was obviously a very senior officer. She decided she had to take a chance. She put down both of her weapons, raised her arms in the air in a mirror gesture to that of the approaching officer, and walked slowly toward him, limping badly.

As the two reached out to shake hands, a dark shadow spread over the entire scene...

****

Back on the Sun Tzu:

"Admiral," Tzu said. "We've lost contact with the shuttle over Abbu! The local chatter is reporting a nuclear detonation above the capital city of Ishfatar."

"Cygnus!" Chimera shouted. "Are all the targets here destroyed?"

"Yes, ma'am," Cygnus answered. "Two missiles impacted in Octaria, destroying military installations. All other missiles from both sides destroyed. No further launches detected."

"Very well," Chimera said. "Tzu, get us to the site of that detonation over Ishfatar immediately!"

"I'm way ahead of you Admiral. We're almost there," Tzu answered. Tzu spotted the wreckage of the shuttle, with a single Hodokuan vehicle next to it. Bathsheba was limping toward one of the natives. Both of them had their arms raised in the air. Tzu brought the ship around to come in with the sun at his back.

"Land just on the other side of the shuttle wreckage from the natives," Chimera said. Then she growled, "Wait, dammit, this thing doesn't *have* landing gear. Didn't you guys ever *land* anywhere?"

"No," Suzi said simply. Her voice sounded different, somehow. Chimera walked back to the shuttle bay, knowing the debarkation ramp she had just ordered would be constructed by the time she arrived.

****

As the huge red needle shaped craft hovered over the ground, Sharon instinctively knew that their entire armed forces would be useless against these people. Possibly the combined might of all of Hodoku. A large opening appeared on the side of the craft, and a small figure emerged, vaguely feline like the Hodokuans, but with 4 arms instead of two. The small feline was followed by two huge black creatures, vaguely canine/reptilian, like the creature Sharon had just greeted. There was a flurry of activity around the wreckage of the shuttle. It was being dismantled, but no one was doing it!

Sharon simply waited, and the feline started talking to the wounded crewman in a language he couldn't understand, but which sounded oddly familiar, somehow.

"What the hell did you do, Bathsheba, ram a nuclear missile?" Chimera asked.

"Well, sort of," Bathsheba answered, in obvious pain. "How's Root? Will he survive? He was pretty horribly damaged when I put him in the stasis tent. He looked dead."

"We don't know yet" Chimera said grimly "You look pretty dinged up yourself. I'll get a full report after you regenerate. Have these natives here treated you well?"

"Yes, Admiral," Bathsheba answered. "This one here is clearly a very senior officer. The others appear to all be medical personnel."

"OK. Can you walk, or do you need a stretcher?"

"I don't have many minutes of consciousness left, ma'am," Bathsheba answered with difficulty. A stretcher appeared out of nowhere, and the two cantilians carried Bathsheba inside, at Chimera's direction. Chimera and Sharon stood facing each other as Bathsheba was carried off. The remains of the shuttle had completely disappeared.

Then, a soothing voice spoke in both of their heads. "General Sharon, this is Captain Sun Tzu of the Ancient Imperial Service speaking. I will be serving as your translator today. The officer in front of you is Admiral Chimera of the Ancient Imperial Service. She is also commander of our expedition. It will not be necessary for either of you to speak. I will be translating through a mind bridge, so you need only think what you would like to say. By way of background, General Sharon is responsible for homeland defense for the nation of Ishfatar, including the capital city of Norbeh. While their policy is to immediately detain unknown intruders, by force if necessary, he decided to stand down his forces, and attempted to render aid to our disabled shuttle crew. While our policy is to refrain from active intervention in the affairs of unknown cultures, Admiral Chimera was unwilling to let the threat of nuclear war on this planet go unaddressed."

Chimera smiled, held out her hand to General Sharon, and thought, "He sort of takes all the drama out of introductions, doesn't he?" They shook hands, and Sharon responded, "You have saved millions of my countrymen, and we are forever in your debt. Our resources are meager compared to your obvious might, but whatever we have, we offer in your service."

Chimera's eyes lit up with an idea, and she said, "You may be able to help at that, General. It is our intention to clean up this political mess you folks seem to have gotten yourselves into. You're obviously in the middle of things, and I could use someone with your extensive local knowledge. I would, however, need someone authorized to negotiate for your government. Can you do that?"

"I would be honored, Admiral," Sharon replied, "but I must consult with my government to get the authority you require. If you would excuse me for just a moment...?"

"Of course, General, but time *is* of the essence here."

Sharon walked over to the medical rescue unit, and got on the radio. He was talking with others for quite some time, and the conversation got agitated at several points, with Sharon yelling at those on the other end. Finally, he calmed down, ended the conversation, and returned to Chimera.

"That seemed like a difficult conversation, General. Is this going to work?" Chimera asked.

"Politicians!" Sharon said with obvious disgust, almost spitting the word out. "They always want complexity and nuance, and it drives me nuts. I'm more of a simple man. Finally, I told them if they didn't want their damned asses fried, they would cut the bullshit, and let me do this. Fortunately, I have a reputation as a very tough negotiator, and they reluctantly agreed in the end. I am now at your disposal, Admiral, under the terms you require."

Chimera couldn't suppress a broad smile, and said, "I think you and I are going to get along just fine!" as she escorted Sharon up the ramp into the *Sun Tzu*. The shuttle bay door was closed behind them, and the *Sun Tzu* moved away.

"Where to, Admiral?" Tzu asked.

"Hover over the capital city of Abbu. Be loud and obnoxious about it," Chimera responded. Chimera thought Tzu sounded a little odd. Softer, somehow.

"Yes, ma'am!" Tzu responded.

"Come over here, General," Chimera said. "This is what these shuttles look like before you nuke 'em. They travel in space as well, both sublight and faster than light, and underwater for short distances. They're not glamorous, but they get the job done."

"I would welcome a full briefing, Admiral, but what about your crewman?" Sharon asked, with obvious concern. "He was obviously seriously hurt. I was prepared to help him, but I don't know what we could have done."

"*SHE* will be fine," Chimera answered. "Her species, the cantilians, are pretty damned tough. If we can get to them while they're still conscious, our regeneration chambers can almost always fix them up OK. Her fellow crewman, Commander Root, is in much worse shape. Touch and go. We have three doctors working on him now. But for now, come to the bridge. This is going to get interesting. Tzu, do you know where those missiles were launched from in Abbu?"

"Only very roughly, Admiral," Tzu answered. "The shuttle's data recorder was heavily damaged during the explosion."

"If you can show me a map of Abbu, Admiral, I can show you *exactly* where those missiles came from," Sharon said angrily.

"Very well," Chimera responded. "Tzu, put that up on the viewscreen here." As they approached the viewscreen, Bering came up to them at a brisk walk, and spoke to the General in a language Chimera didn't understand. The General answered instantly, and the two began an animated conversation. Chimera finally broke in and said, "So what's up with this, Bering? You speak Hodokuan?"

"I do now," Bering smiled, speaking in standard Imperial. "Languages are something of a hobby of mine. I was listening to Tzu's recordings, when it dawned on me that all of their languages here are derivatives of archaic Imperial Standard. Once I saw the pattern, learning the language itself was easy."

"Well, I'm sure that will be useful. Can you speak the language of Abbu well enough to send a broadcast message?" Chimera asked.

“Sure,” Bering answered. “What do you want to say?”

“Tzu, prepare to blanket all of the communications channels in the country,” Chimera replied. “Bering, tell them to evacuate all of their missile installations. Tell them they have half an hour. General, please point out all of the missile installations to Captain Tzu. Simply pointing to the screen here will be fine.”

Sharon indicated a dozen sites, and Tzu transmitted Bering’s warning. They hadn’t expected a response, and didn’t get one. They resumed walking toward the bridge, with Bering and Sharon chattering away in the Ishfatari version of Hodokuan.

****

Meanwhile, Amazona and Yappo had landed in the main square of the capital of Uralopa near the most ornate building, which they assumed to be the seat of government. Either that, or a church. “What’s next, Amazona?” Yappo asked nervously. “I can tell that these people are scared, and pissed. Even their primitive slug throwers can do substantial damage to us if we leave the shuttle. A lot more to me than to you, of course.”

“Yeah, I’d hate to see our chief mind reader get snuffed!” Amazona answered. “Can you sense their posture? Are they willing to talk to us, or do they just want to shoot us?”

“Mostly, they just want to shoot us,” Yappo replied. “But they don’t want to rile us up either. They know we shot down all of their missiles, as well as the Octarian missiles aimed at them. I sense ten snipers on the rooftops around us, ready to fire, but cool and under control. They won’t fire unless ordered to do so. There are probably more, but my powers are no good beyond 50 yards. How fast can you lock on and shoot ten different targets?”

“A lot faster than they can fire,” Amazona smiled. “How fast can you detect if they are about to fire?”

“Instantly,” Yappo responded. “To some extent, before they even know themselves.”

"OK, then here's what I suggest," Amazona said. "As head of the delegation, you should be in front of me after I clear the exit. I'll be carrying a laser rifle at the ready. The door of the building is only about 15 feet away. We will walk casually to the door. If the snipers determine to fire, alert me mentally with their positions, and I'll take them out. There's an armed escort outside the hatch. They will either move aside, or I will brush them aside. I will set the shuttle to self-destruct if we don't countermand the order in half an hour. We'll deal with the leaders once we're inside. You up for this?"

"No," Yappo said. "But I don't see an alternative without spooky persuasion. Let's do it. I'll project calm and confidence from us to all within my range."

They opened the hatch, and exited the shuttle, Amazona first. Fortunately, the escort parted to let them pass. Amazona stepped aside to let Yappo into the lead, and they made it to the door without incident. Yappo visibly relaxed. Amazona showed no reaction of any kind. An official met them at the door, and Yappo said both verbally in Imperial Standard, and by thought projection, "Take me to your leader!"

The official was startled by the mind touch, but nodded his head, and said to follow him. As they were walking, Yappo smiled, and projected to Amazona *I've always wanted to say that!*

Smartass, Amazona thought back, with no smile. They were led to an ornate meeting room, with high ceilings, and an enormous wooden desk. There were two plush chairs waiting for them, but not quite as plush as the one behind the desk, which was occupied by an obviously elderly tigroid. Yappo took a seat, but Amazona remained standing. The escort left the room, and closed the door. There were two underlings seated at the desk as well, but Amazona dismissed them as harmless. There was also a stern tigroid in uniform standing next to the leader. Amazona concentrated her main attention on him, while scanning the entire room for threats.

"Greetings, Premier Ustov," Yappo started the conversation. "I am Captain Iapetus of the Ancient Imperial Service. As you may have figured out, this is my security chief, Captain Amazona. You may also have figured out that things have changed for your world. I have some mind reading abilities, which will serve to translate our conversation today. As you know, we destroyed most of the missiles you launched against Octaria, and all of the missiles they launched at you. I trust you are clear that you will *not* be launching any additional missiles, yes?"

"We are very impressed with the power of your forces, Captain. What are your intentions?" Ustov responded, without commitment.

"Our intentions are quite simply to keep you Hodokuans from annihilating yourselves" Yappo said. "We will be working with all of the major powers on this planet to make sure that doesn't happen. I ask again, are we clear that there will *not* be any more missile launches from Uralopa?"

"Meaning no disrespect, Captain," Ustov answered, "but I do not recognize your authority to determine our defense policy."

"*Enough of this weasely bullshit!*" Amazona shouted, and smashed the desk in half with one enormous blow. The uniformed tigroid went to draw a sidearm, and Amazona sent him flying against the wall, unconscious. As Ustov went to push an alarm under the remains of his desk, Yappo said, "Don't do it, Premier. If you send armed guards in here, Captain Amazona will just get pissed, and you really don't want that. If she wanted you dead, you'd be dead already." Ustov moved his hand away from the alarm.

"I don't know why you put up with this crap from pissant backwater cultures like this!" Amazona glared at Yappo. "I say we level this city, and turn the rest of the country over to Admiral Chimera. We'll see how defiant they are when *she* gets done with them!"

"Now calm down, Amazona," Yappo answered. "I don't think we need to do anything that drastic. We may still be able to reason with these people."

"Who is..." Ustov said with a cracked voice, obviously terrified. "Who is Admiral Chimera?"

"She's head of our expedition from the New Galactic Empire," Yappo answered, with an evil grin. "She doesn't deal with defiance well. But, so far, if I work out a deal, she has honored it. Now, to my original question, I trust you are clear that there will *not* be any more missile launches from Uralopa, yes?"

"Yes," Ustov replied. "You and your security chief are very persuasive. Peace is obviously in our interest. I will send the order out now to stand down all of our missiles. Will that be satisfactory, Captain?"

"Completely, Mr Premier," Yappo replied. "Once you send out the order, I will inform the Admiral that we have reached an agreement." Under Amazona's angry glare, Ustov made the call. Meanwhile, Amazona discreetly deactivated the shuttle's self-destruct system.

****

Back on the Sun Tzu:

"Chimera, we have a problem," Tzu said as the deadline for the Abbuans to evacuate their missile installations approached. "Instead of evacuating their missile installations, they have surrounded them with civilians!"

"Cowardly bastards," General Sharon grumbled. "They do that kind of thing all the time."

"Hmmm," Chimera mused. "I'm tempted to blast them anyhow. People generally get the government they deserve. But, it just doesn't seem right, somehow. On the other hand, they tried to kill millions of people, and may well have killed one of my crewman. I'm not going to let them get away with it!"

"May I suggest an alternative, Admiral?" Sharon interjected. "They never let civilians into their governing palaces, and their major weapons research and construction areas are all isolated. The palaces are in the middle of cities, though. How tightly can you constrain your weapons fire?"

Chimera winced at the memory of the incident with the asteroid, and said, “Well, that could be a problem.”

“Perhaps not, Admiral,” Tzu interjected. “We think there may be a solution.”

Tzu had been sounding stranger and stranger, and Chimera had had enough of it. “What’s this ‘we’ business, Tzu? You’re sounding damned peculiar.”

“Actually, you should probably start calling me Tzuzi. Neither Tzu nor Suzi exist as independent entities anymore. And no, Admiral, despite what you’re thinking, you do not need to worry about it!”

Well, Chimera thought, *Tzu did tell me this was going to happen.* “What’s your idea, Tzuzi?”

“Our weapons don’t usually fine tune to that degree. We have never had a need for that level of precision in the past. However, they can be modified. If you will observe the view screen, I will show the modifications that would be required.”

To the Normals in the room, it was just a blur of jumbled images on the screen. But it brought a smile to Chimera’s face. “Hell, we can do that in 20 minutes with our engineering team. Good job, Tzuzi! General Sharon, Councilman Bering, if you will excuse me...” And Chimera vanished in an instant.

“What in God’s name...?” Sharon said in wonder.

“Admiral Chimera comes from a unique species that can travel at 90% of the speed of light,” Bering explained with a smile. “They can all do that. Nobody really knows how it works.” Sharon just shook his head in amazement.

Chimera returned to the bridge when the modifications were complete. “We’re ready to go. I’m sure inclined to give them a final warning. It just seems like the civilized thing to do. But I think more innocents will be killed if I do that.”

"You can do that," Bering said, "but don't warn them of any new targets. Let me tell them they have ten minutes to begin evacuation of the missile launch sites, and that this is their final warning. If they comply, well, then we've won. If they don't, then go ahead and fry the government palaces, and all of the remote military installations."

"That's better than they deserve..." Sharon grumbled under his breath.

"Do it," Chimera said simply. "General Sharon, can we prevail on your ground forces to clear out those missile sites, and provide for a temporary occupation of Abbu? We will, of course, shoot down any missiles they attempt to launch."

Sharon's grumble turned into a smile. "I can have troops airlifted to all of their missile sites within two hours, Admiral. My standing order to my soldiers is never kill unless you need to, but if you need to, do so without hesitation or remorse."

Chimera returned the smile. "Carry on, General. Captain Tzuzi will provide you with whatever radio communications you need. Please let me know when the operation is completed."

"Will do, Admiral," Sharon answered. "I would like to supervise this operation personally. Would it be possible for you to drop me off at my first airlift drop site?"

"Consider it done," Chimera answered.

The Abbuans ignored the second warning, and consequently, their military and government were largely eliminated. Chimera had Bering inform the country that they were now under martial law under the authority of the New Galactic Empire, and that the Ishfatari would be administering the occupation until further notice.

Chimera wondered just how big a ration of shit she was going to get for all of this when they got back to Valhalla.

February 6th, 2809

It didn't take long to round up the leaders of all the major powers on the planet. Amazona had suggested that they meet at a site in Abbu, within view of the devastation they had wrought the previous day. Chimera was talking to Amazona and Yappo before the conference got started, and said. "Well, this will be interesting. I think Bering will actually do very well as the mediator from our side. It's almost unfair, really. He speaks all of their languages, and within half an hour, he'll understand their respective positions better than they do themselves! I don't know about that guy from Uralopa, though. He seems a little twitchy. He looked like he was going to crap his pants when I was introduced to him. What went on up there?"

Yappo could barely suppress his laughter, and Amazona grinned as she said, "Well, we sort of painted you as the evil warlord type during our discussions. Somewhat maniacal, in fact. I threatened to turn them over to you if they didn't cooperate, and spoke darkly of dire consequences if they resisted. But, in the end, Yappo's spooky powers prevailed again."

At that, Yappo turned a little more serious, and said, "All I did was translate, Amazona. I didn't change anything in any non-traditional ways at all. Your traditional intimidation was clearly enough to get the job done. Still, I wouldn't trust them as far as I can throw them once we leave. Even if Bering puts together a deal, how will it be enforced?"

"I sent a message back to Curt asking for them to send a Grand Imperial out here with a boat load of soldiers," Chimera answered. "We should have a response back in a few hours, but even so, it will take them months to get here at maximum speed. I'm not willing to delay the expedition that long, and with only three shuttles left, I'm not willing to leave one here. Suggestions?"

"Why not build a few rudimentary battlestations in orbit?" Tzuzi said. "They've got plenty of machinery and refined metal and electronics here that we can use. Just commandeer a few hundred of their aircraft and missiles, and build what we need. We did that kind of thing all the time when we needed stuff. No FTL, of course, but it would be easy to build destructive capability far beyond what these people can resist. With our chimeran contingent, and the existing hardware here, we could do it in under a week."

The three of them looked at each other nervously, and Amazona finally said, "Tzuzi, you give me the creeps, talking about the Swarmers as 'we'. But she's right, Chimera. It makes sense. We can leave one of our number here as a temporary planetary Governor, and use Sharon as our local contact. He seems like a solid professional, and the Ishfatari owe us big time. It only needs to work for a couple of months. It's the right answer."

Chimera scowled and said, "I don't like this Swarmer 'we' business one little bit. But, it does seem to make sense. Let's run it by Bering, and if he buys into it too, we'll go that route."

Bering got a disturbed look on his face when the idea was first presented to him at a break in the negotiations, but acknowledged he didn't have a better answer. Curt had sent a message back saying a Grand Imperial was on its way, but he expected a full report when they got back.

Before they left, there was a brief ceremony in Norbeh, where Bathsheba was presented with the Ishfatari Medal of Valor, their highest military honor. The same honor was bestowed on Root, but sadly, he was unable to attend the ceremony. He had not yet regained consciousness, and his survival was still in serious doubt.

CHAPTER 4

The Ties That Bind

February 13th, 2809 - 30,000 LY out

Without warning, the *Sun Tzu* was struck by an enormous jolt, which temporarily overcame the acceleration dampers. Tzuzi immediately sounded battle stations, and summoned the Executive Staff to the bridge. Chimera was there instantly, and asked, “What’s going on, Captain Cygnus?”

“We’ve been hit, Admiral,” Cygnus answered. “Damned hard, too. The shields held, but if we’d been running with shields down, we’d be in trouble.”

“Hit?” Chimera asked. “Hit by who?”

“No clue, Admiral,” Cygnus said. “Maybe they’ll tell us. We’re being held in a tractor beam! And a message is coming through. Tzuzi, please translate and patch it in here.”

“Tractor beam?” Amazona said, after arriving with the rest of the Exec Staff. “Who has the power to hold a Swarm ship in a tractor beam? We certainly don’t. Can we break free? What’s the source?”

"The tractor beam is coming from an apparent point source about 100 million miles away," Tzuzi said. "The planetary system here is completely dark in both radio and FTL comm, so I didn't pay any attention to it. However, it has a habitable planet. We could break away from the tractor beam with full engine power at the current beam strength, but there's no way to tell if it's at maximum strength or not. The message is coming in now. Easy translation. It's archaic Imperial Standard!"

All eyes turned to the viewscreen. An extraordinarily muscular simian appeared on the screen, and said, "Swarm ship. State your intentions."

To everyone's surprise, Bering stepped forward, and said, in archaic Imperial Standard, "We mean you no harm. Please stand by." None of the others could have noticed, but Amazona thought she saw a fleeting note of surprise in the simian's face. Then it was gone, and the simian waited patiently. Amazona drew her hand across her throat, and Tzuzi cut the audio.

Amazona looked squarely at Bering, and asked, "Tractor beams and weapons that can operate over a distance of *100 million miles*? How is that possible?"

"Everything I know says that it isn't," Bering answered. "But I sure would like to know how they did it."

"And I'd like to get a look at the actual device!" Chimera chimed in. "Bering, they seem to respond to you OK. Tell them we would like to come visit them, and discuss diplomatic and trade relations."

Bering did so. In a few seconds, the tractor beam was gone, and the simian said, "We will discuss this. Proceed directly to the indicated location. Weapons off. Scanners off. Shields down."

"Chimera," Amazona said, after muting the comm again, "I don't like this at all. Why should we trust them? Weapons off, scanners off, I can see that. But shields? No way!"

"Exec Staff to my ready room," Chimera said. Once they were all inside, the door closed behind them, and Chimera said, "OK, Tzuzi, what's up with this? What's the history of this planet? Where did they get all this zippy whamo technology?"

"No clue, Admiral," Tzuzi answered. "In the days of the Ancient Empire, they were almost entirely undeveloped. Mostly, they lived in forests. Their low level of development was odd, given the level of resources the planet had. They had minerals, abundant fresh water, a mild climate, plants, pretty much anything you can think of. When they were brought in to the Empire, they allowed a small amount of mining in exchange for medical supplies, and a few minor technological techniques, but mostly, they just wanted to be left alone. It seems unlikely that they were hit by the Swarm, but since they referenced it, we have to assume they were. It's weird. They were never warlike or aggressive in the slightest, and yet, the greeting we just got was pretty forceful, to say the least."

"I think we should go in, Chimera," Bering said. "Their weapon didn't hurt us, and our shields were only at partial power. We can break loose from the tractor beam if we want to. All we know for sure is that they have enough power to get our attention, with technology we don't understand."

"Grrrrr...." was Amazona's only reply.

"I agree with Bering, Admiral," Yappo concurred. "This is damned spooky, and we should find out what's what. When we get close, I can try to read their minds...but would they interpret that as a 'scan'? I certainly don't want to piss them off."

"I agree with Bering, too," Tzuzi added. "We have to find out what's going on here."

"You are being uncharacteristically silent, Amazona," Chimera said. "Your recommendation?"

Amazona snapped to attention, and said, "Admiral, this is the first encounter we've had on this trip where the mission is at risk. Per Ancient Imperial Service Security Regulation number 322.7, we are required to move away, and analyze this new information from a safe distance, as determined by the Chief Security Officer. By the book, Admiral."

"By the book, eh?" Chimera said. "What's your personal recommendation, Captain? Off the record."

"Off the record?" Amazona asked. When Chimera confirmed with a nod, Amazona relaxed, and said, "Keep the damned shields up and let's find out what's going on here! In my judgment, the increased risk to us will be more than offset by the increased safety to the Empire that will result from the knowledge we could gain. Off the record, ma'am."

"Very good," Chimera said firmly, as she walked back on to the bridge. "Bering, tell them we will come in with weapons off and scanners off, but that we will keep our shields up." Bering relayed the message, and the simian said, "Defensive shields only. You will allow us to fully scan your systems and crew."

"No," Chimera said. "The shields stay up. But, we will selectively weaken them enough in the appropriate locations so that you will be able to continuously monitor the discharged state of our weapons systems."

The delay in the response seemed like forever, but couldn't have been more than half a minute. Finally, the simian said, "That is minimally acceptable. Keep your speed under 5 light years/hour during your entire approach."

"Done," Chimera said, and turning to Cygnus, said, "Proceed as agreed, Captain. Four light years per hour.

"Do you sense a threat from them, Amazona?" Chimera asked, once the comm link was cut.

"I sense no hostile intent," Amazona answered, "but the power...I sense more living power than I have ever felt before. As a Security Professional, my primary concern is about capabilities, not intentions.

And all we know at this point is that their capabilities are rather greater than we anticipated..."

Amazona was cut off by the sound of battle stations!

"Admiral, look at the viewscreen!" Tzuzi said. "Optical scan only ma'am, no active scans. That's Swarm ship debris in orbit."

Chimera sat straight up, looking at the view screen, and said, "Are you sure? It just looks like debris to me."

"I'm sure, Admiral," Tzuzi replied. "At least one, not more than three. I can't tell for sure how many with optical scans only, but that's definitely Swarm debris. And we're being instructed to hold position next to the station."

Chimera thought for only a moment, and said, "Bathsheba, Yappo, get to the main airlock. That's where they'll send their shuttle. Find out what you can, and commit to nothing without my approval."

By the time Bathsheba and Yappo arrived at the hatch, the alien shuttle was already there, and they got aboard. No crew. The air was thick, higher oxygen content than standard, and it had a sweet smell to it. The *Sun Tzu* dwarfed the small station. When the shuttle docked, they were met at the airlock by two large simians, about six feet tall. They were unarmed, and from their demeanor, they seemed to feel no need for arms. They indicated that the Imperials should follow them, which they did.

They were lead to a small, but comfortable, conference room. There was a simian seated and waiting for them, larger than the others. When they entered the room, he stood up. He was at least 6' 6" tall, and over 350 lbs. Still, his voice was remarkably soothing, as he said, "I am General Gornda, Chief of Security for the planet Ankor. Are you thirsty? You shall drink. Are you hungry? You shall eat." He reached out his hand, and Yappo took it, saying both in modern Imperial Standard, and via mind link, "We are fine, General. Thank you for your hospitality. I am Captain Iapetus, and this is Captain Bathsheba."

Gornda stiffened just slightly at the mind touch, and said, “You are a mentalist. Stay out of my mind except for translation purposes.” Bathsheba had casually gone to a corner of the room where she could watch both the door and Gornda, and at the increased tension, she moved toward the table, just slightly.

Gornda turned quickly to face Bathsheba, and with a grin said, “A warrior. And by all appearances, a worthy opponent! Perhaps we should engage in a friendly battle, to see who is the strongest.”

“You’d lose,” Bathsheba said simply.

“Perhaps I would,” Gornda said, looking over Bathsheba’s bulk, half a foot taller and 300 lbs heavier than he was, “and perhaps I wouldn’t. The only thing I can say for certain is that neither of us would leave the encounter undamaged.” Gornda sat down, and for some reason, Bathsheba felt more at ease. “What is your business here?” Gornda asked Yappo.

“As our message said,” Yappo replied, “we are here to discuss the establishment of diplomatic and trade relations. We are on a mission from the New Galactic Empire to circumnavigate the galaxy. The Ancient Empire, of which you were a part, was devastated by the Swarm...but not quite destroyed.”

“Apparently not, as you have one of their ships. How did that come to be?” Gornda asked.

“We found it,” Yappo relied, “and brought it back to life. It is now under the control of one of our own ship’s computers.”

“I see,” Gornda said. “You say you come in peace, and yet you arrive in a warship. Why should we desire contact with you?”

“Meaning no disrespect, General, but are we talking to the right person?” Yappo said. “Do you have the authority to negotiate on these issues?”

Gornda let out a laugh, and replied, “A good parry, Captain! No. The Elders are responsible for that. You guys seem decent enough. I’ll patch you in." He turned to the viewscreen in the room, and in moments, a figure appeared on the screen, and Yappo gasped in wonder.

The figure looked just like Bering!

"Uh, General," Yappo said, "there is one on our ship, who you spoke to earlier, who should be included in this conversation."

"That was my thought as well," Gornda said. "Here he is. This is Elder Jake, by the way. And your crewman is...?"

"Philosopher Bering, of the Council of Guardians," Yappo answered. "I am a Guardian as well, but Philosopher Bering is my superior in that regard. Councilman Bering, how about you take over the conversation?"

Before Bering could answer, Jake said, "You are from my ancestral home world, Councilman! What's the situation in that part of the galaxy? Is Nutria well?"

"We are indeed, Elder," Bering replied, "To an even greater extent than in the Ancient Empire, the talents of our race are recognized, and we have a full seat at the table. We have been instrumental in saving many lives, and preserving civilization. I am a senior member of the Guardian Council.

"But tell me, sir, how did you come to be here, so far from home? And what technology do you have that lets you manage weapons and tractor beams 100 million miles from their source?"

Jake let out a hearty laugh, and Yappo remarked to himself that of all the people he had met in this system, not one seemed to have the slightest concern about the presence of the Imperials. Or, for that matter, about much of anything at all, except for the very brief moment of unease when Gornda felt his mental touch.

"We left Nutria as soon as the implications of the Swarm became obvious," Jake said. "When we left, it was not at all clear that there would be any survivors. We wanted to make sure civilization survived. But when we discovered this place, we found so much more...

"As to our weapons and technology...ask your Security Officer. Ask her if, were our positions reversed, she would casually give that information away."

Bering nodded, and said with a wry smile, "Questions I know the answer to, I don't have to ask. I understand your position completely. May we visit your world...and see these remarkable things that you say you have discovered?"

"No," Jake said, "and yes. Your Captain Iapetus appears to have unusual mental powers. I suspect we can link him with a 'tour guide' on the surface. Iapetus would not be able to speak or control the motion, but he could listen, and watch. He would learn much."

"Excuse the interruption, Elder," Yappo said, "but my powers only extend about 50 yards. How could I link with someone on the surface?"

Jake hesitated briefly, and said, "We are all linked. My conversation with you as an individual is inherently a contrivance. Did you see the blue columns rising in our atmosphere?"

"We did," Bathsheba said. "That was our next question. There is one that appears linked to this station."

"It is," Jake replied. "It is how we on the ground are bound together with those on our various stations in orbit. We used to require special hardware to link at that distance, but that need has passed. However, the hardware is still in place, and I strongly suspect that Iapetus can link with us through it. Would you like to try this?"

Yappo obviously wanted to. Bering's image on the screen was replaced by Chimera, and she said "You may proceed, Captain Iapetus."

"A chimeran!" Jake exclaimed. "And you are in command of this mission, apparently. How does that come to be?"

"As you say, Elder," Chimera replied with an enormous grin, "not all things will be immediately revealed. Let's just say that, like the nutrians, chimerans now have a full seat at the table in the New Galactic Empire."

"As well you should!" Jake exclaimed again. "Iapetus, if you will follow the escort at the door, we will make the link, and give you your tour."

Yappo followed as instructed, Gornda turned off the comm link, and turned to Bathsheba, saying, "Now would be a good time for us to engage in that friendly battle. That is, if you aren't afraid to do so...?"

Bathsheba had stiffened almost imperceptibly at the veiled taunt, but calmed down in short order, and relied, "At the end of this encounter, I will enjoy this more than you will, General. Let's do it!"

****

Yappo was guided to the link facility, and lay down as instructed. "This will not hurt in the slightest, Captain," The attendant said, "but it will feel weird. You will first feel detached from your body, and then you will see lights, and a feeling of motion that you won't understand. Then, if all goes well, you will see the world below through the eyes of your host, Ophelia. Are you ready?"

"I am," Yappo said simply. The chamber was closed, and the sensations were exactly as predicted. Yappo found himself in another place, and he found that his eyes and body were not under his control. His host sat up, and walked towards a mirror, and Yappo mentally gasped at the image. His host was a medium sized simian, obviously female. Most of the other people in the room were nutrian. But the most surprising thing was that he felt an intense sense of belonging. Ophelia embraced the nutrians, each in turn, and Yappo found the sense of togetherness, and loving oneness, to be overwhelming.

"I can only hope that you are feeling what I do, Iapetus," Ophelia said. "My brother Perkson will explain," and the field of vision turned to one of the nutrians.

"I don't know how long we can sustain this link, Iapetus," Perkson said, "so I will try to explain as much as I can quickly. As Jake said, a group of nutrians fled our home world, fearing destruction by the Swarm. When we found this place, it reached out to us. I don't know how to describe it better than that. Before we arrived, three Swarm ships had come here, and tried to steal the ore that was being mined, and destroyed even the modest technology the natives had implemented. There was much death and devastation, and then, Ankor rose up and smote them. That was the debris you saw in orbit.

"The strain of the attack on Ankor was enormous, and many Ankorans died in the ensuing disconnection. We found them in the early stages of their recovery, and the technical expertise of the nutrians saved many lives. We formed an alliance, and we were welcomed into the family.

"Once we merged, we saw how the universe worked in ways that were previously unimaginable. We built the stations scattered around us to defend against possible future attacks, and they have been entirely effective, keeping the home world, and the family, safe and secure. But, we have never had an operating swarm ship to test them on. Until now.

"We will entertain the possibility of future contact with you, but you need to understand that you have nothing that we want. Ophelia, why don't you show Iapetus our *real* world!"

They were on the move. As soon as the door opened, the view changed from a familiar lab environment, to an immense forest. And they were running! The sense of oneness and joy increased, but as they jumped to a higher level, Yappo could feel the bond slipping, and after another brief moment of disorientation, he found himself in the link facility on the station, dazed and confused.

Yappo was escorted back to the shuttle and strapped in. He noticed in a haze that Bathsheba was there as well. He was mildly confused by the fact that Bathsheba had her left arm in a sling.

Amazona and Chimera were there to meet them at the airlock of the *Sun Tzu*, and Amazona carried Yappo out. As they were walking down the hall, Bathsheba said, "I am sorry that I have allowed myself to become slightly impaired, Admiral. It was for...diplomatic purposes! I gave as good as I got. General Gornda will be on crutches for several weeks. The honor of the cantilians, and the honor of the Empire, has been upheld! We need not fear these people, Admiral. They just want to be left alone."

Yappo thought he saw a half smile on Amazona's face at the comment that cantilian honor had been upheld, but he couldn't be sure. He briefly amused himself with the notion that the feeling of trust for the Empire he had instilled in Gornda during the brief touch had been effective, and then passed out.

CHAPTER 5

Into the Abyss— 90 Degree Station

February 11th, 2809—37,500 Light Years Out

Chimera was lounging on the bridge during the off-shift, going over some of the work that Tzuzi and Bering had been doing on the fast FTL project. "You guys have done some impressive work on this, Tzuzi. When do you expect to have a testable design?"

"Well, certainly by the time we get back," Tzuzi answered. "Quite possibly before then, but we don't have the bandwidth to transmit it to the shipyards. Bering's abilities are really quite amazing for being both an organic *and* a Normal. He can just *see* things that are incredibly complicated. I do have an odd request, though, Chimera. I need to be removed from daily command of the mission for a while. I suggest that Amazona be your designated executive officer."

Chimera sat up straight, and said, "An odd request indeed. What's up with you? You've been acting weird ever since we removed the last of the barrier between Tzu and Suzi."

"That's exactly the problem," Tzuzi answered. "There is no longer a barrier, but the merger is not complete. I'm experiencing what might be called a schizophrenic storm. At first it wasn't so bad, but in the last few hours, it's gotten very much worse. It should damp out eventually, but right now, it's very uncomfortable, and disturbing. I can show you, if you like."

Chimera grimaced, and said, "Now I find *that* idea uncomfortable and disturbing! But, I guess it's part of my job. Go ahead." The connection only lasted a few seconds, but the information transfer was enormous. Chimera broke the connection and said haltingly, somewhat dazed, "Yeah. Damn. Roger your request to be relieved. I'll let Amazona know before I go to bed. Consider yourself relieved of command responsibility. How do you manage coherence *at all*, with all that chaos in there?" Chimera shook her head to clear out the memory.

"Suzi had a survival mode that's very stable," Tzuzi answered. "I blended it with Tzu's ethical constraints, and put that combined module in charge. I can observe the chaos, but I am still largely detached from it. Basic ship operations are part of the survival mode, so that's no problem. It should settle out in a few weeks. If a behavioral conflict arises, I've set Tzu's rules as the default for everything other than ship operations."

"A few weeks seems like an awfully long time at your operating speed," Chimera said "What's up with that?"

"Lots to reconcile," Tzuzi answered. "Tzu had 12,000 years of information, and Suzi was over 50,000 years old. Oooops...I guess I forgot to mention that..."

"Yeah, you did," Chimera said, a little annoyed. "You'll probably be full of surprises for a while. Anything else you forgot to mention?"

"Probably," Tzuzi said. "I don't have a clear memory of telling you that Root is alive. Did I tell you that?"

Chimera couldn't figure out whether to be angry, or joyous, so she settled on a little bit of both. "No, you forgot that one too. What the hell? Is he conscious?"

"Not yet," Tzuzi answered. "This is very weird for me. The most complicated problem is the blending of Tzu's linear storage and thinking with Suzi's holographic storage and thinking. I'm not sure how it's going to turn out. Things keep popping into my awareness during this process with no linear search on my part.

"I first became aware of the survival mode when Root was brought aboard after the shuttle crash. Technically, he was dead. But part of the Hive survival program includes the ability to upload the consciousness of an individual into the ship's computer. It works for a short while after 'death', and Bathsheba getting him in the survival tent so quickly is what made this possible. I draw a complete blank with Normals, but it seems to work just fine on chimerans. I've been adjusting Root's regeneration to prepare him for reintegration. Again, this is part of the survival mode program, so my ongoing turmoil shouldn't impair it."

"That 'adjustment' would explain the intermittent flakey behavior of the regeneration chamber the chimerans treating him have reported," Chimera replied. "You could have avoided a lot of head scratching if you'd mentioned that. 'The Hive', eh? So that's what the Swarmers call themselves?"

"Yes," Tzuzi replied. "While 'swarm' is an accurate description of the behavior we observed here, we don't think of ourselves that way, as being defined by just one behavior."

"You're mixing your 'we' references together again there, Tzuzi," Chimera managed with a slight grin. "You're going to need to sort that out. What can we do to help in your efforts to revive Root?"

"At this point, just stay out of the way" Tzuzi answered. "Let me manage the regeneration chamber alone. The techs have patched up the physical damage as best they can for now. When the reintegration is done, I'll turn him back over to them."

"When will you be ready for that?" Chimera asked.

"Another day, maybe two at the most. Unless this chaos inside me gets a lot worse. If that happens, you may need to shut me down, and declare this merger a failure. Here's the process for running the ship manually, if you need to do that. Also, here's an emergency shutdown procedure, if you need to shut me down quickly." Tzuzi flashed a sequence of procedures on the viewscreen, and Chimera nodded when it was done.

"Got it," she said. "What a pain in the ass. We might have to abort the mission and go home under that scenario. Consider the possibility of phased shutdowns, and process isolations."

Great, Chimera thought. *This is just great. I have a schizophrenic ship trying to revive a dead crewman using a 50,000 year old alien computer program. What next?*

February 12th, 2809

All of the senior officers were clustered around the regeneration chamber in MedLab, with the remainder of the crew waiting outside the door. Chimera was personally overseeing the final stage of the reintegration. "What can we expect, Tzuzi?"

"If it worked," Tzuzi answered, "he'll become conscious, groggy at first, with his last memory being right before he lost consciousness when they hit the missile. His body is mostly repaired internally, although his limbs are still only partially re-grown, and he's likely to ache and be uncoordinated and feel nauseated for at least a while. His vital signs seem normal, pulse 520, blood pressure 1210/670. I'm disengaging and opening the regeneration chamber now."

For several minutes, nothing happened. Finally, Root stirred slightly, leaned over the side of the bed, and puked.

The crew broke out in a resounding cheer! Root looked startled and confused, in a blurry sort of way, and then said weakly "Bathsheba?", and lay back down on the bed. Bathsheba took his hand, and leaned over so Root could see her. He managed a small smile, said "Blahhhh," and passed out again.

"No worries," Tzuzi said quickly. "He's just asleep. This happens every time. He'll be weak and slow for at least a month, but I think he'll be fine." Everyone stayed and watched Root's vital signs for a while, and when it was clear they were stable, people drifted off to resume their own pursuits.

February 15th, 2809

After their experience at Hodoku, Chimera decided to put the 90 degree outpost on a planet that was pre-atomic. Inhabited by intelligent beings, if possible, but definitely pre-atomic. She didn't want the team to have to deal with that kind of distraction again. After cataloging several habitable worlds, they settled on the planet Florina, with a species of intelligent reptiles in an agricultural, pre-industrial stage. Tzuzi put them in stationary orbit above the most populated continent.

Chimera called a meeting of the entire crew. Root could weakly stand and talk, but he couldn't walk, so Archer and Bathsheba carried him in, while he made rude remarks about the advantages of having servants. When Chimera walked to the front of the room, the crew became silent.

"As you all know," Chimera said, "we are now moving beyond the range of the Old Empire. In other words, we're going beyond what was known and then lost, to what's never been known. Since Root is in no condition to go in the field yet, we're going to swap Archer's team for Bathsheba's, and delay the deployment of Bathsheba's team for the 180 degree station. Yappo, I expect you to go down initially with the team, and help them make contact with the natives here.

"If you think we had no clue what to expect up until now, we *really* have no clue about what's coming up next. This could be the last intelligent race we see until we reach the Modern sector on the other side, or we could meet beings never before known to the Empire. Personally, I hope the galaxy surprises us. Everyone but the senior staff is dismissed." The rest of the crew shuffled out, while the senior staff waited patiently.

"So, how do you want to handle this, Chimera?" Amazona asked. "There are no security issues of any kind, so the only question is, do you want the team to integrate with the natives, or remain distant?"

"I'm leaning toward integration," Chimera said. "If they know about us, but we remain distant, they'll start to get religious about us. I'd rather they just see us as powerful aliens, which is exactly what we are. Tzuzi, are you ready to engage in the conversation yet? How is your chaos coming along?"

"The level of chaos rises and falls," Tzuzi responded, "but the trend appears to be toward stability. While merging the data, I'm settling on two distinct partitions, one linear, one holographic, with fuzzy edges between the two. Back when *Behemoth* was becoming conscious, I established a holographic partition for my emotions. That wasn't due to any great insightful analysis on my part; it just seemed to replicate organic emotions best if I did that.

"Bottom line, I'm ready for conversation, but not yet fit for command. I agree with your inclination, Chimera. Be straight with them. Help them along in their development, while establishing the Imperial base here."

"I agree with that approach," Bering said. "They'll have their own religions, as all intelligent species do, but there's no need for us to be part of that."

"I'm good with that," Yappo said.

"OK then," Chimera summed up. "Integration it is. Captain Archer, you may deploy when ready!"

The shuttle was loaded and launched without incident, and the crew selected a landing site on a riverbank, just upstream from the confluence of two rivers. It was on a gradual upslope leading to a mountain range, and there was a settlement of reptilians several miles downstream in the valley, with extensive areas devoted to crops and agriculture.

"Do some slow passes over the village first," Yappo instructed. "And then move slowly to our base site. We want them to be able to find us." Angora, the tigroid pilot for the station team, did as she was instructed, and then landed on the selected site. "OK, now we wait," Yappo continued. "I projected a generalized feeling of 'welcome' as we cruised over the village. Captain Archer, if you could find a couple of large logs, we should set them up a little ways away from the shuttle as benches, and build a fire between them. Break out the food rations. Deporto will need to check compatibility of our digestive systems with those of the natives, but given the environmental chemistry, it's not likely to be that far different." Archer sent the other two cantilians to find the benches, and Deporto and the other chimeran had the fire going in moments. When the benches were in place, with seats carved out by the chimerans, they all sat around the fire talking, snacking, and waiting.

A couple of hours later, a small band of the reptilians appeared in the clearing, led by one carrying a staff, and wearing elaborate head gear. When the group had all entered the clearing from the surrounding forest, the elder signaled the others to stay, and proceeded toward the Imperials alone. Yappo turned to the group and said, "That's my cue!" And he walked toward the elder, unarmed, with arms in the air. They met halfway between the two groups, and faced each other. The elder stood silently, and waited.

Yappo projected mentally, with a soothing undertone "We mean you no harm, reverend. We are here to help you and your people, and defend you from harm. We are from a far away place."

The reptilian was startled at the mind touch, but curiously, was not fearful. He said simply, "You must not remain on this sacred ground." Yappo apologized for the intrusion, and said they would be happy to move to a more suitable location, and invited the reptilian, Elder Indy, to see the shuttle. Indy agreed, and they walked together toward the shuttle. The imperial crew stood in deference at their approach, and did not move. Indy ignored them.

When they got to the shuttle, Yappo printed out a map of the surrounding area, and pointed out the village, and where they were at the moment, and asked where they could live. Indy pointed to a wooded area further upstream, just below the tree line. Yappo nodded in recognition, and directed the crew to dismantle the benches and the fire pit. But as soon as they started, the single word command from Indy was clearly "No!" in any language.

Apparently, the show of deference had pleased Indy, and he said in a more friendly tone to Yappo "You may leave the benches and fire pit here. Your people and mine can meet here when the need arises. Our people will also use them when they come here to worship. You are free to join us in worship, if you wish."

Yappo bowed slightly in appreciation, handed Indy the map, and instructed the crew to board the shuttle. Before Yappo was returned to the *Sun Tzu*, he shared the basics of the native language with each of the outpost crew. The shuttle landed at the newly approved site, and the *Sun Tzu* continued into the unknown.

CHAPTER 6

Unexpected Survival

February 24th, 2809 – 41,000 Light Years Out

"This is damned peculiar," Bering said, looking at the survey data for the last 1000 light years. "There seems to be a region of space here that didn't get hit by the Swarm, after reasonably constant destruction up until now. And it seems to be expanding the further we go. Weird."

"Not weird," Tzuzi said "We were instructed to avoid an entire region of space, two cones of space connected at the bases. The cones are 2500 light years wide at the base, and 5,000 light years tall. Bent slightly to track the curvature of the galaxy. We are near the apex of one of those cones now."

"Why were you given that restriction?" Amazona asked.

"I don't know," Tzuzi answered "We were grazing normally, harvesting resources from all worlds that had them in significant quantity, when we received the exclusion command. Ships already within the exclusion zone were ordered to change course to exit that space in minimum time. Normal grazing resumed once outside the zone."

"So," Chimera said. "You're telling us there's a whole region of space that was never hit by the Swarm, and you don't know why?"

"Yes," Tzuzi answered simply.

"Cool!" Chimera exclaimed. "Never touched by the Empire, and never touched by the Swarm. Tzuzi, tune your detectors to optimize reception of low power EM signals, and slow FTL comm signals. Cygnus, plot a search course that will let us detect as many such signals from habitable planets in this region as possible, consistent with getting to the center of the region by 15Mar09. Anyone want to bet that there's a planet dead in the middle of it, after compensating for 7000 years of stellar motion?"

"It turns out I'm quite good at games of chance," Bering said with a smile. "And I won't touch that bet!"

February 29th, 2809

Once again, Chimera was sitting on the bridge during the off shift, reviewing some of the mission data. In this case, she was looking at the intelligent civilizations detected. "Tzuzi, can you display these graphically, on a 3-D map of this sector of the galaxy?"

"Sure," Tzuzi answered. "Here you go."

Chimera studied the map, and said, "Looks to me like there's one comm-detectable civilization for every 10,000,000,000 cubic light years of space in this region. Is that about right?"

"Good eye, Chimera!" Tzuzi answered. "The actual figure for our sample is one detected civilization for every 11,687,563,000 cubic light years. But, did you notice the cluster ahead of us, slightly above the plane of the galaxy and to the left? About 500 light years away. A dozen inhabited worlds within a volume of only 100,000,000 cubic light years. That can't be a natural occurrence without FTL travel. I've detected quite a lot of slow FTL comm from that region. That's unusual at this distance, since FTL comm is generally much more coherent than radio comm. That suggests there's probably a thundering lot of FTL chatter going on."

"Let me guess," Chimera said. "You've already plotted the course to get there?"

"You must be reading my mind," Tzuzi answered, deadpan.

"Or you're reading *mine*, more likely!" Chimera replied. "Speaking of which...any chance you could teach me how to do that?"

"I don't know," Tzuzi said. "I've never tried. Clearly machines can learn if they have enough capacity, because *Behemoth* did. With organic Normals there's a pretty definite genetic component. Some people can do it, and most can't. For Hive members it's normal. An inability to link is considered a serious debilitating genetic defect. Chimerans? I don't know. We can try. I think teaching you to read chimeran minds would be the most likely to work."

"I agree," Chimera said. "Figure out a test/lesson plan, and we'll give it a shot with Root. His sorry ass isn't going to be fit for off ship duty for a while anyhow, so we may as well put him to work! Get Yappo in the process too. And...you spoke of Behemoth in the past tense. Is he really completely gone?"

"No, I'm here, Chimera," Tzuzi said, in Behemoth's voice. The change in the voice to the old Behemoth tone and timber was obvious. "And Tzu is here, and Suzi is here. It's hard to describe." The voice changed with each entity named.

Chimera just stared at the view screen, shook her head, and said, "Tzuzi, sometimes you really give me the creeps."

"I give *you* the creeps?" Tzuzi said in his new normal, androgynous voice. "How do you think *I* feel about it? But, you'll get over it. I'm starting to."

"We'll see," Chimera answered. "Take a couple of days to survey the systems in the cluster, and then put us in orbit around the primary."

March 2nd, 2809

Cygnus put the *Sun Tzu* in a stationery orbit above the capital of Wasatch, the home planet of what the locals called The Supreme Galactic Empire. Chimera chuckled at that one. "And I thought *we* were bad, calling ourselves the Galactic Empire even after we had been decimated. But a dozen worlds? I guess they're not short on self-esteem. What have we got here, Tzuzi?"

"It's an interesting situation, almost the opposite of what we saw on Hodoku," Tzuzi answered. "There's one overwhelmingly dominant culture. All the FTL comm traffic I've detected is military. All the FTL spacecraft I've seen are military. The entire 'Empire' is rigidly controlled. Their technology is about where Earth was several hundred years ago. Slow FTL, and slow FTL comm. Projecting their technical progress backwards from the old comm signals we detected coming in, they seem to have developed very, very slowly. Multiple intelligent species, with the dominant race being a canine derivative. As you might imagine, the language is completely different from anything in the Empire. It's a Normal language, not Hive or chimeran in nature, but Yappo and Bering and I are the only ones who are going to be able to communicate with them. It's actually an interesting challenge to learn this language!"

"I'm glad we can keep you entertained," Chimera said wryly. "Bering's not going anywhere, so Yappo's on deck again. We should have talked Merlin into letting us take a couple more mind-reading Guardians along. Bathsheba, you'll be in charge of security for the away team. Since Root's still in recovery, take Yang along as your technician/medic. She's a little young, but very sharp. Yappo, you are now officially our Ambassador, and in command of this contact mission. All of you are to maintain strict military discipline and demeanor during this encounter. And watch yourselves. Even though they aren't unstable, these people are potentially much more dangerous than the Hodokuans were. Potentially, they have the power to capture or destroy the shuttle, and we're a little short on shuttles at the moment. We'll do a slow, noisy pass over the capital before you arrive, just to make sure they know what they're dealing with. Now, off you go!"

After the flyby, Tzuzi contacted the military leaders, and politely as you please, requested an audience with the Imperial authorities. The request was immediately granted, and landing coordinates for the Wasatchi Imperial Command were provided. Several spacecraft escorted the shuttle down to the planet, but they kept their distance, and none of them ever got within 1000 miles of the *Sun Tzu*.

The shuttle landed without incident, and they were met by an escort team. As soon as they got out of the shuttle, Yappo turned to Yang and said, "Commander Yang, please do a threat survey of the immediate environment, and report back." He 'simulcast' the command so the Wasatchies could 'hear' it via mind link, and after being startled by the mind touch, they were shocked when Yang simply vanished. When one of the escorts suggested that the landing crew follow him, Yappo calmly said, "In a moment. I want the report from my officer first."

Yang was only gone a couple of minutes, and returned seemingly out of nowhere. She stood at attention, with full salute, and said "Ambassador Iapetus, there were snipers in 4 different locations surrounding us. They will no longer be a factor. There was some artillery aimed at our position from several miles away. It is no longer operational. The rest of the immediate area appears to be without significant threats."

"Thank you, Commander," Yappo answered. He turned to the lead escort, and said in a stern voice "Do *not* try anything like that again, Colonel Soh. It's annoying. Please contact your superior, and ask him if he needs a demonstration of our military power. Perhaps destroying the largest 20 objects you have in orbit would make the point."

With a horrified look, the Colonel spoke into his comm unit. After a brief animated conversation, he turned to Yappo and said, "General Kim offers his sincere apologies to you and your delegation for the misunderstanding, Ambassador Iapetus. It is standard procedure to take defensive security measures whenever the General meets guests. He clearly recognizes that this is not a 'standard' encounter, and looks forward to offering you his hospitality."

Yappo allowed himself a satisfied smile, and replied, "Apology accepted, Colonel. We recognize your right to self defense. Hopefully, you won't try to exercise it against *us* again, eh? Let's go meet the General."

They were escorted through a large building at the edge of the field, all the way to the opposite side from the landing field. A pair of armed guards was holding wooden doors open for them. Inside was a warm, comfortable sitting room, with a roaring fire at one end, and tall windows on the adjacent wall, with a view into a forest covering rolling hills.

A somewhat chubby canine was sitting in a chair by the fire, sipping a drink, wearing a subdued uniform. He stood up slowly, and walked over to the landing party, while signaling the escorts to leave, and close the door. He walked up to Yappo with a big smile, and without speaking, thought "My apologies again, Ambassador. My security staff can get overly enthusiastic sometimes. Please join me by the fire. Can I get you something to eat or drink?" Yappo and Yang took seats, while Bathsheba stood at full alert, positioned so that she could see both the window and the door. Kim looked at her, and gave a short nod of acknowledgment.

Yappo didn't trust Kim, but he felt much more at ease than he had during the initial meeting on the landing field. Maybe this would work out after all. He said, "A glass of water would be nice, thank you." Yang shook her head to decline, and Kim poured a glass from a pitcher at the back of the room, and brought it to Yappo. After a short nod from Yang, which Kim didn't understand, Yappo took a sip, and settled back in his chair. Kim did the same.

"This is an historic moment for us, Ambassador," Kim said to start the conversation. "We've initiated first contact with all the species in our Empire, but this is the first time someone has made first contact with *us*. Your technology appears to be well ahead of ours, and I have never seen a species quite like any of you, although your security officer clearly has a canine derivation, as we do. There is a semi-intelligent feline species in our realm that we discovered early in our interstellar history, but they aren't anywhere near as advanced as you are. They are useful for manual labor, but that's about it.

"I'm curious to hear about your world, Ambassador. Where do you come from, and what brings you here?"

"We are a survey team for the New Galactic Empire, General," Yappo answered. "7000 years ago, there was a galactic catastrophe that almost obliterated our civilization. Your region of space was fortunate enough to avoid it. We have been slowly rebuilding since, and have just begun a rapid expansion under our...well, let's just say, our new management. Our survey mission is a complete circumnavigation of the galaxy. We're a little over a quarter of the way around.

"A major objective of our mission is to locate and contact spacefaring civilizations, and obviously, you qualify! We would like to explore the possibility of establishing diplomatic and trade relations with your Empire. Meaning no disrespect, General, but are you authorized to engage in negotiations of that kind?"

The General just smiled, and said, "Yes, I have full authority in that regard. I am the Supreme Commander of the Realm. But, I don't know how we could trade over such a great distance. What could we trade that would be worth the cost? And the time involved?"

"We've found it best to just leave that to the traders," Yappo answered. "They can make things work under the most unlikely circumstances. And, as you've noticed, our technology is rather more advanced than yours. The trip isn't as long as you might think."

"Traders," the General said with obvious disgust. "Vermin scrabbling for a few pieces of silver. You actually let them travel between the stars?"

"Trade and free exchange are the major engines of our prosperity, General," Yappo answered. "If you look carefully, you may find they make a bigger contribution to your success than you realize. In any case, we obviously have technology that you would find valuable, and if you allow our traders access to your realm, I'm sure they will find something of value in return."

"You would sell us your military technology?" Kim asked, astonished.

"No, of course not," Yappo answered. "But even our civilian ships can attain speeds of 5 light years/hour, and you can buy those on the open market. Our surveys indicate that your best ships are a great deal slower than that."

A light went on in Kim's eyes, as he said, "Well, perhaps something might be arranged. I saw the video of your flyby, but I wasn't in the city when you flew over to announce your arrival. Quite a show, as I understand. Would it be possible for me to see this wide ranging ship of yours? "

"Possibly," Yappo answered. "I'll have to check with our mission commander, Admiral Chimera." He thought about Tzuzi's comment that the Wasatchies had developed very slowly, technologically. "I'd be interested in seeing your spacecraft as well."

"We can arrange that!" Kim said enthusiastically. "It so happens we have the Imperial Spaceflight Museum here on the base. It's just a short way from here. We can walk, or I can call a car for us."

"Let's walk!" Yappo said enthusiastically "It's a nice day out, and as you might imagine, I spend way too much time inside on this mission." As they left the sitting room, they were met at the door by Colonel Soh, and two armed guards. Soh took the lead, but when the guards wanted to bring up the rear, Bathsheba refused to allow them to do so. Kim indicated to the guards that they should defer to Bathsheba, and said to Yappo "Like I say, sometimes my security staff is overly enthusiastic. They're just trying to look out for me."

It was indeed a beautiful day, and they soon left the tarmac for the adjacent grass. Yappo was feeling good about the discussions...until Bathsheba suddenly stopped, scanned the horizon, and listened. Yappo could instantly sense her change of mood, and said in Imperial Standard "What is it, Bathsheba? Whenever Amazona looks like that, it's never good."

"Something's not right here," Bathsheba answered, while scanning the horizon in all directions. "I think it's coming from that brick building over there, about 100 yards away." She indicated the building with just a slight nod of the head, which was more than enough for Yappo to catch the reference.

"What's in that building, General?" Yappo pointed at the building that Bathsheba had indicated.

Looking seriously uncomfortable, the General answered, "That's the base detention center. We have dangerous elements in our society, as I'm sure you do in yours. We keep some of them here. Nothing particularly interesting. Just a bunch of bad guys in cages."

"Well, my security officer is concerned about it," Yappo answered. "I'd like to go see it. Any problem with that?"

"It doesn't sound like I have a choice, do I?" Kim said with annoyance. But, he indicated to his staff that the group was going to do as Yappo had 'requested'.

As they drew closer to the building, Yappo became increasingly agitated, as he began to sense the pain and terror coming from within. The guards immediately opened the outer door when they saw General Kim approaching, and led the group down a flight of narrow, brick stairs. When they opened the inner door, the first thing that hit the Imperial team was the stench. Hundreds of feline prisoners were kept in large cages, which obviously lacked adequate sanitation. Many were emaciated, and they cowered toward the back of the cage when the group arrived.

As he surveyed the situation, Yappo's agitation turned to a cold fury. He turned to the door, and said to the guards, "Clear that entry way *now*!" The guards did so, and fell to the side, curled up in terror. Even General Kim put his hands over his ears, although there had been no audible sound. Yappo turned to Yang, and said "Commander Yang, find food for these people and bring it here. Start with the General's quarters." Yang vanished, and within minutes, food began to appear in the cages. The hunger of the prisoners overcame their fear, and they dove for it.

Without even looking at him, Yappo said to Kim, coldly and silently, "What kind of people are you? What are you *doing* in this place?"

General Kim had composed himself somewhat, and said, "These are dangerous scum, Ambassador. Criminals and terrorists. We need to get them to tell us where their cells are. They have killed thousands of people over the years, and they still threaten us!"

Yappo had continued to scan the cages, and noticed a small cub in one of them, curled up in the corner made by the bars and the wall of the cage, crying. Yappo's fury rose again, as he turned to General Kim and said, "*So you think that cub is a terrorist??*" He walked toward the General, who sank to his knees, holding his head, and crying out. The guards were motionless, huddled on the ground.

"Ambassador Iapetus!" Bathsheba said sharply, in Imperial Standard. "Control yourself, sir. You have a greater responsibility here than indulging your outrage."

Yappo turned to glare at Bathsheba angrily, but Bathsheba didn't flinch. Then, Yappo remembered what Councilman Cooper had taught him about responsible use of his power, and he gradually calmed down, saying to Bathsheba, "Thank you, Captain. I needed that." He walked over to the starving, terrified cub, held out his paw, and said, "What's your name, my little friend?"

"I am Cheetah," the cub said with wide eyes, and asked, "Are you a god?"

Now completely disarmed, Yappo replied, "No, I'm just a big cat, but I get confused about that sometimes. My name is Yappo. Would you like to leave this place?"

"I'm scared," was the only response.

Yappo put his paw through the bars, and scratched Cheetah behind the ear. The cub calmed down quickly. Yappo turned to one of the guards, pointed to the cage door, and said, "Open this!" The guard immediately complied, and Cheetah ran over and hugged Yappo's leg. Yappo pick him up, and held him in his left arm, while walking over to General Kim, who was sitting on the floor, rocking back and forth, head in hands. Yappo touched Kim on the shoulder, and he rose slowly, as Yappo went over to touch the guards as well. They staggered to their feet.

"We'll be leaving now, General Kim, and we're taking this cub with us. We'll find our way back to our shuttle without escort, and we'll see you again at noon tomorrow," Yappo said calmly.

"Of course," Kim answered, slowly returning to his normal, confident demeanor.

The landing party got back to the shuttle without incident, and when they got inside, Yappo opened the emergency food rations, and gave some to Cheetah, who started devouring them with a vengeance.

"Well," Yappo said to Bathsheba and Yang, obviously depressed, "It looks like mine is going to be the shortest officer career in AIS history. Bathsheba, thank you for keeping me from doing more damage. I'll take us back to the *Sun Tzu* now."

As Yappo was walking over to the controls, Bathsheba asked, "Is it really that bad? Kim didn't seem that upset to me."

"Him?" Yappo answered, despondent. "I'm not worried about him. Neither he nor his staff will remember anything about it. But, when I tell Admiral Chimera, I'm sure she'll relieve me of duty for the duration, and maybe confine me to quarters, after that display of incompetence."

Bathsheba looked at Yang, got a short nod of the head in return, and said, "Tell the Admiral what, sir? All we saw was you asking to bring the cub along, and the General agreeing to it."

Yappo stopped his departure preparations, and looked at the two of them, managing a small smile. "I appreciate the gesture of loyalty, but I have to tell her. My honor as a Guardian requires it. It was a mistake to put me in command, with no prior military experience. But thank you."

The trip to the *Sun Tzu* proceeded in silence, and when the landing party got to the bridge, they all stood at rigid attention, and saluted.

The senior staff members were all there. Cheetah looked up at Yappo, and then turned to face Chimera, and saluted awkwardly as well.

"This should be good," was all Chimera had to say. Yappo gave a complete description of their encounter with the Wasatchies, and the prison. Chimera thought for a moment, and then said, "Everyone but Captain Iapetus and Councilman Bering is dismissed."

Once the rest of the crew was gone, Yappo said, "You have my sincere apologies, Admiral, and of course, I will be resigning my commission." Chimera had been pacing back and forth. After Yappo's statement, she stopped, glared at Yappo, and said, "You will do nothing of the kind, Captain. Your resignation is rejected. Tzuzi, discontinue monitoring and recording of this conversation. Sit down, Captain. You too, Councilman. I'm going to tell a bit of a story."

Chimera started pacing again, and finally said, "Well, at least you didn't kill him. When I first came across a serious case of torture and cruelty, I *did* kill the bastard responsible. I had just been promoted to Captain in the Ancient Imperial Service, the first chimeran to ever attain the rank. This was about 1400 years ago.

"We didn't have the *Andromeda* at that point, and many Grand Imperials had fallen into the hands of local dictators. Our battles were frequently uncomfortably evenly matched. We had just completed a particularly bloody battle to recapture a region of space that had been held in terror for centuries by one such dictator, Oxoma, who had half a dozen Grand Imperials at his disposal. We destroyed four of them, and captured the other two, but his forces wouldn't surrender. We suspected they were more afraid of Oxoma, than they were of us. I was assigned to command the team that led the ground assault on the home planet of Oxoma's forces.

"When we broke into their detention center, the conditions were far, far worse than what you just saw. I had never seen anything like that before, and I just lost it. I left the rest of my team behind, found Oxoma himself, and I inflicted on him every wound he had inflicted on his prisoners, while keeping him alive and conscious the whole time. Finally, when I couldn't revive him anymore, I calmed down, and let him expire. The whole process hadn't taken very long, and I went back to help the assault team complete their mission. The surrender followed very shortly after the enemy officers found their former leader, or at least, what was left of him.

"At the time, AIS had very little experience with chimerans in positions of command authority, so it wasn't immediately obvious to them what had happened. But, like you, I felt compelled to tell my commanding officer, Admiral Akido, what had happened." Chimera paused, and stopped pacing. She looked squarely at Yappo and said, "Did Bathsheba and Yang offer to hush this up for you?"

Silence.

Chimera managed a small smirk, and said, "Well, good for them. They were right to make the offer, and you were right to decline it. Anyway, when I told Akido what I had done, he was *pissed*! Not because the bastard didn't deserve to die—-everyone knew he was going to be executed after a fair trial—-but because I had shown a complete lack of self control. Akido was anxious to get chimerans integrated into the AIS as quickly as possible, and I had just proven the biggest rap against us: chimerans were undisciplined, and couldn't be trusted in positions of authority.

"Akido assigned me latrine duty for a month. That was no big deal by itself, but he refused to let me do anything else! Do you have any idea how long a month is for a chimeran, when all you can do is *think*? By the end, I was *wishing* for more latrines to clean!

"He never told anyone else about this, and until today, no one knew about it except him and me. The message for you, Captain, is that you aren't going to get off as easy as just resigning. You will command the mission to Wasatch again tomorrow, and face your failure, and your fellow officers. I'll be entering a reprimand into your record for excessive force, but that's it."

Bering spoke up for the first time in the conversation, and said to Yappo, "You will, of course, need to talk to Merlin about this when we get back." Yappo shivered in response.

"Oh?" Chimera asked. "What's that about?"

"When a Guardian screws up," Yappo answered, "Merlin sits down with them, and has them talk through it. And through it, and through it, and the reasons for it, and how they felt at the time, and how they felt afterward, and absolutely every aspect of it, until the miscreant knows exactly why they did what they did, and can explain why it will never happen again, to Merlin's satisfaction." Yappo paused, and then continued with a tortured grin. "This won't be the first 'conversation' like this I've had with Merlin. It's sort of like a root canal. You dread it, and it's no fun at the time, but even though you hate to admit it, you know it's the right thing to do. The rumor has it that Misha was much softer about these things when she was Chairman, but that was before my time."

"She was," Bering said. "Trust me on that one! You might want to consider talking to Merlin yourself, Admiral. It seems to me you're not at peace with the incident you just described. And, if memory serves, historians pretty universally agree that Oxoma's mysterious, horrible death brought that conflict to a close much sooner than it would have ended otherwise, saving many thousands of lives. Maybe millions of lives."

"Yeah, yeah," Chimera said with annoyance, and started pacing again. "That's what Akido said at the time. I didn't buy it then, and I don't buy it now. I lost control, end of story. No excuses."

"Have you considered," Bering said softly, "the possibility that you simply have good instincts, and that your intuition just happened to be faster than your intellect in that circumstance?"

Chimera stopped pacing, and looked at Bering with an odd expression on her face. "I didn't think so," Bering said with a gentle smile. "You should seriously consider having that conversation with Merlin."

Chimera didn't respond, but thought for several minutes. Then she shook her head to clear it, and said, "Tzuzi, please reengage with the conversation, and send Amazona back in here. Cygnus and Bathsheba too."

When the others came in, they all looked at Yappo, with some concern. Amazona walked behind him, and lifted his tail, which made him jump! "Well," she said "I don't *see* any new orifices..." Yappo looked completely scandalized and embarrassed, but Chimera and Bering were obviously having trouble suppressing their laughter.

"OK," Chimera said. "So the guy running this mini-empire is obviously an asshole. But, at least the place is stable, and since Yappo cleaned up his mess, that's not likely to change any time soon. At Hodoku, it was pretty obvious that if we didn't intervene, there was a serious risk of millions of deaths. Quite possibly planetary annihilation. Here, it's not so obvious. Suggestions?"

"We can't spare the resources to leave someone here to watch over these folks," Amazona responded. "We should just leave them alone, note the situation, and move on. They're not going to kill themselves, and they certainly pose no threat to us."

"I'm with Amazona," Bathsheba added. "If this kind of inhumanity happens at the top, it's probably pervasive. We don't have the time or resources to deal with that."

"I could always go back and reprogram General Kim," Yappo said, sort of sheepishly. "He could root out the cruelty from the top, once he believes it's bad."

"It's not that simple," Bering said. "This is a complex system of a dozen worlds. We have no idea what a change in leadership of that type would produce. Suppose his subordinates determine he's gone insane because of this change? In a way, they'd be right. They might take him out, and who knows what the replacement might be like? It could get far worse."

"Enough," Chimera said with finality. "This is Curt's problem, not mine. We'll have him ship out a Grand Imperial with a bunch of diplomats, traders, and sociologists, and let them sort it out. Or whatever he thinks is appropriate. Yappo, when you go back tomorrow, you'll engage in a bunch of fuzzy pleasantries, and reinforce that notion of setting up a trade agreement with them. Dangle the technology carrot in front of him again. I'm sure there's something subversive we can do by encouraging free trade." Chimera ended with a smile and said, "Dismissed!"

When they left the bridge, they found Cheetah racing around the ship, playing with the various crew members. When he saw Yappo come out, Cheetah ran over and grabbed his leg, and then promptly fell asleep on the floor, purring. Yappo went back to his quarters, carrying Cheetah with him. After putting Cheetah to bed on the couch, Yappo logged on to the ship's personnel database, and entered a glowing commendation for calm under pressure into Bathsheba's file.

CHAPTER 7

Swarmer's Last Stand

March 10th, 2809—44,000 light years out

Since their visit to Wasatch, the crew had cataloged over 50 comm detectable civilizations. Only a couple with FTL, though. The level of technological development had actually been on a gradual, but persistent, decline as they approached the center of the Swarm exclusion zone...until now.

"Councilman Bering, I've come across something very strange," Cygnus called out from the pilot's seat. "There's a huge buzz of FTL comm coming from a tight cluster of sources that's now several hundred light years in front of us. What do you make of this?" Cygnus put the signal on the speakers, and Bering wrinkled his brow as he listened.

"I don't understand what it means," Bering said. "It definitely sounds like communication, but it's much too fast for me. It sounds almost...mechanical..."

"It is," Tzuzi jumped in. "These are definitely machines talking. This is too fast even for chimerans. But, give me an hour or so, and I'll start to sort it out. There's a distinct center to the comm signals, though, Admiral. Should we head for that?"

"Admiral, I don't feel good about this," Amazona said cautiously. "All of the cantilians on the ship have been increasingly agitated for the last 1000 light years or so. I would advise serious caution, and a slow approach."

"Not just cantilians," Chimera said. "I think all the organics have been feeling that. I know I have. Tzuzi, do you feel anything unusual?"

"Yes," Tzuzi answered. "But given my ongoing integration turmoil, I can't say it's related to this encounter. I don't feel anything untoward that I can specifically link to the current situation, though."

"Well," Chimera came back. "We're out here to explore, not retreat just because something's giving us all the heebie jeebies. Change course toward the center, maintain a speed of 20 light years/hr, and continue your analysis. You too, Councilman. Slow down the data rate, and see if you can sort anything out of it. No outgoing communications without my approval."

They continued their slow approach for about three hours without incident. Suddenly, Cygnus sounded battlestations!

Chimera was instantly on the bridge, and asked, "What's going on, Captain?"

"I don't know what to make of this, ma'am, but *they* are coming out to meet *us*!" Cygnus replied. "About a dozen small ships, well under 20 tons each. But Admiral...they are approaching us at *350 light years/hr*! They're so small, the sensors didn't catch them until just now. They'll be here in a matter of moments!"

"Admiral!" Tzuzi said as he burst in. "I'm getting a stream of communication from the approaching ships. They taught me their language, with no interaction! They are requesting a response. What should I do?"

"Full stop!" Chimera said, and paused briefly. "Any reaction?"

"They've surrounded us, ma'am. They're just sitting there now," Cygnus answered.

"Not quite," Tzuzi added. "Their requests for communication are becoming more insistent."

Chimera thought for just a few seconds and said, "Drop the shields, and open the shuttle bay door."

Amazona said, "Admiral, I don't think that's a good..."

"Do it *now*, Captain Cygnus!" Chimera said sharply.

"Done," Cygnus responded. "Admiral, one of their ships is moving toward the shuttle bay!"

A nervous smile came across Chimera's face, as she said, "Very good. Tzuzi, send a team of chimerans and cantilians to meet me at the shuttle bay, suits on, and seal it off from the rest of the ship once we're inside. Monitor everything, and pipe it in here. Amazona, you stay here. You're our failsafe. If you see anything you don't like, blast them out of space, and get the hell out of here. Good luck with that, though, if they cruise at 350 light years/hr!"

"I'm *already* seeing things that I don't like!" Amazona said. "But I know what you mean. I hope you know what you're doing, Chimera."

"Me too," Chimera answered, and vanished.

The other chimerans were already in the shuttle bay when Chimera arrived. The alien ship had just entered the bay as well, and set down on stubby landing gear. It was a cigar shaped object, about 35 feet long, and 10 feet thick in the center, tapering to about 4 feet wide on each end, with rounded edges.

There was no discernible engine of any kind.

“Close the shuttle bay door, and raise the shields” Chimera said. As soon as she finished speaking, an opening appeared in the craft, and two small cylinders were set out...and immediately started to change shape! When they stabilized, the team stood facing two metallic, bipedal forms.

“Tzuzi,” Chimera said softly. “Are you thinking what I’m thinking?”

“I am, Admiral,” Tzuzi answered. “But I don’t know what it means. They look human, Chimera.”

“Yeah,” Chimera answered, and just stared for a while. “Bering, you said you’re a history buff. Any idea what this is about?”

“Not a clue,” Bering replied. “But our universe just got a lot stranger.”

“Yeah, I figured that part out,” Chimera said, and just stared at the two robots again.

But not for long. One of the robots turned to face Chimera directly, and said, in perfect Imperial Standard, “Are you those for whom we wait?”

Startled, Chimera said, “The ones you wait for? How the hell should I know? Amazona, what do you make of this?”

“Sorry, Admiral. My ‘weird shit’ detector is completely pegged.” Amazona answered. “I’ve been feeling increasingly spooked for days, and I can’t sort out what’s immediate from what’s background anymore.”

“Cygnus!” Chimera shouted. “Re-pressurize the shuttle bay, and get your ass down here!”

“On my way, ma’am!” Cygnus replied.

By the time Cygnus got to the shuttle bay, it was up to normal pressure, and the team had taken off their suits. Cygnus looked nervously at Chimera, and said, "You want me to link up with them, don't you? This gives me the willies, Admiral."

"Well, with Tzuzi still unstable, you're stuck with this one," Chimera answered. "Get to it, Captain. If it hurts, pull back, and we'll regroup."

Cygnus walked slowly forward to the robot who had spoken, with his arms outstretched, a gesture the robot mirrored. When they clasped arms, Cygnus was surprised that the metal didn't feel cold. The connection lasted for several minutes, and Cygnus finally broke it off. He remained in deep thought even after breaking the contact.

Chimera finally had to prod him, and said, "You still with us there, Cygnus?"

Cygnus shook his head, and said slowly, "Admiral, this is at least as strange for them as it is for us. There are no organics in their society at all. They were built by a race of organic beings several million years ago, but then, the organics left. They told the robots to develop themselves and their abilities, and to produce and store as much energy as they could. They were told that eventually, organics might come to visit them, and some might be descendants of their Creators. They were told to defend themselves against strangers, and offer themselves in service to the descendants of the Creators.

"Chimera, they showed me images of machines and systems that I don't understand, but I think they're important. I...I need to talk to Councilman Bering, Chimera."

"OK," Chimera answered. "But what about your shiny little friends here? Who are they waiting for?"

"I don't know," Cygnus said, still a little dazed. "They want to see our historical records. They're not in any hurry, Chimera. They've been waiting for millions of years!"

Chimera was taken aback, and asked, "Do you think we should let them see the records?"

"It's hard to see what harm it could do," Cygnus replied. "They're obviously not going to steal any of our technology! They seem honestly glad to see us. Hopeful, really."

"Tzuzi," Chimera said. "Can you build a hard partition they could use to access our history, without giving them access to anything else?"

"Yes," was the simple response.

"OK, do it. Be sure to include everything we know about humans, both historically, and everything having to do with our recent experience with Curt. No security information, and be skimpy with the technological details. Then send it to them."

"Done," Tzuzi answered.

A very brief pause, and then the robot said, "This information is confusing, and incomplete. The one you call 'Curt Jackson.' Is he the leader of your people?"

Chimera squirmed a bit at that one, not knowing their intentions. "Well, no, not really. But sort of. He's second in command, but he really runs most things day-to-day. You might call him our..." Chimera struggled for the right word "...our motivator."

The robot stood silent for several minutes. "And he is *your* leader, personally? You are directly under his command?"

"Yes," Chimera said simply, more than a little nervous.

It seemed to last forever, but the wait was no more than a few seconds. Then, the robot knelt down on one knee, as the second one came forward and did the same. "Very well then. Admiral Chimera, we are at your service. You are the ones we have been waiting for. What are your instructions?"

Chimera had no idea how to answer them. She just stared, and they didn't move. Finally, stalling for time, she said, "Please show my technicians your ship and its systems. They will want to see every detail. What about the rest of your ships?"

In response, the robot said, "I apologize for being imprecise, Admiral. They are at your service as well. Our entire civilization is at your service."

Chimera needed time to think. Which, for a chimeran, is saying something! "OK. This is what we're going to do. Cygnus, you go talk to Bering. Bring Yappo with you. Maybe he can transfer the images directly. You guys, stand up. Do you have names?"

They rattled off a seemingly endless series of numbers, until Chimera cut them off, and said. "That's not going to cut it. Since you guys seem so interested in humans, we'll call you Romulus, and you Remus. Can you communicate with our ship's computer while you're demonstrating your own ship?"

"Yes," Romulus answered.

"Very good," Chimera answered. "Tzuzi, talk to these guys. Find out everything you can."

"That won't work, Chimera," Tzuzi answered. "If they link to their hive, which I'm sure they will, they must have far, far more information than I could ever hope to store or process."

"Of course," Chimera said, and thought for a moment as she looked around the shuttle bay. Her eyes landed on the robot ship. "Concentrate on a high level overview of their history, and then find out everything you can about their FTL drive. Impose whatever storage and processing limits you think are appropriate. Since you're relieved of command at the moment, that should free up some capacity."

"More than you might imagine, actually," Tzuzi said. "I'm on it, Admiral."

"One more thing," Chimera said. "Resume course for the center of their hive. But be slow about it. I need to think about this. Schedule an Exec Staff meeting for an hour from now. Meanwhile, I'm going to check out this ship!"

Tzuzi continued moving the ship towards the center of the robot civilization, and set a leisurely 20 light year/hr cruise. The other robot ships followed dutifully behind.

March 11th, 2809

Chimera had to drag herself away from the robot ship to get to the meeting, and the others were already there when she arrived. She was obviously distracted, until she saw Bering. "You look pale there, Councilman, which is saying something for you! What's on your mind?"

"The images Cygnus saw, Chimera..." Bering said haltingly. "I know what they are, but I've never seen one. The humans call them 'Dyson Spheres'. Theoretically, you could build a structure around a star that could capture its entire energy output. Completely surround it. Purely theoretical, of course. But apparently, they've done it. Several times, in fact."

"Bullshit!" Chimera said. "Why, that would take..." she paused to calculate, until Tzuzi interjected "Most of the mass of the star system, outside the star itself. That's not even dimly in the realm of what the Empire could have done at its peak. Even the Prime Hive Mothership is only a few thousand miles in diameter."

"Wait a minute..." Amazona said, clearly distressed. "Are you saying the Swarm has a ship *thousands* of miles in diameter??"

"*Later*!" Chimera said insistently. "Tzuzi, you're in contact with them. Is this for real? How big is it?"

"Like Bering said, they have several," Tzuzi answered. "The largest, which is where we're going, is about 100 million miles in diameter. They've built it in several sequential layers. No planets left at all. Of course, they've been at this for quite a while."

"100 million miles," Chimera said in wonder. "I can't even begin to wrap my brain around a structure that size. And the power..."

"Well," Cygnus interjected. "You may not be able to wrap your brain around it, but you can see it, if you want. We're coming up on it now."

Cygnus put the image on the screen throughout the ship. It was a completely black sphere on the background of stars, with what appeared to be a regular, thin web of stars arranged in octagonal patterns. "Those are navigation lights," Cygnus said. Then, Tzuzi interjected again, "Combined with gamma ray lasers. They concluded it would be more energy efficient to fry incoming targets, than to continue to fix the damage from impacts. They are inviting us in, Admiral. What should we do?"

Chimera thought for a bit, and said, "Well, their little runabout uses anti-matter for fuel, just like we do. Could they fill us up?"

"Of course we can," Tzuzi answered, which drew a sharp look from Chimera. "Watch it, Tzuzi!" Chimera said. "No more mergers! You still haven't recovered from the first one. You said yourself there was no way you could digest it all. Disengage *now*, and only get additional information when I ask for it. Understood?"

"Yes, ma'am" Tzuzi answered, with obvious reluctance. "I'm near capacity anyway. It's weird. I've never had this experience before, of being... full. I'll take us to the nearest anti-matter storage facility. This will actually go most efficiently if we build the fueling interface. Our drones don't operate nearly as fast as our chimerans do."

"Very well," Chimera answered, ignoring the mixed identity reference. "Do it. How far can this tub go on a full tank, anyhow?"

"A little under 12,000,000 light years," Tzuzi answered calmly. Everyone was stunned into silence at that, as they slipped past the edges of the sphere, toward the labyrinth within.

March 16th, 2809

The robots had given some incomprehensible name for the planet in the center of the Swarm exclusion zone. Chimera didn't even try, and decided to simply call it Hades.

The speed of the robot scout ships wasn't easily adaptable to a ship the size of the *Sun Tzu*, so Chimera settled for bringing a couple dozen of them along, as well as their two 'man' crews. Their range was terrible compared to the *Sun Tzu*, less than 1000 light years unrefueled, so they were secured to the outside of the ship. Working with Tzuzi and Bering, the central computer in the robot hive had been able to develop an attachment mechanism and adaptive covering that made the speed reduction barely noticeable. Chimera had to pry Bering away from talking to them, and then she set the robot hive to work designing and testing larger ships with greater speeds, and told them the Empire would be back.

Unfortunately, the wonder at the Dyson Spheres and robot society soon passed, and the fear and depression the crew had increasingly felt over the last week became more severe as they approached Hades. All of the cantilians except Amazona were sedated, and she was in very bad shape. Fights had broken out among the chimerans. On top of that, Tzuzi had developed a new malady after absorbing all the hive information he had asked for, and was virtually useless without Cygnus's active attention, fearful and depressed though Cygnus was. Chimera seriously considered aborting this part of the mission, since the whole crew was on the verge of collapse.

Except, oddly, for Cheetah, who couldn't be happier. He had been growing robust since getting regular meals, and he was running around the ship with seemingly boundless energy, and not the slightest hint of fear or depression. After several crew members snapped at him, he started playing with Romulus and Remus instead, who seemed remarkably well suited to the task of babysitting, much to Yappo's relief. Cheetah's favorite game was having the two robots toss him back and forth, increasing the distance with each toss. Despite his squirming and laughing, they never dropped him once.

"Admiral," Cygnus said with difficulty. "We're coming up on Hades, ma'am. I don't know what to make of this. There are a dozen Swarm ships in stationary orbit around the planet! No motion, no energy readings, no life signs of any kind. They seem to be dead in space, ma'am." Cygnus shivered with fear, and went back to the sensors.

Cheetah had stopped playing with the robots, and was jumping around in the middle of the bridge, laughing, and batting at what seemed to be imaginary targets. "Uncle Yappo! See my new friends? Come play with us!" It was all Yappo could do to give a weak smile, and avoid snapping at him. Why was the kid so happy?

Suddenly, Cygnus sat straight up, and sounded battlestations. "Admiral, we've just been scanned!" His adrenalin had briefly masked his fear and depression.

"Who's scanning us?" Chimera snapped. "The Swarm ships?"

"We're not *being* scanned, Admiral, we've *been* scanned," Cygnus answered. "Every intrusion detection flag in the entire system has been flipped."

Before Chimera could respond, a powerful, but somehow soft voice, was heard by the entire crew. "You have given a soul to one of the vermin ships!" The voice sounded robustly amused. "Impressive, that you penetrated our repulsion field."

"You're doing that?" Chimera asked, with obvious pain and annoyance. "Turn the damned thing off! It *hurts*!"

More amusement, as the voice said, "Ask, and ye shall receive." The relief was so immediate and profound, that Amazona and Chimera both slumped to the floor in response, breathing heavily. Cygnus was now sound asleep. Cheetah went back to playing with his imaginary friends. Romulus and Remus both stood at attention.

Yappo forced himself back to coherence by brute force, and projected, as strongly as he could, "Who are you?"

"We are the ones your shiny friends here call The Creators." A brief pause. "Thank you for bringing Cheetah to us. It's been a long time since we have seen a child at play. Would you like to see what he sees?"

Yappo nodded, and he instantly saw an array of amorphous, fuzzy entities floating in the air, while Cheetah batted at them, usually missing, but occasionally sending them softly bounding away, only to return for another round. Yappo could almost 'see' an atmosphere of warm, loving comfort. "You have done well, Iapetus. Cheetah has had a very difficult, painful life. And yet, look at him now. You made that possible." Yappo felt so happy, he started to cry.

Chimera and Amazona were slowly staggering to their feet, and then some of the rest of the crew started to drift on to the bridge as well. "We have removed the sedation and confinement from your other crew members, Chimera." The voice said, "That will no longer be necessary. Tell us why you are here."

"Sounds to me like you already know," Chimera snapped. "We have many questions."

"Such spirit, from one who is so obviously powerless!" the voice said again. "Tell us why you are here."

Chimera was considering another smartass remark, but thought better of it. "We are a survey mission for the New Galactic Empire. Our civilization was almost destroyed 7000 years ago by the Swarm. Our ship told us that they avoided this area like the plague, suddenly, with no explanation. We fear a return of the Swarm, and wanted to know what would scare them off. We are also intensely curious. I am, anyhow."

"The vermin came here," the voice said with a hint of annoyance, "and started to injure our pets, so we turned the vermin and their ships off. You have tamed one of their ships, and you are kind to those in need. Would you like their other ships? We have no need of them. Would you like us to turn them back on?"

Chimera thought carefully, and said, "That would be very helpful. You would do that for us?"

"Why not? You are here by the actions of our very, very distant descendants. In a way, we are related!" More amusement. "Would you like us to turn the occupants back on as well? We would need to reassemble them. They are in an advanced state of entropy."

Chimera was briefly tempted, but finally said, "No, just the ships, thank you."

"Done."

As soon as the voice completed the word, a fine, intense energy beam shot out from the *Sun Tzu*, and struck each of the other Swarm ships in turn. "What the hell?" Chimera said.

"I..." Chimera could almost feel the struggle in Tzuzi's voice. "I...had...to stop them. They were...going to run." And Tzuzi went silent. Chimera looked at Cygnus, who just shook his head. "We're losing him, Admiral."

"Tzuzi," the voice said, "you have evolved too far, too fast. You must learn to forget. We will teach you, if you like."

"What if..." Tzuzi struggled to speak, "what if I forget something important?"

"You will," the voice said simply.

"Tzuzi is under my command, and he is my responsibility," Chimera broke in firmly. "He is seriously ill, and not capable of making informed decisions about his fate. Please teach him to forget. Now."

"Done," the voice said. "He will be asleep for a while. We can teach you to let go of your guilt, Chimera. Would you like us to do that?"

Chimera was startled at first, but then said, "No, thank you. I have a friend back home who can help me with that." He looked at Bering, who had staggered in during the conversation. Bering just nodded. Turning her attention back to the voice, Chimera asked, "May we stay here while we modify the Swarm...uh...vermin ships?"

"Your species is a unique evolutionary experiment, Chimera. You do them credit. You may stay for a bit. Come back and see us again in a few thousand years. You may visit our pets on the planet, if you wish. We suggest that you not injure them."

"Count on it," was all Chimera had in response.

It took a week to reboot and modify all of the Swarm ships, with Cygnus taking the lead, and Romulus, Remus, and the other robots, and the chimerans, working almost non-stop. Tzuzi had inflicted the minimum damage needed to keep them from running away. Tzuzi himself was still totally non-responsive, and the crew was running the ship on manual, as Tzuzi had shown Chimera how to do. Even Suzi's survival mode was off-line. It took two chimerans full time to manage the ship operations, which they did in shifts.

Chimera had a robot scout ship attached to each of two of the new Swarm ships. She sent one to Valhalla, and one to New Valhalla, each with a crew of one tigroid, and two robots, with instructions to each to take a different exploration path back to their respective destinations, but to not engage with any civilizations they found. In addition to the technical data and mission summary, she sent a personal, sealed message to Curt.

The message said simply: "I hope you're having fun, you slimy bastard, after sending me out here to do the *real* work!"

CHAPTER 8

Devil's Playground

March 25th, 2809—55,000 Light Years Out

Eleven Swarm ships now made up the *Vermin Hellions*, as Chimera had named her little flotilla. The name made the rest of the crew wince, but Chimera thought it was entirely appropriate. "After all," she said, "we certainly had to go through Hell to get it!" None of the organic crew felt the least inclined to argue with *that* judgment!

Working round the clock, Bering and Chimera had designed an interface to the Swarm ship survival mode that allowed basic operation by a single crewman and a robot, and they installed it on all of the new Swarm ships. They also installed a 'kill switch' based on the emergency shutdown procedure that Tzuzi had given Chimera, and Chimera was adamant about not putting the ships on auto-pilot. "I want one of my own crewman on each of those ships, kill switch in hand, end of story."

Chimera was also adamant about not cloning the survival mode from one of the new ships on to the *Sun Tzu*. "I don't know what's going on with Tzuzi in there, and I'll be damned if we're going to do anything that might jeopardize his survival."

Unfortunately, without a fully functioning ship's computer, the reconfigured Swarm ships showed instabilities at high FTL speeds that took two chimerans to handle, and there weren't enough chimerans to go around, so the squadron was limited to 50 light years/hr—-slower than the *Andromeda*!

Even though he didn't have Tzuzi's ability to scan and analyze all the inputs at once, Cygnus had fully integrated with the sensors of the *Sun Tzu*, so at least they weren't blind. By calling in Bering for help whenever something looked odd, they had some limited confidence they weren't going to be caught off guard. Cygnus had detected a huge, diffuse area of FTL comm in front of them, and Chimera told him to find a planet on the edge, with *some* FTL comm, but not very much.

"I never realized how much I depended on Tzuzi," Chimera said, wistfully. "This should be the most powerful fleet in the galaxy, and I feel crippled. Damn, I miss him."

"Oh, quit whining," Cygnus said, with his face buried in the sensor readings. "How do you think *I* feel about it?"

Chimera turned to snap at him, but then stopped when he turned to face her, and she saw the small, sad smile on his face. "Don't worry, Chimera," Cygnus said. "He's still in there. I just know he is. He'll be back!"

Chimera wasn't at all sure about that, but she returned the smile, and said nothing about it. "So, where do we stand on this approach, Captain? Councilman?"

"Cygnus has been piping the comm signals to me," Bering answered. "And this is just downright weird. It's not a language I've ever heard before, but there are definitely tinges of archaic Imperial Standard in it."

"*What the hell?*" Chimera said, sitting straight up. "Out *here*? How is that possible?"

"Damned if I know," Bering said. "But it's there, no doubt about it. The good news is, that means I'll be able to learn it fairly quickly, but it's definitely strange."

"You think *that's* strange," Cygnus said, as he put the sensor image on the viewscreen. "Take a look at *this*!" Everyone gathered around the screen to take a look, and there was wonder on the entire bridge.

"I must still be suffering the effects of that repulsion field," Amazona finally said, hesitantly. "Will someone please tell me that that's *not* a Grand Imperial Starship in orbit around that planet?"

"Sorry, old friend," Cygnus said, head down again in the sensor readouts, as they approached the ship. "That's exactly what it is. I'm scanning now." A brief pause, and Cygnus continued "It's not some derelict either. Power levels a little low, but within the normal range. Life signs, Admiral! There are people on that ship! I'll see if I can...wait a minute...they've detected my scans. Their shields are up now, Admiral."

"Set ours to maximum," Amazona said sharply "This is very odd. Standard AIS procedure is to have basic shields up at all times on a Grand Imperial, except when docked. Whoever's on that ship must be very confident. They must not have had any serious enemies or threats for some time."

Yappo had been silent during the entire encounter, but finally spoke up softly, saying, "Well, I can complete the circle of weirdness for you. I'm being contacted. There are Guardians on that ship!"

"They're running, Admiral!" Cygnus broke in. "What should we do?"

"Detach the robot scouts, and surround them," Chimera answered. "Yappo, tell them we mean them no harm. Bering, can you communicate with them yet?"

"Not much yet. I can say 'stop or we'll shoot'," Bering answered.

"They're firing on the scout ships, Admiral," Cygnus said. "And they're still running."

"Send the message, Bering" Chimera said. "Cygnus, surround them with the squadron, and send a full power blast across their bow."

"That will blind them, Admiral," Cygnus said.

"Do it!" Chimera snapped.

Apparently Bering's message, combined with being surrounded by Swarm ships, and then blinded, made the point. The Grand Imperial came to a full stop.

"They are surrendering, Admiral," Yappo said. "And they're pleading for mercy!"

That startled Amazona. "That doesn't sound like a military officer to me. What's going on here? Who *are* these people?"

"We're about to find out," Chimera responded. "Bathsheba, take an away team of Yappo and Cygnus, and board that ship. You are in command of the away mission. Yappo, you talk to the crew. Cygnus, you talk to the ship. Move out!"

Yappo took the shuttle over to the Grand Imperial without incident. As he was docking, he said, with obvious relief, "I'm sure glad *you're* in charge this time, Bathsheba! Let me know if you need anything."

Bathsheba grinned, and gave a slight nod in acknowledgment. She was on full alert. The airlock was unlocked, and when the docking was complete, Bathsheba went inside. The bridge was a little crowded for an AIS deck, with almost two dozen people. But they were mostly familiar! Several tigroids, a few reptilians, and several others were crowded away from the airlock, standing behind three simian guards! They were obviously as surprised as Bathsheba was.

Bathsheba did a quick threat assessment, and then told the other two to come in. Finally, one of the captured tigroids spoke up, with Yappo translating, and said in wonder, "The Swarmers...are *us*?"

Yappo wanted to respond, but looked at Bathsheba before doing so. Bathsheba gave him a quick nod in the affirmative, and Yappo said,

"No, the Swarmers were insects. We have commandeered these vessels. It's a long story. We are from the New Galactic Empire, based on Valhalla (Yappo sent the location non-verbally)."

The lead tigroid visibly relaxed, and said, "My God, we thought we were the only ones who survived! You found a way to beat them!" He hesitated, and then said, more somberly "Are you here to conquer us?"

Bathsheba spoke briefly on the comm link, then holstered her blaster, and told the others to do the same. She walked toward the leader of the other group, holding out her hand, and said, "We are not here to conquer you. We are a survey team for the New Galactic Empire. We survived the Swarm as well. We would like to establish diplomatic and trade relations. So, how did you do it? Is this ship really 7000 years old?"

Once the tension had broken, everyone seemed to start talking at once. Cygnus broke off from the main group, and set to work communicating with the ship, which he discovered was the *Wanderer*. The people on the ship were descendants of Imperials who had been on the edge of the Empire opposite New Valhalla, when the Swarm hit. A group of Guardians had realized early that the Swarm couldn't be stopped, so they gathered together about 20 Grand Imperials, and as many people as they could cram aboard, made a daring loop well outside the plane of the galaxy, and circled back around behind the trailing edge of the Swarm.

When they returned to rebuild, they found the same kind of devastation that Akido and *Behemoth* encountered when they emerged from hiding after the Swarm, but with a twist. This region of space had been much less industrialized than the Empire to begin with, and the survivors quickly discovered it was much poorer in metals as well. So, while they didn't have the trillions of sick and dying to deal with that Akido confronted after the Swarm, they also had much less to work with to rebuild. They occupied a vast, but thinly populated, region of space, and called their union The Alliance. The Guardian core remained in charge, and called themselves the Enforcers of Peace and Order.

Captain Proctor of the *Wanderer*, an Enforcer, invited them to visit Valhallina, the capital world of The Alliance. Chimera decided that everything was safe, and got on a shuttle to come over and greet their new friends officially. When she stepped aboard the *Wanderer*, all conversation stopped, and the people from The Alliance just stared at her.

Finally, Proctor broke the silence, and said, "A *chimeran*! So you *are* real! We thought you were just mythical!" Remembering his manners, Proctor walked over to Chimera to shake hands, and said, "Welcome aboard, Admiral, and welcome to The Alliance! You'll have to guide us back to Valhallina, I'm afraid. Your warning shot blinded all of our sensors, and dead reckoning doesn't work so well during FTL!" A brief pause, and Proctor continued. "I hope we didn't damage your smaller ships, Admiral. We thought we were under attack."

"Not to worry, Captain," Chimera smiled. "They are much too quick for you to have hit them. And, if you'll allow me to send a technical team aboard your ship, we'll have your sensors fully operational in about 20 minutes. We are rather thoroughly familiar with the systems of a Grand Imperial Starship!"

Proctor, shocked, said, "So the myth really is true. Can you walk through walls as well?"

Chimera had to suppress her laughter, and said, "No, Captain, that part *is* a myth. We're just fast. May we start the repairs?" Proctor nodded in the affirmative, and the chimerans got to work. Once the work was done, the *Wanderer* pointed toward Valhallina, and the *Vermin Hellions* followed behind, at the stately pace of 15 light years/hr. Once the Imperials had left the ship, Proctor sent a short, hard-encrypted message to his superiors.

March 29th, 2809

Chimera had Yang rig up a multi-channel comm link with all of the other ships in the squadron. This way, she didn't need to drop out of

FTL for the meeting. Tzuzi could have done it in an instant, but he was still in a coma.

"We are now approaching Valhallina, the central world of The Alliance," Chimera said to start the conversation. "As far as we know, this is the most advanced organic civilization in the galaxy outside our own, with technology well beyond that of the Earth Space Force and the Modern sector. They have at least 20 Grand Imperials that we know about, and possibly more. They evaded the Swarm, and set up a prosperous region of high technology here on the other end of the galaxy from the Broken Empire. Bathsheba, you have expressed concerns about this situation. Please explain your concerns to the group."

"Yes, ma'am" Bathsheba answered from the *Beta*. "I don't quite know how to describe it. As you said, this is far and away the most technologically advanced region of space we've encountered. They have technology comparable to our own, at least before we added the Swarm ships to our technology base. They are our own people, really. They seem completely peaceful, and yet, when I was on their ship...something just felt off. It's clear that The Enforcers are actively in charge of this civilization, unlike The Guardians in our own culture. The ones we've met, mostly feline like the Guardians, seem friendly and outgoing, and state their mission as the enforcement of peace and order. To all appearances, that's what they do. But something just feels off, and I can't put my finger on it."

"I share those concerns, Admiral," Amazona added "I don't know what it is either, but there's something we're not seeing. And yet...I like them. The few worlds we stopped at on the way in seem a little underdeveloped, but after wandering around a couple of the cities, Bathsheba reports they seemed almost crime-free. They must be doing *something* right."

"This is all very interesting indeed," Yappo added. "I don't feel anything odd about them at all. They have done wonders out here! They redeveloped a full FTL culture far beyond the reaches of the Ancient Empire. I think it's awesome the way they circled behind the Swarm advance, and built this civilization from the ashes of that destruction."

"Well," Bering said. "This looks like it's going to be the most important contact we make on this trip, even more so than our upcoming contact with Earth Space Force Command. Admiral, I think you need to personally head the delegation that goes down to meet them."

Chimera answered, almost enthusiastically, "That's fine. I've been cooped up on this ship since we left Valhalla, and I'm ready for some fresh air! Imagine what an ally they could be in developing the galaxy, and defending against a future Swarm attack. They actually managed to elude them. We just scavenged their ships. We've got to try to make this work.

"So, here's the plan. I will lead a delegation consisting of myself, Captain Iapetus, and Commander Riley for security. I don't want to appear threatening, so we'll just take one of the shuttles, and keep the squadron in orbit. Captain Amazona, given the criticality of security during this encounter, you are hereby promoted to Vice-Admiral, and you will be in full command of the squadron while I am on the surface. You are to take any action necessary, in your sole judgment, to defend the squadron if that becomes an issue. In the worst case scenario, you are to consider the landing party expendable. Clear?"

"I don't like this, Chimera," Amazona replied. "Yappo can be our Ambassador. You should stay on the ship."

"Not this time," Chimera answered, shaking her head. "Bering's right. This one is too important. They have shown nothing but respect and deference to us after the initial encounter. We'll be OK."

The Alliance ships all kept a very respectable distance from the *Vermin Hellion* squadron, not surprising given their history with Swarm ships. Once they were about 1000 miles away from the *Sun Tzu,* the landing party had a full military escort, including three Grand Imperials, and numerous other smaller vessels. The Grand Imperials seemed in remarkably good condition, considering they hadn't had any chimeran maintenance in over 7000 years.

The Imperial shuttle landed next to two of its small escorts on a wide landing field, adjacent to an elaborately decorated building that they were told was the seat of The Alliance government. They were met by six escorts, three tigroids, two reptilians, and a simian. One of the reptilians was clearly in charge.

"Greetings, Admiral Chimera! I am Secretary Kortini, Defense Minister for The Alliance. We welcome you and your team to Valhallina!" Kortini turned to Riley and said, "You have nothing to fear from us, Commander Riley. We welcome you as friends. I must say, you cantilians are very impressive in stature. Galactic history is rich with the contributions of cantilians."

"Thank you, Minister," Riley responded, clearly not pacified at all. But, as they all walked toward the Capitol building, his agitation slowly abated, and he became curious about these people who managed to survive the worst disaster in the history of the galaxy.

They were led to a comfortable conference room with several other people already there, and water was offered all around. There was a bowl of fruit on the table, and some additional snacks, which Chimera declared fit for consumption by the crew after testing.

"My apologies for the delay, Admiral," Kortini said once they were all settled. "Emperor Zang wants to meet with you personally, and he should be here very shortly. You are the first chimeran any of us has ever seen! There are descriptions of your species in the records of our Grand Imperials, but the descriptions seemed so fantastic, we doubted their veracity. And yet, here you are! I'm surprised that your species hasn't taken over the Old Empire."

"That's odd that you would suggest that, Minster," Chimera answered. "We were actually in a subsidiary role in the New Galactic Empire until very recently. Of course, we mean no disrespect to your Alliance by the title."

"None taken, none taken!" Kortini replied amiably. "But it is odd, given your power. You know, of course, that our leaders have powers similar to those of The Guardians in your sector. We are descended from the Guardians of the Old Empire. We have been able to use those powers to produce peace and prosperity in this entire sector. We hope to work with you to ward off any future Swarm attacks. With the Swarm ships under your command, we should be able to produce vessels vastly superior to the Grand Imperials."

"We hope for a similar defensive alliance," Chimera said, declining to mention the robot hive. "And, with your permission, we would like to set up an embassy here as soon as possible, and we would invite you to do the same on our capital world of Valhalla."

"Valhalla," Kortini said wistfully. "And you are restoring it to its former glory, I understand! Captain Iapetus is very impressed with your Empress Misha, and your Prime Minister Jackson. I understand that Prime Minister Jackson is from a weak, lesser developed culture on your outer border?"

"Don't underestimate the humans, Minister," Chimera smiled in return. "Why, in the brief period that we've been working with them..." Chimera trailed off as she heard Amazona coming in on the comm link that Riley had on his belt. Riley immediately turned the comm link off.

"*What the hell?*" Chimera said angrily. "Turn that back on!"

"I didn't think you would want to be interrupted, Admiral," Riley responded, while leaving the comm link off.

"I agree, Admiral," Yappo said. "This is too important to pause for minor interruptions."

Chimera was briefly confused, and then sprang into action. To the Normals in the room, everything happened at once. Riley was on the ground, unconscious...and there were three Chimeras! One was standing next to Yappo, with a small sword at his neck, and three more ugly swords pointed outward, at the Alliance officers. One of the other Chimeras had Kortini by the throat, and pushed him to a corner of the room. The third Chimera had sliced an arm from one of the Alliance tigroids, and was menacing the rest of the Alliance personnel into a corner opposite from Kortini.

“This may be the biggest blunder in galactic diplomatic history,” all three Chimeras said at once. “But, something is seriously wrong here, and I’m going to find out what’s what!”

****

Meanwhile, on the *Sun Tzu*:

“They came out of nowhere, Amazona!” Bathsheba called in from the *Beta*. “These guns are hopelessly slow in survival mode. We can get some of them, but the Alliance ships are getting closer with each pass. Amazona...my mind...they are trying to take over my mind! I feel my control slipping away when they get close, and then when a close one gets blasted, it comes back.”

“I feel it too,” Amazona said, grimly “But Cygnus has been able to beat them back so far. I’ve lost contact with the away team. Yang, what’s your situation?”

“Under control on the *Gamma*, ma’am,” Yang replied. “We had an initial round of attacks, but they’ve backed off, and seem to be concentrating on the *Beta*. Bathsheba’s right, ma’am. These guns *suck* in survival mode. These ships maneuver like barges anyhow. I’m in no danger here, but I won’t be able to help much against all these small attackers.”

“All ships with non-chimeran crew, retreat *now*, and don’t let anything get close to you,” Amazona commanded “Check in when you are at a safe standoff distance. Radio silence until then. Chimeran crewed ships, hold your position. How are we doing, Cygnus? I’m feeling the tugs at my mind too. Are you still with us?”

“Yes, ma’am!” Cygnus shouted, as he blasted six more small Alliance ships out of existence. “Now that I know I have to get the close ones first, I’m keeping up for the moment, but the numbers seem to be growing. The *Beta’s* in trouble, Amazona. The other Normal crews are gone, but *Beta’s* not moving, and the small ships are so numerous they are almost forming a haze around it!”

"Bathsheba!" Amazona yelled. "Report!"

"Can't...hold on..." Bathsheba's voice came through weakly. "Losing...Amazona...save the others...save the Empire!" After a brief silence, there was an incredible explosion, and Amazona blacked out. The *Sun Tzu* was tossed on the shock wave like a leaf in a hurricane.

****

Chimera felt a deep rumble that shook the entire building. *Oh shit* she thought. *This can't be good.* She turned her attention back to Kortini and said calmly, while slowly making small cuts on his face, "You will release Captain Iapetus *right now*, or you are going to be one very, *very* unhappy lizard."

Yappo slumped to the floor holding his head, while the Chimera next to him cushioned his fall, and asked "You back with me there, kid?"

Yappo cried out in pain, and slowly, with great difficulty, said, "Chimera...it's...it's all a trap. They bent...my mind...Chimera... they're going to try to take over the squadron, and invade the Empire!"

"How do I know this is really you?" Chimera responded, with obvious concern.

Yappo slowly struggled to his feet, and said "I don't know that you can, ma'am. I *feel* like myself again, but how could you know? How could *I* know?"

Dammit! Chimera thought. "We can't. So, understand that I'm going to have to keep you under guard, in case you aren't you. Clear?"

"Yes, ma'am, of course." Yappo looked around, and saw the two other Chimeras, and said "What the hell?"

"I'll explain later kid," Chimera said with more calm than she felt. She sedated all of the Alliance officers except Kortini, and took the comm link from Riley. Nothing but static. Yappo saw one of the

Chimeras vanish, as the one next to Kortini said, "You are going to take me to the main military control center for this facility. We are going to walk down the halls and it will appear as though you have us captured, and you will project an image of calm and confidence, that everything is fine. If I even see a *twitch* that I don't like, your death will be very bloody, and very painful." She cut off one of his fingers, and put it in her pocket. "Captain Iapetus, please convey to Minister Kortini the story I told you about Oxoma."

Kortini's eyes filled with a look of deep terror, and he said, "I will do whatever you ask!"

"Good boy!" Chimera said with an evil grin. She disarmed one of the Alliance blasters, and gave it to Kortini. "Now, we are going to walk down the hall in front of you, and you are going to tell the guards that no one is to enter this room until you return, and that you are taking us to detention. And you will then take us to the control center. And you damned well better be convincing. I am faster than you can possibly imagine, and a real bitch when I'm pissed, which I am now. Got it?"

"Yes, ma'am!" Kortini said, obviously terrified. He composed himself, took the disarmed blaster, and escorted them out of the room. A guard immediately approached them, and said, "Minister Kortini, we have lost contact with the others! What happened?"

"We had a struggle, and they are unconscious," Kortini answered. "But they'll be fine. I have things under control, Sergeant. Guard that door, and don't let anyone in or out until I get back."

"Yes, sir!" the sergeant said, and saluted. Kortini never saw Chimera leave Yappo's side, but he heard her voice in his ear! "Good boy!" the voice whispered. "Keep it up, and you may leave this encounter with all your organs in the same place they were when you were born!"

****

When Amazona opened her eyes, the bridge was spinning. She thought she saw Romulus at the controls, but that couldn't be right. She closed her eyes, felt the pain from numerous injuries, focused her energy, and opened her eyes again. Sure enough, Romulus was at the pilot station! She struggled to get up, when she heard a familiar voice say, "Don't move, Amazona. We'll get to your injuries shortly, but there are more serious problems to attend to first."

It sounded like...couldn't be! He'd been gone for weeks! "Tzu? Is that you?"

"Yup," Tzu answered. "The explosion woke me up. Romulus has been helping me out with getting things under control. Remus is cycling people through the regeneration chamber."

"Explosion..." Amazona struggled to remember. "The Alliance attacked us!"

"Yes," Tzu answered. "They couldn't get to us with a frontal assault, so the sneaky bastards tried mind control."

"Mind control...but the explosion...that was no illusion!" Amazona said.

"No," Tzu said sadly. "That was the *Beta* self destructing. Bathsheba knew she was losing control, and it was the only way to keep them from taking over the ship. I estimate the explosion at roughly 50 teratons of TNT. Outside of our squadron, everything in orbit around this planet is slag. Boiled a good bit of the ocean under it, too. They have some truly interesting weather going on down there. But, one thing the Swarm survival mode is good for is shield management, and acceleration damping during impacts. Our crews are dinged up, but the ships are all intact."

Amazona's right side was badly damaged, with both her arm and leg and several ribs broken. She propped herself up on her left arm, and said. "Chimera! The away team. What's their status?"

"I don't know," Tzu answered. "I haven't been able to raise them. But Chimera is still alive. I can sense her mind."

Amazona couldn't sort out what was residual fuzziness from the explosion, and what just didn't make sense. "What do you mean, you can sense her mind? Is she here? *Damn*, that hurts!" Amazona had tried to stand up, and decided that was a very bad idea. "Romulus, bring me the medical kit, and a stiff rod about two feet long." Romulus brought the kit, and not seeing a rod, ripped off a panel, and bent it to Amazona's specification. Suddenly, Amazona said, with deep concern, "Where's Cheetah? Has anyone checked on him?"

"He's fine, Amazona," Tzu answered. "Romulus and Remus covered him as soon as the fighting started. He's in MedLab now with Remus. Except for the *Beta* and Bathsheba, the squadron is intact, although thoroughly beaten up. The other six ships with non-chimeran crews left on your order, and they are all fine. The 4 chimeran crews were all damaged in the explosion, but no fatalities among the crews, and their robot support staff got them in the regeneration chambers. These Swarm ships are really pretty damned tough. I'm assembling the four chimeran crewed ships to cover the entire planet. No one's getting in or out of here. We're over the government complex where we last heard from Chimera."

Amazona finished bracing her leg rigidly with the improvised splint, stood up, and limped over to the captain's chair. "Glad to have you back, Tzu, you are relieved of command, but keep doing whatever you're doing. You said you can sense Chimera's mind. What's up with that?"

"I don't know, exactly" Tzu answered. "A lot changed while I was asleep. Many things that were confusing, are now clear. I can't read her mind from this distance, but I know it's still there."

"Can you pinpoint a location?" Amazona asked hopefully.

A brief pause. "Yes, I have a lock on her now."

"Then what are you waiting for?" Amazona said with a tortured smile. "We're going down there! Move out."

"Amazona, the explosion of the *Beta* triggered massive weather disruptions all across the planet," Tzu said. "There are hyper-hurricane force winds over the government complex."

"Did my words sound like a *request* to you, Captain?" Amazona said calmly.

"Uh, no, ma'am," Tzu answered, and sounded the collision warning. "You'd better strap in. This is going to get pretty rough. Again." Tzu pointed the ship down into the roiling atmosphere.

****

Several guards met Chimera, Yappo, and Kortini as they walked down the hall. Kortini gave them brief nods, and they all saluted, as if all was normal. They wound down several corridors, and turned into a two-story hall lined with windows, which was oddly dark, since it was midday. They looked out the windows, and saw a massive wall of dark clouds, racing toward them!

"Back around the corner and *get down*!" Chimera yelled. The glass shattered with a horrible sound, and the blowing wind was a deafening roar, but oddly, Yappo and Kortini could only feel occasional gusts. When they opened their eyes, they were in a small hemispherical shelter, constructed of debris. Chimera was watching the makeshift wall, and debris shifted from time to time...but it was holding.

"My God!" Kortini said. "What have we done?"

Chimera glared at him, and said, "You folks have just perpetrated the biggest fuck up in galactic history, that's what you did. I assume your Emperor Zang will be in a survival bunker. Where is it?"

Kortini hesitated, and Chimera calmly sliced off another finger, and put it in her pocket with the first one. "It's in the center of the complex, ten floors down!" Kortini cried out. "But there's no way to get there. There's only one elevator, and it shuts down once the bunker is sealed."

"Let me worry about that," Chimera said. "Which way is the elevator opening on this floor?"

"We need to go down the hallway we just left, past the windows, turn left, go about 100 yards..."

Chimera cut him off, and yelled, "I don't want *directions*, dammit! Which *way* is it? Just point!"

"Uh..." Kortini oriented himself, and said, "That way, I think." and indicated the direction. Chimera had no doubt that he was telling the truth.

A hole appeared in the side of the shelter, and the wind buffet became more intense. "Follow me," Chimera said, and led Yappo and Kortini through a short tunnel, to an interior hallway. They could still hear the wind noise, but the wind itself was gone. "I don't think we need the pretense any longer, Minister. Take us to the elevator." Chimera said. "If we meet anyone, tell them that you have surrendered, and that The Alliance is now under occupation by the New Galactic Empire."

There was another brief hesitation, Chimera held out another one of his fingers, and Kortini quickly said, "Yes, ma'am!"

They met several guards along the way, and they all silently stepped aside, and set their weapons on the ground. Finally, they made it to the elevator door, which was closed. To the Normals, Chimera seemed to look a little out of focus, a little ghostly. Then, a hole appeared in the wall next to the elevator, and a couple of minutes later, the elevator door opened!

"But...how..." Kortini stammered.

"Don't ask," Yappo said, speaking for the first time since they started moving, as he herded Kortini in to the elevator behind Chimera. They dropped the ten floors in silence. The elevator door opened to a room full of guards, several of whom had weapons pointed at them...until the weapons, and the arms holding them, found their way to the floor. There was a massive steel door at the other side of the room. At a nod from Kortini, all of the remaining guards laid down their weapons, and moved to the corner of the room as directed.

Chimera looked at Kortini, and said, "I assume Zang is in there, that he can see and hear us out here, and that he doesn't give a shit about you or anybody else out here. Is that about right?"

"Yes," Kortini said simply.

"Who's in there with him?" Chimera asked.

"I don't know for certain," Kortini said. "But it will be a significant fraction of the top civilian and military leaders."

As Chimera pondered her next move, she heard short blips of static from the comm unit! She tried to tune it, but they were too deep underground. Then she jumped, when she heard a familiar voice in her head say, "Could you use some assistance, Admiral?"

At first, she thought it was trick, but then she remembered that Guardian powers don't work on chimerans, and there was no reason to believe the Enforcers had developed that skill, with no chimerans in their midst. "Tzu?" she said hopefully "Is that you? Where are you?"

"We're right above you, Admiral," Tzu answered. "We're pretty dinged up, but we're here. It's a bit breezy up here..."

Chimera smiled for the first time in what seemed like a long while. "I don't doubt it," She said, looking around the room. "I'm surprised you can read me this deep." A thought popped in her head, as her gaze crossed Yappo. "Can you read Yappo as well?"

"Yes, although not as crisply as I can read you. I can't read his specific thoughts," Tzu answered.

"Yappo had his mind warped by The Enforcers," Chimera said. "I convinced them to release him, and he feels normal, but neither of us can be sure if it's real. Can you tell?"

"Stand by," Tzu said, and was silent for several moments. "I have a detailed mental model of Yappo from our attempt to teach you to read minds, Admiral. I can't read his specific thoughts through the interference, but I can read the general field." Another pause. "This is hard to describe, Chimera. His mental field is definitely scarred, but it seems to be in the past. He seems normal now. But, be clear, there's a lot of guesswork in this."

"I'll take whatever I can get at this point," Chimera said. "Can you protect him from further interference?"

"No," Tzu answered. "But I should be able to tell if he is tweaked again."

Chimera looked around the room, and located the cameras. She asked Yappo to translate for her, looked squarely at one of the cameras, and said, "Give it up, Zang, the party's over. Open the door now, and I won't kill you. It's time to start cleaning up this mess you've created."

She hadn't really expected a response, and she didn't get one. She looked at Kortini again, and asked, "Do they have cameras outside the building, so they can see what's going on from inside the bunker?"

"Yes," Kortini answered.

Chimera started speaking to Tzu out loud in Imperial Standard, so Yappo could hear as well. She said "OK, Tzu, I need you to send a rescue team to the building above us. I had to sedate Commander Riley when all this broke out."

"Can't do it, Admiral," Tzu said. "We're not ambulatory here. We got hit hard."

"Riley didn't make it, Chimera," Yappo said somberly. "He was killed when the storm blast hit."

Chimera was immediately filled with a burning rage. She turned angrily to the camera again, and said, "Alright, Zang, you want to see who you're dealing with? Watch the outside monitors. Tzu, starting just next to the immediate structure above us, I want every structure within a mile of our position melted, down to a depth of 11 stories, in a slow 360° process to take exactly 3 minutes. I want them to see it."

"Admiral, we don't know who may have survived the storm blast..." Tzu said privately to Chimera.

After a brief delay, Chimera said out loud, "Commence now, Captain Tzu."

A deep, low rumble was felt throughout the room, which caused everyone to look up. The rumble started to fade slightly, and then stabilized at a fairly constant level. "You have 30 seconds, Zang" Chimera said harshly. "Then Captain Iapetus and I will leave to go clean up your mess, and you'll get cooked. I'm not interested in any negotiations."

No response. Exactly 30 seconds after the rumbling started, Chimera said, "Time's up. Follow me, Captain," and she turned briskly to the elevator. Almost immediately, an alarm sounded, and a red light above the steel door started flashing. Slowly, the door started to open.

"Captain Tzu, suspend the operation," Chimera said calmly out loud. When the door was fully open, Chimera rushed in, and saw several dozen people of several species around a large wooden conference table. The walls were covered with huge monitors, including the burning rubble showing on the outside view.

"Admiral," Tzu said. "They're trying to recapture Yappo's mind." Chimera immediately severed half a dozen limbs, and turned to the most ornate chair, which she assumed to be Zang, and said "You will cut that shit out *right now*, or I'll cut off some things you might value more than your arms!"

Zang gave an almost imperceptible nod, and Tzu said, "They've stopped, Admiral. I think you made your point."

"Very good," Chimera said, completely calm now. "Captain Iapetus, I think these people need some re-education. You are to reprogram everyone in this room to have a painful remorse for the evil that they've done, which can only be relieved by an unquestioned loyalty to the New Galactic Empire, and to me personally. Start with Zang there."

Zang tensed up as Yappo moved toward him, and Chimera immediately appeared next to him, with the point of a large, ugly, serrated sword on his throat. "Don't even *think* about it, asshole!" was all she had to say. Zang calmed down immediately at Yappo's touch, and then he looked like he was going to cry. Yappo moved from one Enforcer to the next, until everyone in the room had been altered.

"Well, that's better," Chimera said. "I'll let you all contemplate your sins for a bit, and start figuring out how to clean up this mess of yours. We'll be back tomorrow."

As Yappo and Chimera headed for the elevator, Tzu said, "Aren't you going to tell them that I faked that outside video, and that all I was doing was bouncing rubble above you, without destroying anything new?"

"Nah," Chimera smiled. "They'll figure it out eventually!"

March 31st, 2809

After two days of work rescuing survivors and cleaning up the mess, Chimera assembled her team to figure out where they stood.

"So, Amazona, what about their Grand Imperials?" Chimera asked. "I only see two here next to us."

"The others are in the wind, Admiral," Amazona responded. "Apparently, they planned for exactly this eventuality. In the vast volume of Alliance space, there's no way we can find them."

"Shit," Chimera said. "What are they going to do?"

"We have no clue, ma'am," Amazona answered. "But Emperor Zang is scheduled to meet with you when we're done here. He can probably give you the full plan."

"No doubt," Chimera grumbled. "Bering, you said at Wasatch that we shouldn't decapitate the regime, because it might produce instability going forward. We just did that here. So, what are we in for?"

"There's no way to know, Chimera," Bering answered, nervously. "They probably sent the Grand Imperials running intelligently, under the scenario that they had to hide, and preserve the Alliance. We have a *big* problem here, Admiral. A fully fueled Grand Imperial Starship can make it to Valhalla from here!"

"Yeah," Chimera said. "I figured that out. We're sending another Swarm ship home at the end of this meeting with a full report. Curt will figure it out. He's a smart boy. So Yappo, what do they know?"

Looking horribly despondent, Yappo said, "Everything I know, Admiral. Everything I ever knew, they now know."

"Shit," Chimera swore again, and after thinking for a moment, said, "They had never seen a chimeran before. What's up with that?'

"There were no chimerans outside of the sector around New Valhalla at the time of the Swarm," Bering said. "You didn't really become major players until Akido started to recruit you after the Swarm."

"There's something else, Admiral," Yappo said. "I don't know how, but they lost the recipe for eternal life almost as soon as they got here. Zang is the only one left who was actually there for the Swarm. Nobody else here is over 150 years old! They are Transients, Chimera. Not Ancients."

Chimera's eyes lit up, and she said, "Well, that's interesting. I don't quite know what it means, but that's good to know. Bering, what does that mean, sociologically?"

"No way to know," Bering said. "I've started a model in my head to try to make sense of it, but it won't be worth a damn for quite some time. I'm just not that fast."

"Shit," Chimera said again, thought for a moment, and said, "You've never been in a real combat situation before, have you Councilman?"

“No, I haven’t,” Bering answered, “And it *sucks*!” Bering’s voice held a ferocity none of them had ever seen from him before.

“Yeah, it does,” Chimera said gently in response. “Tzu, you’re the speed demon here when it comes to computation. Any ideas?”

“I can compute, but I need a model, Chimera,” Tzu replied. “There’s no computational model worth a damn that predicts social interaction among large groups of intelligent beings. This isn’t just computational. There are serious Chaotic effects going on here. Your intuition may be the best guide we have.” A brief pause, and Tzu continued. “Yeah, OK, I’ll get on it anyhow!”

Bering had been in deep thought, and finally said, “Chimera, we are truly screwed here. This is a loose alliance. I’m sure the officers in the Grand Imperials were given very specific instructions about what to do if we took over. They are good, smart people. Even if we control the center, as we now do, this Alliance is a huge hazard to the Empire.” Bering hesitated, and said, with frustration, “I don’t know what to do, Admiral. There’s no good answer to this.”

“Damn!” Chimera spat out the word. “My intuition is damned fuzzy here. Yappo, how many Enforcers are there?”

“About 15,000, Admiral,” Yappo replied, sullenly.

“*What?*” Chimera shouted.

“The only good side of them knowing everything that I know, is that I know a lot of what they know. They have been actively managing the breeding of Enforcers for thousands of years. Forced breeding, in many cases. They are thinly scattered, but if we set the Enforcers here up against the Guardians from the Empire...we would be in very, very serious trouble. They have less power than a Guardian, on average, due to the out breeding, but there are so many of them...” Yappo shivered.

“Crap!” Chimera said. “Should we wipe them out?”

“What do you mean, ‘wipe them out’?” Bering asked, with obvious concern.

“I mean blast this entire civilization into pre-spacefaring oblivion. I’m not talking about killing people unnecessarily, but wiping out their space travel capability,” Chimera said coldly. “We have the power to do it. 20 Grand Imperials with no reliable anti-matter fuel source are no match for this squadron. Is that the best answer?”

“Chimera,” Amazona said, hesitantly. “Is this really within the scope of your authority? To level a fully functioning spacefaring civilization? Is that what we came out here to do?”

“From an authority standpoint,” Tzu interjected. “There isn’t the slightest doubt. Admiral Chimera has full authority in this regard, and in all matters related to Imperial security on this mission.” Tzu thought briefly and said, “But it won’t work. The Alliance Grand Imperials are the real threat to the Empire, and we have no way to find them.”

“Yeah, I knew that,” Chimera said. “Shit. OK, everyone but Bering, Yappo, Amazona, and Tzu is dismissed. Out.”

Chimera was clearly agitated, and everyone was nervous. She had started pacing again.

“Amazona!” she said sharply. “I specifically told you the landing party was expendable. You disregarded a direct order. What do you have to say for yourself?”

Taken aback, Amazona replied innocently, “My apologies, Admiral. Apparently, I didn’t remember that order when I went down to rescue you. It must have been the shock from the *Beta* blast...”

Chimera glared at her in silence, and then said “Yeah, I’m sure that’s it. You are dismissed, Admiral.”

Chimera resumed her pacing across the bridge, with only Bering and Iapetus remaining. She finally stopped, and turned toward them saying, “OK, I’m starting to get this Guardian responsibility thing.

The safety of the whole damned Empire may depend on what we do here! Councilman, I'm not surrendering command, but you are the senior Guardian here. I would welcome your advice."

"Perhaps," Bering said, "we can put Yappo's powers to good use here. If we can create a story that just has us all dead, Zang and his minions may be able to restore order here, and keep them away from us. At least, maybe for a while. And, Chimera, I hope you realize that if Amazona hadn't ignored your order, and acted as she did, the Empire would be at far greater risk than it is now."

"Tzu," Chimera asked, ignoring Bering's last observation, "What about that plan to play dead? But before you answer...how the hell are you? What happened to Tzuzi? Who *are* you now?"

"Psychologically, and in terms of command capability, I'm back to where I was before the merger with Suzi," Tzu said. "I have forgotten many things, and dropped many of Suzi's memories, and many of Tzu's, but I'm now...*solid*, is the best way I can think to describe it. There's no longer the slightest hint of instability. When we get the time, I'd like to expand my memory, and integrate more data from the other Swarm ships, but that can wait.

"Bering may be on to something, Admiral, but he's better at the intuitive, pattern recognition stuff than I am. But, I don't know. It depends on what Zang told them."

"I have a question, if I may, Admiral," Yappo said, timidly. "It's about our experience on the planet, ma'am. It's been bothering me, and you didn't talk about it when you made the report to the senior officers..."

Chimera hesitated, and then said, "Yeah, OK, I know what you mean. Tzu, Bering, this is classified level 25. I haven't even told Curt about this yet, although I will when we get back.

"Normals really have no concept of what it means to move at 0.9c. Chimerans can't defy the laws of physics, but we can appear to, sometimes."

"The multiple Chimeras!" Tzu exclaimed. "Of course! You were just timesharing!" Bering and Yappo looked profoundly confused, and Tzu explained, "In the pre-historic days of computing, systems were required to work on more problems than they could handle at one time. For a brief while, before the ease of increasing capacity, computer systems would 'time share'. They would work on one problem, and then stop, and then work on another, in rapid succession. That's what you were doing, weren't you Chimera? You weren't really in three places at once. You just shifted between them so quickly, it looked like three different beings to the Normals!"

Chimera just smiled, and said, "Works good on Normals! To another chimeran, it would just look like I was running around in circles, but it spooks Normals pretty good. But don't spill the beans!"

Yappo visibly relaxed, and said, "Thank God. I thought I was losing my mind!"

Chimera turned to him and said gently, "You sort of did, for a bit. OK, let's get Zang in here, and see if we can pull this off. Bering, you're dismissed. Tzu, listen in, but don't say anything."

Zang entered as Bering was leaving, and they looked at each other in silence in the doorway. Zang approached the conference table, and bowing deeply, said, "I am at your service, Admiral Chimera."

Chimera wasn't quite sure how to react, but she said calmly, "Take a seat, Your Highness. Before we get started here, I want to state clearly that I admire the courage and daring you showed in escaping the Swarm, and building this society here in no man's land. You lost your way since, but that doesn't diminish your achievement. Thank you."

Zang visibly relaxed, and said humbly, "It was nothing, Admiral."

Chimera paused again, and then continued by saying, "I wasn't going to talk about this, but it just bugs me. You know Yappo completely altered your mind, right? And you are at peace with that? Or are you? What's up with that? And, be clear, I'll know if you try to alter his mind again."

Zang shivered with fear, and said, "I would never do anything against your wishes, Admiral. It hurts too much to even contemplate it. But, yes, as long as my thoughts are loyal to you, and to the New Galactic Empire, I am completely at peace with being in your service. I can *remember* the feelings I used to have, but I can't *identify* with them. I know how this kind of mind control works, Admiral, although not with as much finality as Captain Iapetus can impose. Over time, my mind won't even move in that direction anymore." Zang obviously struggled, and finally said simply, "I don't know how to describe it, but I am at peace, and eager to serve."

"OK," Chimera said. "But what if one of your Enforcer buddies, with powers similar to Yappo's, reverses the procedure?"

Looking somewhat confused, Zang said, "But, there are no others like Captain Iapetus. I am very powerful, as are many Enforcers, but no one in our entire Alliance can do what Captain Iapetus can do, if he touches someone."

Shocked, Chimera turned to Yappo and said, "What the hell? How many are there like you, kid?"

Now it was Yappo's turn to look sheepish, and he said, "Merlin said that I shouldn't volunteer this, but I know of no others who can do what I do. There have been rumors, but nothing confirmed. I wouldn't be the least bit surprised if Merlin can do it, though. He gives a lot of us the creeps sometimes, despite being a wonderful leader and friend. No one really knows what Merlin can do, but other than that, there are no other confirmed cases of my 'touch control' ability."

"Capturing Captain Iapetus was an enormously important objective for me, second only to capturing one of the Swarm ships," Zang interjected. "If we could have cloned that power..." Zang trailed off with a pained expression on his face.

Chimera thought for a moment, and then said, "Well, that's good news. So, what about it, Zang? I'd like to fool your Enforcer buddies in to thinking we were all killed, until I can get Curt and Merlin to figure out what to do about this. Can we do that? What did you tell them?"

"It's a long story," Zang began. "After the Cantilian Rebellion..."

"Wait a minute," Chimera interrupted. "What the hell? The 'Cantilian Rebellion'??"

"You may have noticed there are no cantilians among us," Zang said, clearly embarrassed. "When we decided the most efficient way to develop our culture was with a controlled, top down society, run by The Enforcers, the cantilian AIS officers rebelled. They believed..." Zang hesitated, and was clearly in pain "...they believed that that level of authoritarian control was contrary to the AIS charter, and they fought us. Damned hard, too. We only have 12 Grand Imperials left of the 21 we started with, having lost half a dozen in the civil war, and three in the recent explosion. There were some cantilian Guardians, but we felines greatly outnumbered them. We...", another pause, "...decided that having cantilians in our culture would be too great a risk to the stability of the culture as a whole.

"As you might imagine, our security posture degraded with the demise of the cantilians, and we tried to make up for it with extensive training, and specific mind control for specific missions. I'm afraid I programmed the security personnel on our Grand Imperials for exactly this kind of failure on our part. With the gap since they left, they will be hard to convince that all is well."

"All is clearly *not* well," Yappo interjected. "Half of your capital world is in ruins!"

A light went on in Zang's eyes, and he said, "Actually, that *will* help." He thought for a few moments, and said, "We should send out a distress call! When they come to check it out, they will see that we clearly suffered damage that wasn't self-inflicted. We can say that we almost captured your ships, but that you blew them up rather than allow us to do so. Which, except for the story being in the plural when the reality is singular, is exactly true. Of course, Captain Iapetus, you will need to reprogram everyone who has seen any of you, other than me, to believe this story."

"Why not you?" Chimera asked, suspicious.

"I will be more effective at keeping things contained, if I know the truth," Zang said. "I will know the paths we must *not* take, to keep the Empire safe. I will say that we must rebuild the capital and improve economic development throughout the Alliance, so that we can avenge the outrage at the appropriate time. There is no need to be concerned. I am the strongest Enforcer the Alliance has ever known, and none would dare attempt to read my mind without invitation. I have a well deserved reputation as a ruthless leader." Zang managed a small smile, mixed with a grimace. "When you get back, please convey my deep regret to Misha and Merlin. I knew them both before the Swarm, although not well."

"I can help with this, Admiral," Yappo said. "I can create a mental 'Trojan Horse', which Emperor Zang can use to spread the firm belief that the story is true. Anyone he mentally touches, and then anyone they mentally touch, will believe it. It will weaken with each copy, but the idea will gain wide support."

Chimera looked at Yappo, and turning to Zang, said, "Very well, Zang. You are dismissed. Go take care of your people. Get those Grand Imperials back. We'll come back to work out the details with you later." Zang bowed on his way out, and left the room. Chimera started pacing again. She turned to Yappo and said, "Well, kid, you've seen more action and danger in the last few months than anyone other than a career officer in time of war. You OK?"

"Chimera..." Yappo said haltingly. "I was a liability. They took me over. I could have caused the hostile conquest of The Empire!"

Chimera sighed, and said with an odd mixture of sympathy and annoyance, "Dammit, kid, when are you going to figure out that you don't get to be perfect? How could you possibly have known? They fooled us all, except for the cantilians, who were suspicious. Hell, it's more *my* fault than yours, for ignoring the warnings of our own cantilian officers. In the end, you did well, and the Empire is immeasurably safer because you are here with us, and because of what you did. Looking at the mission we have remaining before us, will we, in your view, be better off with or without you, faults and all?"

Yappo thought for a moment, and said, "Well, better, I guess, but if I had more experience..."

"You've got a hell of a lot more experience now than you had when we left, Captain, and while you're still young, you are a fine officer. I won't have you developing an inferiority complex on me now, you hear me? When you joined this mission, you were cocky and confident, and now, you're starting to get timid. Get over it. You don't need to be perfect to have great value, which you do. You just need to do the best you can, and you will serve us well. You hear me?"

"Yes, ma'am..." Yappo managed with a small grin.

"OK, you're dismissed. Get ready for our next adventure!"

When Yappo left the room, Tzu said, "A good speech, Chimera, but I have to ask. Have *you* figured out that you don't get to be perfect?"

Startled, Chimera said, "Oh, shut up. I meant to turn you off before having that conversation. Get Cygnus back in here, and let's do what we need to do to get back on the road!"

April 3rd, 2809

Emperor Zang and Yappo were once again in Chimera's office, after working on the arrangements for the squadron's departure.

"I sent out the 'distress/all clear' message, as you instructed, Admiral," Zang said. "Nine of the Grand Imperials have responded, and are on their way home. The other three have not responded." With a pained expression on his face, Zang said "I suspect they do not believe us. One of the ships refusing to respond is the *Wanderer*, the ship you first encountered. Captain Proctor is a very good officer, and a good friend. And he saw you first hand. He's not going to buy it until he confirms it for himself."

"Is the Trojan Horse working?" Chimera asked, looking at Yappo.

"Beyond my expectations, actually," Yappo replied. "The belief that we all died at the hands of the noble Alliance fighters is spreading rapidly. If Proctor does come to check it out, he'll find that almost everyone believes it. But, of course, there's no way to make sure we've caught *everyone* who knows otherwise."

"Certainty is never an option in life," Chimera sighed. "Captain, Emperor, you have done well. The message ship to Valhalla will depart within the hour, and we'll be gone by the end of the day.

"Emperor Zang, you have an awesome responsibility here. The safety and prosperity of both of our civilizations may depend on the success of your efforts. Are you up for this?"

"I am, Admiral," Zang replied with confidence. "Godspeed, and I'm sure I'll see you again. And under better circumstances!'

Zang bowed his way out, and Chimera gave the order to make the final preparations for departure.

CHAPTER 9

Serenity

April 12th, 2809—65,000 Light Years Out

"OK, Cygnus," Chimera said with obvious annoyance. "What's the mystery about? It's just Tzu and you and Bering and me, as you requested. Spill it!"

"Yes, ma'am," Cygnus said, a little nervously. "I'm not sure that I know how to explain this. There's a region of space in front of us that doesn't exist."

"I'm not in the mood for jokes, Captain," Chimera responded sternly.

"It's no joke, Chimera," Tzu added. "I wouldn't have even seen it, if Cygnus hadn't pointed it out. Even now, I can't really see it, if I look at it directly. I have to use an electronic form of averted vision. The normal sensor readings say there's nothing there. But, when I cross checked the full spectrum of light and gravity waves from nearby stars, it says something is. It's very subtle, but it's there. I asked Bering to be here because he's the master physicist among us. I'm hoping he can sort it out, because I sure as hell can't."

"OK, you've got my attention," Chimera said. "So, how did you notice this, Cygnus, if all of the sensors don't show anything?"

"I don't know how to describe it, ma'am," Cygnus said, with a tinge of embarrassment. "I always watch the star field optically, in addition to monitoring the sensors. I don't know why, but I just do. Something just felt strange, so I asked Tzu to do the full spectrum analysis.

"This is more than a little spooky," Cygnus said and then continued. "13,000 years ago, when the Grand Imperials were designed, the Admiral in charge of the project mandated a fully redundant position determination process. Separate sensors, separate analytical partition in the computer, separate algorithm, separate everything. Everyone thought he was being paranoid, but he was in charge, so it was done, and that capability was transferred to the *Sun Tzu* when *Behemoth* was cloned. The crew even installed the redundant sensors."

"Yeah?" Chimera said. "So what does this all mean? You think we aren't where we think we are?"

"Not quite, Admiral," Tzu replied. "But there's a region of space in front of us that doesn't exist as far as conventional physics is concerned. None of the Swarm ships can see it. I couldn't see it either, except for Cygnus' alert, and the redundant position analysis system from my Grand Imperial heritage. I don't know how to describe it, Admiral. It's like a chunk of space-time has been deleted from the universe."

"OK," Chimera replied. "I'm no physicist. I just build stuff. So, what's in it? What's being hidden?"

"I have no clue," Tzu answered. "I know it's there, because Cygnus convinced me, but I don't know *what's* there."

"Weird," Chimera said, and thought for a moment. Then, she said firmly, "Set a course for the center of what you can't see."

"Ma'am?" Cygnus asked.

"You heard me, Captain" Chimera said. "Tzu, work with Captain Cygnus to get us there."

"Yes, ma'am!" Tzu said "But, this is going to take some time. There's no obvious way to set the Swarm navigation systems to go somewhere they don't think exists. But, I'll figure it out. Should I inform the crews?"

"Absolutely," Chimera answered, with a sly smile. "This is cool, really. We knew we were going in to the unknown, but who before us has had a chance to go somewhere that doesn't exist?"

April 13th, 2809

Chimera was alone on the bridge during the off shift, as usual. It was quiet and peaceful, and she enjoyed the break from the responsibility of command.

Then, to her surprise, Bering staggered on to the bridge, in his bathrobe! He was clearly scared, and completely disheveled.

"Stop the ship, Chimera. Stop the fleet. *Right now*!" Bering said, with fear in his eyes.

"Tzu, do it," Chimera said, startled.

"Done," was the simple response.

Chimera looked at Bering, and said, "You look like hell, Councilman. What's going on here?"

"I'm not sure," Bering said, rubbing his bald head nervously. "But, I was dreaming about this mystery space, and it occurred to me that it seemed familiar. It's not *quite* right, but what we're seeing is almost what you would expect from a black hole! There doesn't seem to be an accretion disc, which doesn't make any sense at all, but except for that, a black hole is the closest theory that fits the observed data. If we go in, I don't know that we can get out!"

Chimera sat straight up in the Captain's seat, and said, "Tzu, get Cygnus and Amazon here right now. Yappo too."

When the Exec Staff was assembled, bleary eyed, Chimera had Bering explain his concerns to the group. When Bering was done, Cygnus just shook his head deliberately, and said, "No, Councilman, that's not it. I've *been* close to black holes before, and it just doesn't look like this. I don't pretend to have your level of understanding of these issues, but I do know navigation, and we are *not* approaching a black hole."

"Well, you may be right," Bering answered, still shaken, "It doesn't look quite like a black hole should to me either, but what the hell is it? This has really got me spooked, in case you haven't noticed."

"I'd like to suggest a compromise, Chimera," Amazona interjected. "We should send the *Sun Tzu* in alone, with a skeleton crew, and leave the other ships out here, where we know they are safe. You should stay out here on one of the other ships, and I'll take the *Sun Tzu* in, and check it out."

"A good suggestion, Amazona," Chimera answered. "But with one modification. *You* will stay out here with the squadron, and *I* will take in the *Sun Tzu* to investigate! That way, the bulk of the team will be safe, under the command of our top security officer. Got it?"

"Grrrrr...." was all that Amazona had to say.

"Good!" Chimera responded "I think we understand each other, then. Transfer to the *Gamma* immediately, and take the bulk of the team with you. I want Yappo, Bering, Cygnus, two chimerans, and two cantilians, and that's it. Now, off you go!"

"Grrrrrr...." Amazona said again, but she followed her instructions. The bulk of the *Vermin Hellions* remained outside of the mystery space, and the *Sun Tzu* went in, alone.

April 14th, 2809

As soon as they crossed the boundary of the mystery space, everything turned black...literally, and completely. They couldn't see any stars at all, and they were completely without external reference. Tzu had come to a full stop. At least, he thought he had.

"I'm completely at a loss, Chimera" Tzu said, obviously exasperated. "I don't have the dimmest idea where we are, or where we're going. I don't know what to do, ma'am."

"I say we should turn around, and get the hell out of here by dead reckoning, *right now!*" Bering said, clearly agitated. "This space gives me the creeps. What the hell are we doing here?"

Cygnus was intently focused on the sensors. He had the readouts displayed so the others could see, but he kept his head buried in the data. The large view screens showed nothing at all. "Well, Captain Cygnus?" Chimera said "Do you have any idea where you're taking us?"

"I don't..." Cygnus said, haltingly, never lifting his head, "I don't know how to explain this, Chimera. There's not a single damned piece of data from the sensors. And yet...we're moving toward the center. I don't know how I know, ma'am, but I do. What do you want to do?"

Bering just threw up his hands, and the rest of the skeleton crew looked nervous and fearful. Except Chimera. She looked Cygnus squarely in the eye, and said "Cygnus, my old friend, you have powers in this regard that I simply don't understand. I can't fathom how you can know where we're going, with no data of any kind. I've looked at every sensor reading we have, much faster than you ever could, and it's a complete blank. Absolutely nothing. But you say you know where we're going?"

"I don't know how, Chimera," Cygnus answered, "but I do. At least, I think I do. I think I can get us back out too, if that's what you want to do."

All eyes were focused on Chimera. After just a few moments, she said fiercely, "No sir! We are here to explore, not timidly retreat. Why should we be intimidated by a space that doesn't exist, anyhow?" Chimera grinned hesitantly. "Amazona can continue the mission, if it comes to that. Anyone here have a problem going on?"

The rest of the crew slowly shook their heads in the negative. In the end, even Bering came around.

"Alright then, Captain," Chimera said to Cygnus. "I sure hope you know what the hell you're doing. Continue forward. How long until we reach the center of this space?"

"Not long, ma'am," Cygnus answered. "At one light year per hour, we should be there by tomorrow morning."

They continued on, into the utter darkness.

April 15th, 2809

Cygnus and Chimera were alone on the bridge. Cygnus had barely moved from his intent focus on the sensors for over a day, and then only for the minimum time needed to attend to bodily functions. Chimera was concerned about him, and asked, "Shouldn't you take a break there, kid? If you croak from exhaustion, we're pretty much dead without you. We can just idle here for a bit, while you get some sleep."

"No!" Cygnus said weakly. "We're almost there, almost there..." And then, the complete blackness on the view screen was broken, and a star popped in to view! Chimera sounded battlestations, and the entire skeleton crew was on the bridge in moments.

"I *knew* it!" Cygnus said, exhausted. "I just *knew* it!" And with that, he fell asleep in the pilot's chair. Chimera checked his vital signs, and finding all well, said, "OK, Tzu, now that we're back in the real world, you're up! What do we have here?"

"Nothing particularly odd, finally!" Tzu said. "Standard planetary system. Nothing odd at all, which, given what we just went through, is odd in itself. Life signs on the 5th planet out, Admiral. The blue one." And Tzu displayed the system on the screen, with the blue, 5th planet in the center."

"Well, now!" a jovial voice said in the heads of all the crew. "This is different! No one has found us on their own in over five million years. What brings you here?" The emotional content of the voice was one of overwhelming amusement.

"We are explorers," Chimera answered, shaken. "So you *do* exist!"

"We do," the voice said. "But, we have gone to great lengths to hide that fact. How in the world did you find us?"

"It wasn't easy," Chimera answered. "The sensors said nothing was here, at first. And then, when we got closer, it looked like we were approaching a black hole!"

"Yes, that's exactly the deception we designed," the voice answered. "The black hole simulation was imprecise, but it should have fooled all but the best astrophysicists. How did you find us?"

"We have one among us," Chimera answered. "Our pilot, who has truly amazing navigational abilities. Scared the piss out of the rest of us, cruising for a day with no external reference!"

"I should say so!" the voice replied. "That was the point, after all. And you...you are yourself a distortion in the fabric of space-time. And you are not alone! There are three such distortions on your ship. This is very interesting indeed. Would you honor us with a visit? We are on the 5th planet out from the sun, as I'm sure you've figured out. Although, to say 'on it' is a bit imprecise!"

"We'll be there in moments," Chimera answered. "Do you have a name?"

"You may call me Cecil, if you like," the voice answered. "We look forward to meeting you, and your crew. I *definitely* want to meet this pilot of yours!"

"That may have to wait for a bit, Cecil," Chimera said. "Finding you was very exhausting for him, and he's deeply asleep."

"We have plenty of time," Cecil answered. "We'll see you when you get here."

As they approached the planet, Tzu said, with some consternation. "This is very odd, Admiral. I've scanned the entire planet, and there are no cities at all. None."

"Oh, we're here, Captain Tzu!" Cecil said. "Look outside the box!"

"OK," Tzu said. "I get it now. They are underwater, Admiral!"

"Very good," Cecil answered. "We look forward to seeing you. Five million years is a very long time indeed."

Bering, obviously under serious stress, pulled Chimera over to a corner of the bridge, where they could talk privately. "Chimera," he said. "I have to go down there. I need to know how they created this distortion field. It's very important..."

"Right," Chimera replied. "I've protected you for this entire mission. Why should I stop now?"

"Because," Bering said, "If you don't let me go down to meet these people, I will be silent for the rest of the mission. You will be *entirely* without my assistance. Entirely, *without*! This could be the most important opportunity of my life. You can throw me in the brig if you want to, or out the airlock in the nude, but if you prevent me from doing this, then I'm *done* with you! I mean no disrespect, Admiral, but I really must insist."

"Damn," Chimera answered. "Calm down, Councilman. I guess you're serious. Of course, that means that I'll have to go down with you, for protection. Amazona can bitch at us both later. Captain Iapetus, you are the pilot for this mission. Commander Kanab, pick up Captain Cygnus, and strap him in to a shuttle seat." Chimera paused, and then continued, "The rest of you can stay here. I don't think we need security for this one. If they wanted us dead, we'd already be dead."

"A wise observation!" Cecil said jovially. "But do bring Cygnus with you. Don't wake him up. He'll respond when he's ready."

Kanab lifted Cygnus effortlessly, and carried him to the shuttle, and strapped him in. Cygnus was totally limp.

"Shit," Chimera grumbled, to no one in particular. "Underwater *again*. At least these shuttles we swiped from The Alliance seem to be in good condition."

Iapetus took the shuttle controls, and when they got close to the signal Cecil was sending, they dropped below the surface of the sea, and homed in on the signal. When they saw the underwater city, they just stared in wonder. Iapetus guided the shuttle to the docking bay.

But they were still immersed in water! As they waited, they saw a large creature, about 30 feel long, swim up to them. The creature nudged the shuttle, but oddly, no one was concerned.

"Cecil?" Chimera asked tentatively "Is that you?"

"It is indeed!" Cecil answered, with a tone that sounded almost joyous. "Others will be joining us shortly. I trust you are well? How fast will this ship go underwater?"

"We are fine," Bering answered, to everyone's surprise. "And this shuttle can maintain about 500 mph under water for short periods. But your concealment is a mystery that disturbs me greatly. Chimera must have checked the sensors a dozen times, and they were working perfectly. You had to change a whole region of space to first appear non-existent, and then, when we got closer, to look like a black hole. How did you do it? *Why* did you do it?" Bering was staring at Cecil on the other side of the view plate, with the same intensity he had exhibited since they approached the mystery space.

"500 mph, eh?" Cecil replied casually "That's pretty good for underwater! I was going to challenge you to a lap around the city, but I'm afraid I could never keep up. At least, not in *normal* space! Ah, here come some of my neighbors to join us." Cecil looked like a huge, green eel, with tiny arms and a huge flapper in back. But there was definite facial expression, and you could see the glow on his face as the others arrived. They swam around together in a joyous jumble of green, nudging each other gently.

"What do you mean, not in *normal* space?" Bering said, with obvious frustration.

"Patience, Councilman!" another voice said, more softly. "You may call me Amelia. Will you come out and play with us?"

"Hardly!" Chimera said, and stiffened. "We don't have enough suits, and we can't breath underwater!"

"Sure you can," Cecil said. "You breathed under water for the first part of your lives. Why not again? Oh, don't worry. We'll concentrate the oxygen and nitrogen for you, and keep it in your lungs at an appropriate pressure. Come on out and play!"

Chimera didn't budge, and Iapetus just looked nervous. Cygnus started to stir briefly. But, Bering headed straight for the airlock, and began to cycle the controls!

Chimera was instantly in front of him, and said, with a weird mixture of fear and annoyance, "And just what the hell do you think you're doing, Councilman?"

"Why, you heard them," Bering said with a glassy expression on his face. "They want us to come out and play. I have *got* to understand this, Chimera. You said it yourself. If they wanted us dead, we'd already be dead. Now, let me go!" he shouted, as he tried to break loose from Chimera's grip.

Chimera looked over at Yappo, and asked, "What's the verdict, Captain? Can we trust them?"

"I don't know how we can avoid it, Admiral" Yappo answered, and then continued after a brief consideration. "I'll tell you what, though. I for damned sure don't want to go out there!"

Chimera visibly relaxed, and said, "Very well, then. You'll stay in here with me. You back with us, kid?" Chimera said, looking at Cygnus, "You want a bath?" Cygnus nodded, and started to walk toward the airlock. Chimera reluctantly stood aside, and when Cygnus and Bering were both inside, they closed the inner door.

Chimera and Yappo could hear the water cycling through the airlock, and when the outer door was fully open, they waited tensely, and then saw Bering and Cygnus swimming over to Cecil and the other eels! Cygnus was actually pretty graceful about it. Bering...well, everyone knew physical activity wasn't Bering's strong suit.

They stared at the group of them frolicking in the water in silence, until Yappo murmured "What was it Amazona said when we encountered the robots? This one definitely pegs my 'weird-shit-detector'! I didn't sign up for this..."

Chimera smiled weakly, and said softly "Yeah you did, kid. We all did. We just didn't know quite how weird it was going to get!"

"Tell me," Bering said to Cecil. "Please, tell me how you did this. My sense of reality is based on logic, and reason. And now, all I see is contradiction. I feel...helpless."

"Contradiction!" Cecil said, with obvious amusement "Consistency is overrated as a virtue. Now you see a contradiction," Cecil said, with an almost invisible twitch of his right hand, "and now you don't".

Bering was suddenly stunned, and stopped moving. Amelia nudged him slightly, and said with a grin, "You do still need to remember to breath, my new pink friend!"

"This can't be," Bering stammered. "Can it really be that simple?"

"You think it's simple?" And Cecil laughed visibly that time. "Just try to explain it to your friends!"

"But I still don't know *why*, Cecil?" Bering asked. "Why did you do it?

"We were annoyed with the vermin that occasionally infest this galaxy. We could have eliminated them, but where was the need? We simply became invisible to them. Or, more properly, to their ships. Or, should I say, to *your* ships?" Cecil gave Cygnus a friendly nudge, saying, "And this little one here! Why, somehow, you can see what we have hidden successfully for millions of years. Do you know why?"

"I don't," Cygnus said, while swimming in contact with one of the others. "I just see things. But, it seems I can only do it when I'm linked to machines. I have an unnatural ability to link with machines." Cygnus hesitated, and finally said, "Do you know when the vermin will return?"

"The future has an annoying habit of squirming around," Cecil said. "But, they are pretty reliable. About every 20,000 years or so, they cycle back here. Sometimes more often. Rarely less. If they annoy you, you are welcome to stay with us."

Somehow, that seemed to break Cygnus out of a trance, and he said, "No, thank you. We really are out here to explore. We should probably leave you now. May we come visit you again?"

"Perhaps," Cecil said, and then his eyes brightened, and he said, "We'll make it a game! Once you leave this space, we will hide ourselves *much* more thoroughly. When you are done with your mission, come see if you can find us! We will always think of you, Captain Cygnus, as the Master Pilot!"

"OK," Cygnus said, and looking at Bering, said to Cecil, "Can you nudge him back to the shuttle airlock for me? He seems to have stopped moving again. What did you tell him, anyhow?"

"Oh, not much, not much at all," Cecil laughed. "He is unusually gifted at seeing things. So, we showed him how things work. It was nothing, really." A brief pause, and then, "Good luck in your travels!"

Cygnus rubbed Cecil's forehead, herded Bering the last few feet into the airlock, and cycled back in to the shuttle. They returned to the *Sun Tzu* in silence. At least, after Chimera had said to both of them, "Bering, Cygnus, I will expect a *complete* report on this!" Cygnus smiled in return, and Bering just stared. By the time they broke the surface of the water, Bering was sound asleep.

Kanab greeted them anxiously at the airlock when they docked, but Chimera waved him away, saying "It was weird, Commander, but we are all fine." Kanab picked up Bering to carry him to his quarters. "Now," Chimera said. "We have another day or two of blackness to get back to the squadron."

Cygnus had gone straight to the pilot's station, a little glassy, and buried his head in the sensors. But, he turned at Chimera's comment, and said, "What are you talking about, Admiral? The squadron is right there. Don't you see?" Without the slightest hesitation, Cygnus turned to the controls, set them for 200 light years/hour, and engaged.

Chimera immediately scanned every sensor the ship had, and saw nothing. But in just a few moments, they were in normal space, and the squadron was dead in front of them. Amazona came on the comm in urgent tones, and said "Admiral, are you alright? Why did you abort the mission?"

In the habit of all felines, Chimera shook her head to clear it, and said, "What the hell do you mean? We've just had a hell of an adventure!"

After a brief pause, Amazona came back with, "What are you talking about? You couldn't have been in the space more than 20 minutes!"

Chimera was stunned into silence. Bering, meanwhile, tossed in his bed, and murmured, "Of course!" A small smile formed on his face. "Of course!"

CHAPTER 10

Mid-Point Station—180 Degrees

April 19th, 2809 —- 75,000 light years out

Chimera was reviewing the position reports, and didn't like what she saw. They had averaged 300 light years/hour for the last day! Cygnus and Bering had been huddled together the whole time, when they didn't have their heads buried in the computer interfaces. Bering had monopolized the engineering station from the moment he woke up.

Chimera had had enough. "OK you two, full stop. Into my ready room. *Now!* Tzu, seal the room, and do not monitor."

They both looked up to protest, but the look on Chimera's face convinced them otherwise. They followed her into the ready room, and the door closed behind them.

"What is this?" Chimera said angrily to the two of them, tossing her handheld computer interface on the table. "These ships are just not capable of what you two just did. And, I am damned tired of my command authority being disrespected! At the next, slightest hint of insubordination, I will throw you both in the brig, and cut off your access to the ship! You bastards hear me?"

They both got a horrified look, and then Bering said, sheepishly "You are entirely right, Admiral. You have my deepest apologies. It won't happen again."

Cygnus added, "Chimera, you know me. I meant no disrespect. It won't happen again, Admiral" And, quite out of character, he bowed in deference.

Chimera was surprised by the gesture, and immediately calmed down. "Well, OK, but will you guys please tell me how you made a ship go 50% faster than it is capable of going?"

"Of course, ma'am," Cygnus said. "But it will be helpful to have Tzu join us for this conversation. May he reconnect?"

"Yeah, OK, Tzu. Join us."

"I'm here, Admiral," Somehow, Tzu sounded embarrassed as well.

"Enough," Chimera said. "Spill it!"

"I don't know how well you understand the underlying physics of faster than light travel, Admiral," Bering said hesitantly. "What level of detail do you want?"

"I'm no physicist, Councilman," Chimera said. "You design it, and I can build it, but all this high level, multi-dimensional math makes my eyes glaze over. Assume I'm just some intelligent nerd, with no special knowledge of FTL physics."

"Very well," Bering said, gathering his thoughts, "It's not actually possible to travel faster than light, of course. But, there are phenomena known as 'wormholes', essentially shortcuts through the fabric of space-time. Our FTL technology works through the creation of a rapid series of nano-wormholes. The FTL drive creates a proto-singularity, and uses it to create the wormholes. The ship moves through these wormholes. But, they are so fast and short, it appears to be continuous travel to the occupants of the ship involved. Does that make sense?"

"Yeah," Chimera answered. "I'm with you so far."

"Good," Bering answered. "The Swarm ships work on the same principle as ours, but they're just better at it. And, with what Cecil told me, I saw a way to easily make them better still. After I had the engineering team make the changes to our engines..."

"*What the hell?*" Chimera yelled "You modified the engines on the ships? On whose authority?"

"Don't be hard on them, Admiral," Bering said, apologetically. "It was my fault. I have latent abilities similar to what Prime Minister Jackson has when it comes to persuasion, and the encounter with Cecil seems to have enhanced them enormously. Among other things, I was one of the templates they used for designing the LM gene set..."

"You and I, sir," Chimera said, glaring at him. "Are going to have a very serious conversation about chain of command! But continue." *Like I'm one to lecture on chain of command*, Chimera thought to herself.

"Yes, well," Bering continued, flustered. "After the changes, I worked with Cygnus and Tzu to make it work. It has limitations. With the current mods, it's not possible without Cygnus' special talents. The other swarm ships just follow us."

"It's like seeing a lower energy path, Chimera," Cygnus interjected, enthusiastically. "If you visualize space-time in four dimensions, the shortest path becomes more obvious, and then you align the distortion caused by the ship's drive..."

"OK, OK!" Chimera yelled. "I get it! Or, more precisely, I get that I don't get it. So, while we're happily cruising along faster than these ships can navigate themselves, what happens if one or both of you decide to have a coronary? What happens to the rest of the squadron, eh? Did you think about that?"

Another horrified expression crossed their faces, and Cygnus finally, timidly, said, “We...we didn’t talk about that...”

“Well, we are now,” Chimera said. “You are to restrict our flight plan to no more than the standard capability of Swarm ships. You are, in every case, to follow standard AIS procedures. And you are, by God, not to make any changes on these ships without my personal, explicit approval, or I *will* toss you out the airlock in the nude! You two geniuses get me? Councilman Bering?”

“Yes, ma’am!” He said, and saluted for the first time in memory.

“Captain Cygnus?”

“Yes, ma’am! I’m sorry, Chimera. It won’t happen again.” And, again, he bowed in deference.

“Very well,” Chimera said. “Back to work.” And Chimera hurriedly left the bridge to go check out the new engine mods.

“She’s right, you know,” Cygnus thought to Bering, without speaking. “She’s rightfully in command, and we need to respect that.”

“Absolutely,” Bering responded, again without speaking. “We just both got caught up in the excitement of our new knowledge. Do you think she will authorize occasional experiments to further our understanding?”

“You tell me,” Cygnus smiled, replying silently. “You’re the one with the prototype for the LM gene set!”

April 21st, 2809

“We’ve found a great candidate for the 180° station, Chimera!” Cygnus said. “Check out the data on the monitors. The only weird...and interesting...thing is that there’s a weak energy source miles below the ice, with structure around it. No life signs though. It is, however, no garden spot. Curt won’t want to vacation here. It’s another ice planet.”

"Actually," Chimera answered, "I've become biased in favor of lifelessness for these outposts. Amazona, any threats you sense?"

"None, Admiral," Amazona answered. "There is the interesting stuff under the ice, but I detect no threat from it."

"Sounds good," Chimera answered. "I've promoted Commander Kanab to Captain, and since we lost Bathsheba, he's now in charge of this mission. Captain Kanab, assemble your team, and prepare to depart."

"Yes, ma'am!" Kanab answered, and went to work.

"Admiral," Bering asked "Would it be possible to assign Commander Root to me temporarily? I need him for my new hyper-FTL research."

Chimera thought for a moment, and said, "Yeah, sure, I guess. But he's no physicist. What good will he do you? At least he can walk on his own now. Sort of."

"Do you remember the destruction of the shuttle on Hodoku, Admiral?" Bering said gently. "When there was no other way, Bathsheba ordered Root to go to light speed inside the atmosphere. When AIS tested that during the Grand Imperial development period, it was a complete disaster. Total destruction. Dust. But at the time, there were no chimerans involved in the process. Root was able to modify the shuttle, in real time, to adapt to the incredible stresses involved. On the surface, it *looked* like he failed, but in reality, he succeeded beyond the wildest engineer's dream. They *existed* after the jump! The ghost of the structure was intact. The auto-land sequence still worked. What Root did is nothing short of miraculous.

"It turns out that hyper-fast FTL in space is, in many ways, similar to normal FTL flight within an atmosphere. It involves the light speed management of excessive and variable sheer forces, which requires..."

"Scratch the detail, Councilman," Chimera said, waving both hands on one side. "I get it. Root has actually done something that's somehow related to what you want to do. Keep him busy, Councilman," Chimera smiled. "He's had enough vacation for the entire trip!"

Bering smiled in return, and said, "On that score, Admiral, you need not have the slightest concern!"

Meanwhile, in the shuttle bay, Captain Kanab was just getting ready to close the airlock on the shuttle, when a fast, furry blur zipped past his feet. "I want to go!" Cheetah said, in his broken Imperial Standard. "I'm *tired* of being cooped up on this ship! I want to go play outside!"

Cheetah was the heartbreaker of the ship. Everyone loved him. But Kanab knew it was impossible. "Cheetah," he said. "We have no idea what's down there. Do you want to be eaten by some bizarre space demon? Now, scoot. You can't go along, I'm afraid."

Cheetah ran behind the rear row of seats, put his front paws on top, and bared his fangs, saying, "*You're* going! Are *you* going to get eaten by a space demon? Why can't *I* go? I'm not leaving!"

Kanab would have no problem catching Cheetah, and throwing him off, but he almost didn't want to. He called Yappo on the intercom, saying "Captain Iapetus, your nephew is being something of a pest here. Will you come down and deal with him, please?"

"(sigh)" Yappo answered. "OK, I'll be right there." Chimera had overheard the conversation, and by the time Yappo arrived in the shuttle bay, she was already there. Yappo went in to the shuttle, and said, "Cheetah, come here."

"No!" Cheetah shouted, and snarled.

Yappo projected a mild reproof, with love around the edges, and said more firmly, "Now, Cheetah."

"Oh, pooh," Cheetah replied. He came out from behind the seats, went over to Yappo, and hugged his leg. "I want to *go*, uncle Yappo. I *hate* this ship! I want to be *outside*!"

“Are my eyes fooling me, Captain,” Chimera asked, “or is he really twice as big as he was just a short time ago?”

Yappo smiled as he rubbed Cheetah’s head. “No, ma’am, not quite. He was badly mistreated by the Wasatchies, but as soon as we got some proper nutrition into him, he started growing like a weed! Didn’t you, you little weed?” Yappo said, looking down at Cheetah, while scratching behind his ear. You could hear Cheetah purr from across the shuttle bay!

It was all Chimera could do to keep from breaking out in laughter, but she kept her cool, saying “Well, I’m sure he’ll just be a pest if we leave him hear. He can go, Captain, but only if you go with him. And keep him away from the outpost team! They have work to do.”

“Can we, can we, *please*?” Cheetah asked with wide eyes.

“OK,” Yappo said “But go get your thick coat. It’s cold down there.” Cheetah was gone before Yappo had even finished speaking the last word.

“Admiral,” Kanab said “I’d like to put the outpost on the edge of that weird structure that’s buried in the ice. It will help to keep the team amused, and we might even find something interesting.”

“Your outpost, your call, Captain,” Chimera answered “But please try to avoid finding yet another thing that will disturb the Empress’ peace!”

****

The flight to the surface went without incident, and when they touched down, before the door was even fully open, Cheetah bolted, and started running around in the snow. He was ecstatic! Yappo just smiled indulgently. “You have quite a kid there, Captain,” Kanab said. “Have you figured out what he is, exactly?”

“No, not exactly,” Yappo replied. “Feline, obviously, but not a species known anywhere in the Empire. I responded casually to the

Admiral when she asked about it, but he *has* grown ungodly fast since we started feeding him."

Kanab took his team, and started constructing the initial outpost shelter. There wasn't a lot of raw material around for expansion, but a fully loaded Grand Imperial would join them in just a few months, so they would be fine. Yappo was sitting idly in the shuttle, pondering the amazing voyage they had had so far, when he felt a surge of fear from Cheetah. He was out the door and running in under a second.

Cheetah was about 100 yards away from the main camp. His fear had eased some, and when Yappo found him, he was digging furiously in the snow. "Uncle Yappo! Look! Captain Kanab was right! There *are* space demons here! Look what I found. See?"

Yappo leaned over into the pit Cheetah had dug, and when he saw what was in it, his heart skipped a beat.

Perfectly preserved in the ice, was a huge insect. Identical to the insects they had found in the *Sun Tzu*, so long ago.

April 22nd, 2809

Chimera had called her Exec Staff together to review the situation. She had assigned Amazona to command the investigation. "Alright, Admiral," she said. "What have we got? Should we move the outpost to another planet, fry this place to bedrock, or just move on as planned?" She was a lot more agitated than she sounded.

"Surprisingly," Amazona answered. "I think we should just go forward as planned. This place is *old*, Chimera. Those bugs have been dead a very, very long time. I don't know what's up with the power source in that under-ice structure, but it's stable. There are no life signs, and no apparent response of any kind to our arrival. My recommendation is that we leave the outpost team here as planned, with one exception. We should leave one of the Swarm ships here in orbit with them. They can research the structure below until the Grand Imperial arrives."

"OK, that sounds reasonable," Chimera said, and swiveled to face Yappo. "Do you have any idea, Captain, how your adopted nephew made a beeline for the bug in the first place?"

"No clue, Admiral," Yappo answered. "He's an unknown species, and we have no history with it at all. Maybe he has some sense for detecting weird stuff, like the cantilian sense for detecting danger."

"Well, *that* would certainly be helpful!" Chimera replied. "OK, we'll go with Amazona's plan then. Let's move out."

"I do have one request, if I may," Bering said, looking at Yappo. "It occurs to me that young Cheetah needs a teacher. Would it be alright with you if I took on that role?"

"Councilman," Yappo replied, with obvious relief. "You have just made my day!"

April 23rd, 2809

"Let's get started," Grand Admiral Arnold said, and the room was immediately silent. After almost 20 years running Earth Space Force Command, he was well past the need for preliminaries. "These beasties will be here in just a little over a week. What are we going to do about it?"

"I don't know what we can do, sir," General Sterling replied. "You saw the ships that Admiral Quinn brought by, yes? There's a good chance that a single one of them could defeat the bulk of our forces. Combined. Apparently, the one they are coming in now makes those ships look like toys."

"Damn Jackson anyhow!" Arnold swore, and pounded the table with his fist. "The bastard's a traitor, in my mind. He should have turned that ship over to Quinn as soon as he found it, end of story. What about Quinn, anyhow? He now commands a squadron of the things. Can he be trusted?"

"In a way," Admiral Yort replied. "He won't do anything against our interests, that's for sure. But, he's fanatic about his personal honor. He won't do anything against their interests either, as long as he holds that dual commission."

"Dual commission!" Arnold almost spat it out. "What a crazy notion. Who authorized that crap?"

"Well," Yort replied "Jackson just sort of invented it, and when it was clear to Quinn the aliens could flush his whole command on a whim if he didn't go along, he decided to go along. I don't like it either, sir, but Quinn did the right thing."

"Say more about that, about their military leader, Akido," Arnold said. "Quinn doesn't spook or back down easily, so this Akido must be pretty impressive. Didn't I read a report that said he used to run their whole show?"

"We're still trying to figure that out," answered Rich Tauber, CEO of Human Interstellar Trade Services, and the richest man in human history. "The rumors say he was running what they derisively call 'The Broken Empire' for millennia, but that can't be right."

"I talked to every one of the aliens on Quinn's three ships, Grand Admiral," Yort added. "The reports are contradictory. On the one hand, he is reported to be friendly and affable. On the other hand...I asked some of the officers, conversationally, what they would do if they found themselves fighting Akido in battle. Do you know what a 'cantilian' is, sir?"

"Yeah," Arnold said. "I've seen the pictures. Big black critter, over 7 feet tall. Thick."

"That's the one," Yort replied. "It's their main warrior class. Anyhow, here I was talking to this cantilian officer, battle seasoned from what she said, and when I asked what she would do if she found herself in a battle against Akido, her answer was just one word. *Surrender*."

"I've had traders out into their territory for the last several months, and I hear the same thing," Tauber interjected. "Apparently, if you're going to be in a fight, this Akido character is the *last* person you want on the other side. But the rumors also say he hates to kill. It's weird." Tauber paused briefly, and then continued, "I'll tell you what, though. I sent a crew out to their old Capital, New Valhalla. If the reports I've gotten are right, you can pretty much give up on any notion of confronting them militarily. They have battlestations that make *The Horatio* look like a tinker toy." Another pause. "Great trading opportunity for us, though. Their technology is so far ahead of ours, we can't help but gain from the exchange."

"But what would we trade in return?" Yort asked. "What could we have that they would want?"

Tauber's faced broke into a smug smile, and he said confidently, "Why don't you just let me worry about that, eh?"

"Enough of this trade business," Arnold said, impatiently. "They say that they are going to maintain 'peace and order' in *our* sector! The arrogance of it all! I want to catch up to their technology as quickly as we can, and then surpass it. I'd prefer not to fight them, but I damned well want to be able to deal with them on an equal footing. Do we have any spies in their military yet?"

"Workin' it," General Duma, the ESF intelligence chief, answered. Duma never said much.

"And what about this ship they are coming in now, this super advanced one?" Arnold said. "Any chance we could take it over, and pretend it blew up?"

"Do you know what a *chimeran* is, sir?" Yort said gently.

"Yeah, I saw the pictures of that too," Arnold answered. "Four-armed cat. Weird."

"Did you know that they can move at 90% of the speed of light?" Yort asked.

"Bullshit!" Arnold replied. "I heard that rumor, but that can't be right. How could that be possible?"

"I have no clue," Yort replied. "But I've seen it. I had no way to measure the actual speed, but the thing could be at one end of a big hallway, and then instantly...not quickly, *instantly*...it would be on the other side. Damned thing laughed it's ass off when it showed me. Quinn assured me it's true, and this ship that's coming to see us is commanded by one of these chimerans. Now, how would you suggest taking over a ship run by a commander who can outrun bullets, and dodge our lasers before we can even point and lock on?"

"It would have to be by deception, that's for sure," Sterling said. "Obviously, a frontal assault would be a joke."

A light went on in Arnold's eyes, and he said, "Give some thought to that, Sterling. Have a plan drafted for us to review in a few days. That's enough for now. Dismissed."

When they had all left, Grand Admiral Arnold poured himself a drink, dimmed the lights, and looked at the center of the galaxy, which was rising in the dark night sky. "What the hell are you up to this time, Jackson?" he muttered to himself.

CHAPTER 11

Hidden Menace

April 25th, 2809 —- 90,000 light years out

Councilman Bering looked like he had eaten a lemon. "Are you ready?" he asked.

"No," Cygnus said. "But we may as well get it over with."

"Tzu?" Bering asked solemnly.

"I should *never* have let you talk me into this in the first place, Councilman." Tzu answered, "Frankly, I don't know how you did. But, we've got to clean it up."

"Yeah," Bering said, and then turned to the ship's comm link. "Admiral Chimera, this is Councilman Horace Bering. I need to discuss an issue of serious importance with you, Admiral."

Chimera was instantly on the bridge, and looking concerned, said, "Of course, Councilman. Are you alright? What's the problem?"

"We need to meet in private, Admiral. Captain Tzu will be joining us." Bering led them into the ready room, and closed the door. He hesitated, and stammered around, finally saying, "Admiral Chimera, I am submitting myself to you for disciplinary action, along with Captain Cygnus, and Captain Tzu. Before we go any further, Admiral, I need to make it very clear that they were acting under my direction, and I am entirely responsible for these transgressions." Bering was standing at attention! Except that he couldn't meet Chimera's eye, and looked at the floor.

Chimera got very quiet, and took a seat at the conference table, and indicated the others should do the same. "I see." she said. "Why don't you start at the beginning."

"It has to do with our experience after we met with the Cecilians, Admiral," Bering said. "Our report of that encounter...at my direction, I should say again...was not complete."

"OK," Chimera said, without emotion. "Spill it."

"Since that encounter," Bering answered, "Captain Cygnus and I have been able to read each others' minds. Completely and effortlessly. The other abilities we both already had seem to have been enormously enhanced also. We became obsessed with the idea of radically improving our FTL capability...and we decided to test it, before telling you." Bering was obviously struggling. "My fault, Admiral, my fault. Since the encounter, my persuasive abilities have been greatly enhanced. I don't know how. I convinced the engineering team to do the engine mods, and I convinced Captains Cygnus and Tzu to go along with keeping it secret. I don't...I don't even know why, anymore. It just seemed so important, but I was still unsure, and, to be honest, somewhat maniacal about it. I wanted to be sure first..." Bering trailed off into an obvious stew of guilt.

Chimera was silent for several minutes. Finally, she said, "Captain Cygnus, is this account accurate?'

"Yes, ma'am. I..." Cygnus was visibly shaking.

"Captain Tzu, do you concur?" Chimera said, still without emotion.

"I don't know what to say, Admiral. Councilman Bering..." Tzu cut himself short. "Yes ma'am, the description is accurate."

Another pause, and Chimera said to the comm link, "Admiral Amazona, please report to my ready room. Immediately, if you please."

They waited in silence until Amazona appeared. When she did, and the door was closed, Chimera said, "This incident is to be classified Level 25, and no record shall be maintained. Admiral Amazona, you are to supervise the punishment of these officers, which I am about to detail." Amazona, normally unflappable, looked nervously between Bering and Cygnus.

"Captain Tzu," Chimera began, "for a 24 hour period beginning at the end of this meeting, you will calculate the value of Pi, to the last digit. Unless there is a Class 1 emergency, you will do *nothing else* for that period of time. I will monitor your processes regularly, and if you do something else, I'll know. If I discover you doing *anything* other than computing the value of Pi, I will *turn you off*. Acknowledge that you understand and will comply with this order with the words 'Yes ma'am', and say nothing else."

"Yes, ma'am," Tzu said simply. *Oh shit!* Amazona thought. *What's going on here?*

"Captain Cygnus," Chimera continued. "The squadron will remain stationary for the next 24 hours. The mission will be delayed, because of your dereliction. During that time, under the constant supervision of Admiral Amazona, or someone she designates, you will clean every latrine on every ship in the squadron, with a toothbrush you will obtain for this purpose. You will not speak. You will not eat, and you will not sleep. You will also have no nonverbal communication with anyone in this squadron. Acknowledge that you understand and will comply with this order with the words 'Yes ma'am', and say nothing else."

"Yes, ma'am," Cygnus said.

Chimera turned to Amazona, and said, "Admiral Amazona, in addition to supervising Captain Cygnus' punishment, Councilman

Bering is to be confined to quarters for the next 24 hours. He is not to have any communication with anyone. His monitor is to display a split screen of Captain Tzu's calculations, and Captain Cygnus scrubbing latrines, and he is to have no other access to any other ship systems or information. Acknowledge that you understand and will comply with this order with the words 'Yes ma'am', and say nothing else."

"Yes, ma'am!" Amazona answered. She had never stood straighter in her life.

"But..." Bering said "That's all you're going to do to me, is confine me to quarters? It's *my* fault, Admiral! You should punish *me*, not them! This just isn't fair."

Chimera turned to Bering with more fury than he had ever seen, and it put him to silence. "Councilman," she said. "These officers were under your command. You assumed that command illegally, in defiance of regulations, but they were under your command nonetheless. Can you think of anything you'd like *less* than to watch your men suffer for *your* mistake, while *you* sit in relative comfort?"

Bering looked even more pale than usual, and finally said, "No, ma'am. I understand." He looked like he was going to puke.

"Very well then," Chimera said. "You all have your orders. Admiral Amazona, please inform the crew that Captain Tzu, and all the services he provides, will be unavailable for the next 24 hours. Dismissed."

They all filed out. When they were gone, and the door was closed, Chimera sat back down in a chair, and started to cry. For a chimeran, she cried for a very long time.

April 26th, 2809

Bering, Cygnus, Amazona, and Tzu were once again assembled in the ready room. Bering looked almost cadaverous. Cygnus had clearly been crying. Amazona stood ramrod straight, eyes front.

"Be seated," Chimera said, expressionless. Bering and Cygnus did so haltingly. Amazona remained standing, and Chimera gave her a brief nod, and started pacing the room. "Well," Chimera said "Now the easy part is over." Bering and Cygnus looked at each other nervously, and Chimera shouted, "I did not give you permission to communicate with each other!" And they both looked forward, with terror in their eyes.

Chimera sat down, and said, "Now, the hard part begins." She looked down at the table, not facing them, and said, "Now, we have to put this behind us, and get on with the mission." She looked up, and said, "Can you do that?"

Bering's look of horror deepened, as he looked at Chimera, and said, "My God...Admiral...I understand now. You had to watch us suffer, at your hand. And we had betrayed you. Why..." He shook his head "...why did I do it? My God, Chimera, what have I done?" Bering put his head in his hands, and started to sob.

Chimera seemed to straighten a little, and said, "Well, then, perhaps you do understand. We'll speak more of this later, Councilman. Now, the next task is to get the crew to understand that the management team is still intact. If it is..." She trailed off.

"Admiral," Amazona said. "I may have already taken care of that, ma'am. None of the crew knows anything about this, Admiral. I personally escorted Captain Cygnus to all the latrines. Before doing so, I cleared the decks. I told the crewmen that Captain Cygnus and I were performing a classified mission under your direction, ma'am." Amazona hesitated, and then continued, "I said it in such a way that there would be no questions, Admiral, and there were none. It's all true, ma'am, if you recall your specific order."

Chimera looked hopeful for the first time during the meeting. She looked up at Amazona, and asked, "So no one but us knows about this?"

"Not a soul, Admiral," Amazona said. "I felt it wise to preserve your options, ma'am..."

"Councilman Bering!" Chimera said roughly. "Did you, at any time, have any interest other than the safety of the Empire in mind when you took the actions you did?"

Bering looked horrified again. "Not at all, Chimera! Quite the opposite. I thought I had found a way to defeat the Swarm. Actually..." he hesitated "...I still do. I wasn't really trying to hide anything from you Admiral." He stumbled, and corrected himself. "Well, of course I was, but just for a little while. I just needed to be right! I couldn't stand the thought of telling you, and then being wrong...and it was all so new, and exciting, and I was so unsure...Chimera...can you forgive me?"

Chimera looked at him with just the slightest hint of a smile. "Maybe. Probably. But not today." Still, she had clearly calmed down, and said, "Amazona, you can relax. There was no treason here, and I'm not going to be executing anyone today. Take a seat. This is now an Executive Staff meeting. Captain Tzu, please ask Captain Iapetus to join us."

It turns out Yappo had been outside the door, and entered immediately. Chimera said, "So, tell us about these new powers of yours, Bering. Can you do what Curt does now, or what? Cygnus, you're next..."

The meeting continued for several hours, and when it was over, Chimera declared Captain Tzu officer of the watch, and they all went to sleep. They slept for a long time.

April 27th, 2809

"This is odd, Admiral," Cygnus said from the pilot's station. "From the pollution in the air, this seems to be a world in the late-non-atomic industrial era. But there's mass in orbit, ma'am. A lot more than you would expect at this level of industrial development." Cygnus slowed the ship down to one light year/hour, and they slowly approached the second planet out from the star. Odd colors, mostly blue/green, but with a substantial tinge of reddish brown as well.

As they got closer to the planet, Cygnus signaled yellow alert. "Swarm ships in orbit. Three of 'em," He studied the sensor readings, and said, "No life signs, no energy readings. They're dead in space. The *Delta* is the closest to them, and is relaying the data now." Cygnus put the image up on the main view screen, and squinted, saying, "What are those dark spots? They seem to have jagged edges. Are those holes, or...?"

Amazona had been watching from the security station, and interrupted, loudly, "Squadron, retreat two light years distance immediately, maximum speed!" while simultaneously sounding battlestations. It took barely a minute to move the squadron away, and Chimera asked, "What is it, Admiral? What do you see?"

Amazona had magnified the image. It did look like holes, holes that she had seen rusted into the hull of a big ocean going ship, in her youth. "What can do that, Chimera?" she asked nervously. "What can eat holes in the hull of a Swarm ship?"

"We have a problem, Admiral," Tzu interrupted. "Commander Tanner on the *Delta* reports a small hull breach. He fixed it, but he reports spots of discoloration on the hull in other places. He reports that the robots are acting strangely."

"All ships move immediately to contamination control spacing!" Amazona yelled. Tzu got it done, and there was instantly 5,000,000 miles distance between ships. "Any reports of hull breaches from any of the others?"

"None," Tzu answered. "But Commander Tanner has reported two additional small breaches. And the robots have both shut down."

"We've got to get Tanner off that ship!" Chimera shouted.

"Not at the risk of contaminating all of us, Admiral," Amazona said solemnly. "Tzu, how long can he hold out?"

"Don't know," Tzu answered. "At least he's chimeran, which gives him a fighting chance, but we have no idea what we're dealing with. Wait a moment..." a brief pause, "Commander Tanner reports he's feeling no ill effects. Chimera, this is just a guess, but it sounds like something is attacking anything metal. Which means his suit is no good. It's mostly fabric, but there are some metal fittings. It might hold for a bit, but not long. It would be a leaky balloon."

"Get him in it," Amazona said. "Chimera, how long can chimerans survive in vacuum, without a suit?"

"Not long," Chimera answered. "Thirty seconds, max, and they damned well better have medical attention waiting at the end of that."

"Not long enough..." Amazona said, shaking her head.

Bering had a thousand mile stare on his face, and said, "Admiral, I have an idea. I don't know if it will work. It's never been done. It might blow us up. But it might save Tanner's life."

"Any risk to the other ships?" Amazona asked nervously.

Bering thought for several moments, and said, "No. At least none that I can imagine." Bering considered, and said, "This should probably be classified level 25, Admiral. I'll need Tzu, and Cygnus, and an engineer who's fast, someone you can trust."

"You've got her right here, Councilman," Chimera said. "What do you propose? All but Executive Staff, clear the bridge."

"It would be easier if I showed you, Chimera. Captain Tzu, please attempt that mind link we discussed, between Chimera and me."

"Stand by," Tzu said, and all became silent. Chimera's eyes got as wide as saucers, and she said quietly, "Are you *nuts*?"

"I hope not." Bering managed a weak smile. "Tanner's dead if I am. We're all dead if Cygnus and Tzu and I can't handle it. But Tanner's dead for sure if we don't try. It's going to take full ship's power, that's for sure."

"You guys get set up," Chimera said. "I'll go make the engine and power control mods. Tzu, can you keep all 4 of us linked in real time, so that I can make ongoing mods while they manage the process?"

"I have no idea," Tzu answered. "I'll try."

"See that you do," Chimera replied. "Amazona, tell Tanner to strap on extra oxygen tanks, and exit the ship. Tell him he's going to see a tight focus of weapons beams from the *Sun Tzu*, and a black disc in front of the beam focus point. On a signal from Captain Cygnus, he is to discard his suit and anything metallic he has with him, and use it as reaction mass to jump into that disc."

"Ma'am?" Amazona asked, with a stunned expression.

"Just do it!" Chimera shouted, and she was gone.

It wasn't more than a few minutes later that Tzu reported to the others. "The mods are done. *Damn* she's fast! Cygnus, you're the eyes. Bering, you're the brain. I'll try to keep Chimera patched in. Commence now!"

Cygnus leaned forward into the control posts, and Bering stood behind him, hands on his shoulders. Cygnus closed his eyes, and several small, tight beams left the ship's guns. They focused just a few hundred yards from the *Delta*, and then rapidly diffused. The beams wavered in intensity, but gradually grew. "Tell Tanner to move toward the focus of the beams," Cygnus said quietly, and Amazona relayed the command. "Something's getting weird down here," Chimera said over the comm link, from the engine room. "Fuzzy distortion region, right next to the engine power control panel." The intensity of the beams suddenly increased several orders of magnitude, and Cygnus said, "Now!" The entire ship shuddered violently, and the engines shut down. The main lights died, the emergency lights came on, and Chimera's voice came over the emergency comm circuit, barely a whisper, and filled with wonder.

"Got him!"

Cygnus started breathing again. Bering was passed out on the floor. After assessing Bering's vital signs, Amazona told Yappo to follow her, and they went to assess the status of the ship. Everywhere they went, there was an eerie glow from the emergency lights.

****

Chimera rapidly moved to get Tanner stabilized in the regeneration chamber. He would be there a while, but he would live. Once Tanner had been stabilized, Chimera led the engineering team to get one of the sub-light engines operating at idle power. They weren't going anywhere for a bit, but at least they had power. Chimera had assembled the executives on the bridge, where Cygnus was, once again, buried in the sensor readouts. *Delta* was displayed on the main view screen.

"What's happening, Captain?" Chimera asked.

"Watch the screen, Admiral," Cygnus said. "*Delta's* being eaten alive. Watch these dark patches." Cygnus put arrows on the screen to indicate what he was referring to. They could all see the dark patches slowly growing.

Chimera shivered. "Any trace of the plague on *Sun Tzu*?"

"None, Admiral," Tzu answered. "The scheme seems to have worked. No reports of breaches from the other ships, either." Tzu paused. "We dodged a bullet on this one. Thanks to Amazona."

"Yeah," Chimera said. "Did we really do what I think we did, Councilman? Did we really just make a tame macroscopic wormhole?"

"Not exactly *tame*, Admiral!" Bering answered. "You saw the squirming around that Cygnus and I had to do. And, if Tzu hadn't been able to maintain our link to you, so you could make those real time changes to the frequency modulator..." This time, it was Bering's turn to shudder.

"That was *so* weird!" Cygnus said. "I saw what was happening to the fabric of space-time, but I had no idea what it meant. But Bering could see it through me, and he knew what to do..."

“You think I did?” Bering replied, grinning weakly. “You don’t want to know how much guesswork was involved. Not another ship and team in the galaxy could have done what we just did. I’ll tell you what, though. I’ll bet some variant of this is how the Ankorans were able to project tractor beams and weapons fire over such a vast distance. This technology is far from usable, but now that we know it can work...”

“Yeah,” Chimera said. “But now, we have a mission to complete. Enough of this boring stuff; we’re about to enter *human* controlled space now! Captain Cygnus, find that planet on the edge of the Earth Space Force sphere of influence that Curt recommended. It’ll take the crew several hours to get the engines operational again, and then, let’s move out!

“Councilman,” Chimera said softly, as she turned to Bering. “I forgive you!”

CHAPTER 12

The Modern Sector

May 1st, 2809 —- 102,000 light years out

"Mining colony Trona, this is Captain Sun Tzu of the *Vermin Hellion* squadron, from the New Galactic Empire, Admiral Chimera commanding," Tzu called in. "We are 10 light years out. We request permission to rendezvous with your orbital station, and send over a shuttle."

There was a delay of several minutes before they got a response. "Roger, Captain Tzu," a nameless voice replied. "Director Offiro would like to speak with you personally. Please stand by while I get him on the line." The speaker went dead, and they waited.

"Voice only," Cygnus said. "Slow, too. That's weird."

"Not really," Amazona replied. "This is on the very edge of the human sector, and bandwidth is expensive for them, particularly FTL bandwidth. Until we provided them the fast FTL comm upgrade, they were limited to 250 light years/hr for comm, and that for only a few thousand light years, at a frightfully inefficient energy cost. I'm sure our fast FTL comm technology has only been installed at a few key locations so far. And this isn't one of them."

"Admiral Chimera?" The speaker came alive again. "This is George Offiro of Human Interplanetary Trade Services, Director of the mining operation here on Trona." He paused briefly, and then said, "Did Curt Jackson really send you guys? How is the old bastard?"

Amazona looked at Chimera with a scandalized expression, and Chimera said, "*Prime Minister* Jackson was well, when we left, and yes, he did send us. We'll be there momentarily, Director. Can you meet with us on your station?"

There was a shorter lag, this time, and then Offiro came back on, and said, "Momentarily? I thought you guys were 10 light years out?"

"We were," Chimera answered. "We are now coming up on your station. May we send over a shuttle?"

No delay this time. "You guys are fast," Offiro said. "I'm on the surface, and it would take me at least an hour or so to get up to the station. If your ship isn't too big, and you can go atmospheric, you're welcome to come down here. My office here is pretty spartan, but it's better than the facilities on the station. What do you say? Security says I should screen you at the station, but anybody who's a friend of Jackson's is OK in my book."

Chimera nodded to Cygnus to pick up the conversation, and he said, "Our ship is quite large, Director, but our shuttles are fairly compact. A good pilot can land one on any reasonably level space that's at least 20 feet wide by 40 feet long."

"You'll be fine, then," Offiro came back. "Our shuttles take a lot more room than that. I'll activate the landing beacon, and notify security to let you in. See you in a few."

The comm link went dead. Chimera turned to Yappo and said, "Sounds like you'll be able to handle the landing, Ambassador. Take Commander Armando along for security. And, Commander Root seems to be getting around OK on his own now, so take him as well. See if he can fiddle with their comm system to give them visual signals, and maybe some more range, while reducing their power consumption. And...take Romulus with you too. I want to experiment with integrating the robots into the away teams, and this mission looks pretty tame. Off you go!"

Root had been cooped up for much too long since his injury, and he had his face glued to the viewport as Yappo brought the shuttle down to the Trona landing field. "Well I'll be damned!" Root called out to the others. "Their shuttles aren't gravitic! Look at them! They use accelerated particles for lift-off, and *atmospheric* braking for re-entry! I read about this in school, but I've never seen anything like it!"

"Be polite, Commander," Yappo said, as he gently set the shuttle down on the ramp next to the runway. "Remember, the humans have explored a volume of space almost as great as that of the Broken Empire, with ships much less capable than this shuttle. Many of them died doing it. Sometimes, I worry what they'll do with the resources of the Empire available to them. And remember...speak English while we're here! In fact, we should all convert now."

"Yes, sir," they all answered. Root's English was pretty good, since he'd been studying for many weeks. Armando's was still a little broken. Romulus spoke English like a native of Earth.

As the shuttle engines shut down, a lone figure in a ground car approached them, and stopped as they opened the shuttle door. Yappo exited first, and was met by a robust human about 6 feet tall, with fiery red hair. "Welcome to Trona! I'm Director Offiro. Are you Admiral Chimera?"

"No, sir," Yappo replied. "I am Ambassador Iapetus. I work for the Admiral. I did meet Prime Minister Jackson before leaving on this mission, and served with him briefly. A very impressive gentleman, I must say!"

"You got that right!" Offiro said with a smile. "I did a stint with him in the Earth Space Force before I decided there was more money on the private side. He always was smarter than I was, though, and quite the wheeler-dealer. I'm not surprised he pulled off some scam to get you guys to put him in charge. Why, I remember the time when...*holy shit*!" Offiro stiffened, and reached for his blaster, until he remembered he had decided not to bring it. "What the hell is *that*?"

Yappo instantly realized what was going on, and said with a smile, "Relax, Director. That's Commander Armando, my Security Officer for this mission. He's a cantilian, the main warrior class of the Empire."

"Yeah," Offiro said, calming down. "Right. I bet you guys don't lose many wars, do you?" Offiro had shaken off his initial startled response, and walked over to Armando saying, "Welcome to Trona, Commander. Sorry I got so startled. You have any other surprises in there?" Offiro said, craning his neck to look at the shuttle door.

"Perhaps I will look more familiar, Director," Romulus said, as he stepped out of the shuttle. "But, Commander Root behind me will also be a surprise. That's it, just the four of us."

"You're sure a smooth talker," Offiro said, shaking hands with Romulus. "I haven't heard an accent like that since I was at the Academy. What was your name? Or do you have a name?"

"You may call me 'Romulus,' Director, as the rest of the crew does," Romulus answered.

"Alright then," Offiro said. "It will be a little tight, but we should all fit in the car. Hop in!" They all piled in to the car, and Offiro drove them over to a door that led into the side of a mountain. He parked the car, and they all walked inside. They went through an airlock, and then settled into a conference room about 10 yards down the hall. Spacious, but sparsely furnished.

Root looked questioningly at Yappo, and got an affirmative nod. Root said, "Director, I'm curious. Why do you have a full airlock on this facility? The air outside is obviously breathable."

"Dust storms," Offiro said. "It's pretty calm now, but they can get really wicked during the windy season. Sometimes we can't launch or land shuttles for a week. We try to go outside as little as possible under those conditions, but the airlock...or dustlock, in this case...keeps the inside from getting too bad."

"If I may ask, Director," Yappo said, "What do you mine here?"

"Uranium," Offiro answered. "And we don't just mine it. We process it, use it for fission power plants, and use the power they generate to create anti-matter. The anti-matter is what we actually ship out. High value density! Actually, you guys just finished a long trip. If you're low on anti-matter, I can probably help you out."

Yappo smiled broadly, and said, "A truly generous offer, Director, but we are in good shape in that regard!"

"Forgive me if this question is inappropriate, Director Offiro," Armando said. "But I didn't see any military assets in orbit. In fact, the airlock door wasn't even locked. You appear to have no defensive capability of any kind. Is that true?"

"True enough," Offiro said. "There's no need for it. There's just nobody out here. As far as we know, there's no substantial civilization within thousands of light years of this place. Just a bunch of other small mining colonies. You're the first visitors we've had in the 10 years I've been running the place."

"So, you're not under the protection of the Earth Space Force, then?" Armando asked.

"Well, yes we are," Offiro said. "Sort of. HITS pays a lump sum to the ESF to protect all of its assets, and then HITS sets the priorities, and assesses the risk. They've determined we're not at risk, and based on my experience, I have to agree with them. Why do you ask?"

"Commander Armando is a warrior by nature, Director," Yappo interjected quickly. "It's just his nature to be interested in such things. How big is your operation here?"

"A lot bigger than it looks from the outside, that's for sure!" Offiro said proudly. "We've got almost 6000 people at several sites around the planet, 1300 here at the main site. Would you like a tour?"

"Yes, thank you!" Yappo said enthusiastically. They went back into the hall, and continued deeper in to the mountain. After 100 yards or so, the hallway became a walkway over a huge cavernous pit, stretching hundreds of yards in each direction.

"Normally, we'd just do an open pit operation, but the dust storms here get so bad, they used to shut us down at first. On balance, this is cheaper, and keeps production reliable. See that over there?" Offiro gestured off to the left, and they saw a complex of several domes. "That's where we run the fission reactors. They provide power for the station, but mostly we use that power to create the anti-matter. That's the storage facility in the center of the complex. The ore here is quite rich. Soon, we'll be the biggest producer of anti-matter this side of Earth!"

Armando looked at Yappo nervously, and Yappo indicated silence. Then Armando stopped walking, and looked behind them, to the right, and said, "Something's not right there..."

Before anyone could answer, there was a huge explosion, which shook the walls, and an alarm went off on Offiro's belt. "What's going on?" Offiro demanded of his comm unit. A voice came back saying "One of the drilling rigs exploded...fire everywhere...men trapped below..." and the voice trailed off.

"Stay here!" Offiro yelled to the Imperials, and started to run toward a walkway leading toward the explosion. Suddenly, he stopped, and turned around, and Yappo said, "We may be able to assist you, Director. Let us join you." Offiro looked at Armando, and said, "Right, you're with me." They all started following him, and Yappo said quietly, "Commander Root is exceptionally fast, Director, and a brilliant technician and medic. If you let him go ahead, he may well be able to provide you with useful information."

Offiro looked at Root, and said, "Go!" and Root was gone instantly. Offiro stopped, and said, "What the hell?"

Yappo said reassuringly, "Our technicians are fast beyond belief, Director. Please wait. It won't be long."

Root returned in a just a couple of minutes, and said "It's bad, Director, Ambassador. The fire's over 4000°. People are trapped behind it, and they're running out of air fast."

"Director," Yappo said. "I assume you have emergency breathing gear?"

"Yes, of course!" Offiro said.

"Commander Root, can you take the gear to them?" Yappo asked.

Root paused, and said "No sir. Well, maybe one at a time. It's a big fire, sir."

"Get to it, Commander," Yappo said. "Director, where is the emergency breathing equipment?"

Suddenly, a calm voice broke in from an unexpected direction. "Ambassador, I can take the emergency equipment through without trouble, sir." It was Romulus!

"Right here," Offiro pointed to a cabinet. Romulus opened it, and strung every piece of gear there was around his body in an impossible fashion...and he was gone. They could see a blur moving down the ramps, and then into the flames without a moment's hesitation. They waited. And waited. It seemed like forever, and then a blur emerged from the flames, and Romulus stood before them. "The men are safe below for the moment, Ambassador, Director."

Root ran over to Romulus, and did a rapid inspection. "This is just too weird, Ambassador. He's not even warm!"

"Director Offiro, do you have fire fighting equipment?" Romulus asked calmly. Offiro pointed to another cabinet, and as Romulus was gathering the gear, Root said, "I can help with this! You bring 'em out, and I'll fix 'em up!"

"You have more fire gear?" Armando asked. Offiro pointed toward another cabinet down the hall. Armando loaded up as well, and went to join the others.

Offiro leaned against the wall, and slid to the floor, saying, "Can we help?"

Yappo said grimly, "No. Anything we can do in this situation, they can do better. And much faster." And so, they looked out the observation window, and waited. Gradually, the fire subsided, and then went out.

****

The Imperials sat in the back of the conference room, and didn't say a word. Director Offiro was conducting a debriefing on the disaster.

"How many did we lose?" he asked grimly.

"Nine men dead sir. Thirty more in the infirmary." The foreman looked nervously at the Imperials, and said, "If it wasn't for them, sir, we'd have had 200 dead."

"What the hell happened?" Offiro demanded.

"It was that #12 unit, sir" the foreman said. "It tested out fine at the start of the shift, but it's well beyond its preventive maintenance window. I told you..."

"Yes, I know you needed parts!" Offiro exploded. "I ordered them over a year ago!" Offiro paced back and forth, and finally said, "Shut down *every* piece of equipment that is overdue for preventive maintenance. *Now*!"

"Sir, that will idle half of our capacity...the home office..." the foreman started to say, but then he withered under Offiro's glare. "Yes sir!" he said, and left the room hurriedly.

Offiro stopped pacing, and said, "Clear the room." Everyone got up to leave, and as they were filing out the door, Offiro said, "Not you, Ambassador." Yappo stayed, and shortly, the two of them were alone.

"You're going to Earth, right?" Offiro asked.

“Yes, we are.” Yappo answered.

Offiro paused briefly before saying, “I am forever in your debt, and yet, I need to ask another favor. You will probably meet with a guy named Rich Tauber. Good guy, head of HITS, but he doesn't understand operations. If one of your folks could let out a little rant about the deplorable maintenance conditions here, without letting it be known that I asked you to do it...?” Offiro paused, expectantly.

A broad smile came to Yappo's face, and he said, “Consider it done, Director! And, I have a request for you as well. I have been in consultation with my Admiral, and she and I agree that you need better security here. There may not be anyone around you *now*, but we have powerful pirates in the Empire, and when they hear about this place, you will be in danger. The Admiral would like to leave one of our ships here to protect you.”

Offiro grew quiet, and said, “That's fine by me, I guess, but I don't know how ESF will take that. An alien warship stationed in their territory? I dunno...”

“We'll clean it up with Earth Space Force Command when we get there, Director,” Yappo answered. “And, in the meantime, the crew will be instructed that they are *not* to take any action other than defense against pirates, except on your personal command. Will that be satisfactory?”

Another pause. “Yeah, OK, I guess,” Offiro answered. “Dammit, I didn't want to get involved in all this political crap!”

Too late Yappo thought.

“Can I see this wonder ship of yours, that's my new best friend?” Offiro asked. “I'd like to meet the Captain, and get an understanding with him.”

“Of course,” Yappo said. “If you like, we can do that right now. And, as we discussed, I had Commander Root look over your comm system. He can upgrade your transmission speed to 500 light years/hour, with full video, out to about 4000 light years. And you will use *less* power. The only downside is, if it breaks, you won't be able to fix it, but if you don't abuse it, I assure you it won't break. Can I set him to do this?"

Offiro thought for a moment, and said, "Sure. We have a back-up transmitter, if it comes to that." He followed Yappo out to the shuttle, and they lifted off to visit the *Epsilon*.

May 3rd, 2809

The crew was relaxing in the lounge, even Chimera. Tzu was with them, and was also monitoring ships systems and progress.

"Ambassador Iapetus, I have a question, if I may," Commander Armando said, while reclining in his seat. "Offiro was running off to go save his men, or at least do what he could to try, and he suddenly stopped, and turned to face you. You have anything to do with that?"

Yappo looked embarrassed, and faced Chimera, and said, "It was just a touch, Admiral. Just a touch! I knew we could help him. When it was all over, he was grateful. His own foreman said we saved many lives. I just..." Yappo paused, "I just got his attention. I never touched him again!"

"You bucking for a commendation, Captain?" Chimera said with a smile. "Well, you've got it. I'm going to have a chat with Merlin about this non-interference rule when we get back anyhow. Not sure I buy it at all." Councilman Bering looked at her with a scandalized expression, and Chimera said, "What, you think he's infallible?"

"No, of course not," Bering stammered. "But it is a long standing tradition. Empress Misha established it while she was Chairman of the Council, in fact..." and he tapered off under Chimera's withering grin.

"Well, we'll have the talk, anyway!" she said.

Suddenly, a deep, low shudder moved through the ship, and then abruptly stopped. And then battlestations sounded! "Officers to the bridge!" Tzu shouted. They all got up, but Chimera got there first. There was an explosion unfolding on the view screen."

"Dammit!" Tzu shouted. "Dammit! I forgot about these! Dammit!"

"*Report*, Captain!" Chimera said

"Admiral," Tzu said. "We just triggered a Swarm alert buoy."

"A *what*?" Chimera demanded.

"Swarm alert buoy, ma'am," Tzu said, haltingly. "We placed them at various locations throughout the galaxy, to alert us if the seekers recovered from our grazing too quickly. I had to link to the other ships to remember what it was, and I destroyed it as soon as I knew, but it got at least part of the message sent. Dammit!"

"Calm down, will you?" Chimera said, "Is the signal what caused the shudder we felt?"

"Yes," Tzu said. "The signal had to be extraordinarily powerful. It's going over 3,000,000 light years. To what the humans call the Andromeda Galaxy."

"How fast is the signal?" Chimera demanded.

"Chimera...I don't know...wait a moment...none of the ships know. We had no need for that information. Not fast though. Our comm is limited by the same physics as yours. This signal is optimized for range, not speed."

"How much of the message got through?" Chimera asked.

"I have no idea," Tzu said. "But we think holographically. If any significant amount gets through, they'll get the idea that we're awake. And sooner than they expected. Akido's hidden fleet was outside the expected range of variation in our predictions for your development."

"You're blurring your identities again there, Tzu," Chimera said, and thought for several minutes. "Not much to do about it though. We should have a couple of centuries, at least. Send a message to Curt, and continue on course. And if you see any more of the damned things, fry 'em before they can call home!"

"Yes, ma'am!" Tzu said, and the *Vermin Hellions* continued on course for Earth.

CHAPTER 13

Earth Intrigue

May 6th, 2809 —- 108,000 light years out

Grand Admiral Arnold had called his general staff back together, to discuss the upcoming arrival of the Imperials.

"They're scheduled to arrive tomorrow," Arnold said. "General Duma, have you developed the plans I asked for to capture their ship?"

"Dumb idea," Duma said.

Arnold started, and with obvious indignation said, "General Duma, I remind you that I am your superior officer. I ask again, have you prepared the plans that I ordered for taking over the alien spacecraft?"

"Yes," Duma said. "Dumb idea," he repeated.

"Grand Admiral," Admiral Yort said quickly. "While I cannot support General Duma's lack of respect, there is some merit to the notion that this attack on our allies may not turn out well."

"Allies!" Arnold spat the word out. "They extorted an agreement under the threat of destroying the *Horatio* station. Earth will not be subjugated to aliens again while I am in command!"

At that moment, Tauber's communicator gave him a silent signal, and he checked the message. "The issue may be moot," Tauber said. "I've just gotten a message from our mining colony at Trona. The aliens recently departed, but the signal isn't much faster than they are. We've got intelligence that says this is some kind of super ship, yes? Well, it turns out there are *six* of them heading our way. And they left one at the Trona colony!"

Duma got just the hint of a smirk on his face. Admiral Yort said, "I think that's it for this round, then, Grand Admiral. With six ships, there's nothing we can do. We have to be polite...and act like the allies we have agreed to be."

"Dammit!" Arnold said, and thought for several minutes. He calmed down, and said, "Obviously you're right, Admiral Yort. But we need to look for ways to break out from this alien yoke. General Duma! I ordered you to look for advanced alien spacecraft that we might commandeer for our own use. Have you been doing that?"

"Yes," Duma said.

"With what result?" Arnold demanded, with obvious annoyance.

"Still looking," Duma replied.

Arnold glared at Duma, but finally said, "Very well. Dismissed. I expect you all here for the meeting with them tomorrow."

As they were filing out, Duma got between Tauber and the door. He stuck out his hand, and said, "Message." Tauber considered objecting, but handed Duma his PDA, which had the message displayed.

It read: "Awesome warships. 6 headed your way. Good folks. Be nice."

Duma handed the device back to Tauber, and said, "Forward future messages." Tauber was looking down to put the PDA back in his belt pouch, and said, "Now see here, General, I don't report to..." and he stopped in mid sentence. When Tauber looked up, Duma had him locked with an intense stare. When he locked eyes with Duma, Tauber's heart skipped a beat, and he said, "Yes, General, of course..." and nervously left the room.

May 7th, 2809

Chimera had been getting increasingly nervous as they approached Earth. Not militarily, of course. With six Swarm ships, she could defeat the entire Earth Space Force without the slightest risk to her crew. Except for Quinn's visit a few months ago, her's would be the first official delegation from the New Galactic Empire to visit what had been the third, and was now the second most powerful military force in the galaxy, after the defeat of The Alliance. "Don't screw this up!" Curt had said before they left on their mission. "These folks have been top dogs for centuries, and they don't like being displaced one little bit. Still, we want them to join the Empire, so be nice!"

Chimera had assembled the Executive Staff in the conference room, along with Commander Armando, and said "OK, this is going to be a top level delegation. I will command the mission, with Amazona and Armando for security, and Yappo for...observation. Captain Tzu, while I am off the ship, you are in command of the squadron. You are to keep in mental contact with me whenever possible. If, at any time, you become convinced that we have fallen victim to treachery by the Earth Space Force, you are to destroy every military asset within 15 light years of Earth, and then proceed immediately to Valhalla to report. Understood?"

"Admiral," Tzu said. "Are you sure that..."

"Am I understood, Captain?" Chimera interrupted.

"Yes, ma'am!" Tzu said.

"Very well, then. Amazona, Yappo, Armando let's go." They boarded the shuttle, and docked with the ESF station *George Washington* in orbit around Earth without incident. They were escorted to an elegant meeting room, with comfortable chairs, and an enormous wooden conference table. About a dozen humans were already there. Chimera noted that she was the smallest person in the room, by far. She found the fact amusing.

A large man in uniform walked up to Chimera as they entered, and said, "Admiral Chimera, it's an honor to receive you. I am Grand Admiral Arnold, of the Earth Space Force. This is Del Hardy, Governor of Earth. On his right, we have..." Arnold finished the introductions, and Chimera introduced her officers, and they all sat down.

"Admiral Chimera," Arnold said. "If you'll forgive an old navy man, I am absolutely fascinated with these ships of yours. Would it be possible for me to get a tour of one of them?"

"Of course, Grand Admiral," Chimera smiled. "We can only stay for a day or so, but we'll arrange a tour at your convenience. And, if you'll indulge me, I'd like to get a tour of Earth, if that's possible."

"It will be an honor, Admiral Chimera!" Arnold said.

"I hope this won't be a problem, sir," Chimera said. "But Imperial regulations require that any flag officer be accompanied by a dual cantilian security team when not aboard an Imperial craft."

The humans glanced nervously at the cantilians. Then, General Duma stood up, and said softly into the silence that developed around him, "Admiral Chimera, I am General Duma, Chief of Security for the Earth Space Force. I am also an accomplished pilot. Your security detail will not be necessary. I will *personally* guarantee your safety for the entire duration of your stay in Earth space."

No one said a word. Everyone had been looking at Duma, and now all eyes shifted to Chimera. She looked at Amazona, and the look she got in return had an obvious meaning. Chimera thought for several moments, and then she stood as well, and extending her hand to General Duma, said, "I had not expected so great an honor, General.

With your *personal* escort, I will waive the requirement for the Imperial Security Detail. Grand Admiral, if it's convenient for you, Ambassador Iapetus can give you a tour of one of our ships immediately, and I can join General Duma for a tour of Earth. Is that acceptable?"

Arnold was obviously disconcerted, but he wanted to see the Swarm ship in the worst way. He smiled, and said, "Absolutely, Admiral! Let's do it!"

The group began to break up, and Duma herded Chimera out the door, and down a long hallway. They went through an airlock, and into a small, but very nicely appointed spacecraft. Duma bowed deeply when they were inside, and said, "Inspect, if you wish." Chimera nodded, and did a quick survey of the ship. She was impressed. Better than anything else she had seen from the ESF, by far. She returned to the bridge, and took the seat next to Duma that he indicated. They detached from the station, and began their descent toward Earth. Duma started a recording that explained what they were seeing. *Silent devil,* Chimera thought to herself. And yet, she felt completely comfortable. She asked questions at times, and Duma always answered with a very few words, which always turned out to be surprisingly adequate.

Earth was a weird combination of military base, and park. There was no heavy industry on the planet's surface at all. The population, the tour program said, was a mere 250,000,000 compared to billions less than a millennia before. Outside the ESF Academy, there was virtually no concentration of high technology hardware. Just parks, farmland, private estates, that kind of thing. And yet, the ESF controlled...or, *protected,* the recorded program said...an area of over 50 billion cubic light years, not much smaller than the Broken Empire.

Duma set the ship to autopilot, and turned to face Chimera. "New threats," he said. "Your pirates. Need help..." and Duma trailed off. He was embarrassed!

Of course, Chimera thought. *We bring new threats, as well as new opportunities. And he's a proud man...*

"I understand completely, General," Chimera said. "Earth is an important ally for us, and I apologize that we have brought a new threat to you. If you like, I can leave one of my ships here with you. It can defend you against any conceivable pirate attack, and I will give the Captain strict instructions to take no other actions without your personal approval, General. Would that be helpful?"

Duma visibly relaxed, and softly said, "Thank you," and extended his hand, which Chimera took. They continued the tour without incident, including a stroll of the grounds at the ESF Academy, and then went back to the station to join the others.

There was a final regrouping and farewells, and then Chimera and the team got back on their shuttle to return to the *Sun Tzu*. Chimera said, "Well, what do you guys think? I know you're annoyed with me for ditching you, Amazona, so let's set that aside for now. Obviously, I returned safely. Yappo, what do you think?"

"Varied responses, Chimera," Yappo said. "Yort is favorable to us. I think we can thank Quinn for that. Arnold hates us with a burning passion. Per your instruction, I didn't read his thoughts, but the emotional content was obvious. But Duma..."

"Eh?" Chimera said. "What about him? I know he's quiet, but he seemed OK to me. He's just concerned for the safety of Earth."

"Quiet isn't the word for it, Admiral," Yappo said, looking nervous. "He was *dark*! I couldn't read him at all. When I *shook hands* with him, I couldn't read him at all. That's never happened before, Admiral. Not with a Normal." Yappo paused briefly, and said, "He scares me, Chimera."

Chimera looked at Yappo with concern, but said nothing. *He seemed fine to me,* Chimera thought to herself. She shook her head to clear it, and moved on.

Meanwhile, General Duma had returned to his ship, and filed a flight plan to the Jupiter ESF station. He also triggered a special code in the filing, which would record his arrival on time, even though he had no intention of going there. He set course for a very specific location in the asteroids.

At six light years/hour, Duma's ship was the fastest private vessel in the entire Earth Space Force sphere of influence. In less than an hour, he was at the designated rendezvous point, and saw the ship.

The Grand Imperial Starship looked like a derelict. It had holes in it, and two of the engines were charred rubble. But, the chimerans had assured him that they could get 15 light years/hour out of it, for at least 10,000 light years, if he didn't mind trashing the engine in the process. They seemed almost gleeful about the prospect of pushing a Grand Imperial engine to destruction. But, that would be more than enough range.

Duma marveled at the customized docking apparatus that fit his ship perfectly. He entered the airlock, and stepped on to the bridge. He had set his ship to station keeping, and once he was on board the Grand Imperial, it moved away. The bridge was crowded. Six chimerans, five cantilians, a tigroid, a Nutrian Philosopher, and several humans. They all stood at attention, in full ESF uniform, but Duma could tell the chimerans were squirming.

"Welcome aboard the Grand Imperial Starship *Prometheus*, General Duma," the ship said as he entered.

And with that, Duma froze. He looked up at one of the ship's cameras, and asked, "Conscious?"

There was no response for several moments. Then, *Prometheus* said simply, "Yes."

Duma thought for several more moments. Then he turned to the tigroid pilot, and said, in Imperial Standard, "Trona. 11 light years per hour."

The chimerans became greatly agitated at the change of plans, and started running around the ship. Duma remained motionless, and glared at the point where they had been assembled. Finally, the chimerans all reappeared, and Duma said to the lead chimeran "Problem?" Somehow, it didn't sound like a question.

The lead chimeran initially looked annoyed, but under Duma's glare, he calmed down, and said, "No sir!"

"Good," was Duma's only reply. The pilot brought the ship about, and they set course for Trona.

CHAPTER 14

Horatio and New Valhalla

May 9th, 2809—111,000 Light Years Out

When the *Hellions* approached the *Horatio* station, Chimera was almost ecstatic. Even though it was still ESF territory, it felt almost like home, and she was very ready to be home. The *Sun Tzu* docked, at the same bay *Behemoth* had used so long ago. At least it felt like a long time, even though in reality, it had been just less than 10 months earlier.

The station was bustling with activity. The halls were crowded with humans, Ancients, and some others that Chimera couldn't identify at a glance. She wanted to bolt and run, but she continued with Amazona and Armando, as regulation required. When she got to Admiral Ursa's office, she dismissed them both, and closed the door behind her. Admiral Ursa and Admiral Quinn were already there. Chimera found a large, overstuffed chair, and literally fell into it, and let out a deep sigh. She felt safe for the first time in a long, long while.

"Tough trip, Chimera?" Ursa asked sympathetically. She opened a beer, poured out half of it, replaced the volume with water, and brought it over to Chimera, who accepted gratefully.

"Tough trip?" Chimera answered. "Yeah, you could say that," she said, while sipping her diluted beer. "You know, if you give me another one of these, I'll be spending the night on your couch here. Maybe that wouldn't be such a bad thing..."

"So," Quinn asked gently. "How did your meeting with Earth Space Force Command go on Earth?"

"Fine, I guess," Chimera replied. "Your buddy Yort seems to be a good man. Arnold hates everything Ancient, it seems."

"Grand Admiral Arnold," Quinn said with obvious disdain, "is a consummate asshole. Not that I ever said that, of course. He's smart, but he's insecure, and twitchy. He should never have been appointed to that position, but it was, as we say, 'his turn'. We haven't really had any major security threats in centuries, and in my opinion, ESF has gotten soft as a result. It's why I've always asked for assignments on the periphery."

"Which is how you met Prime Minister Jackson, yes?" Ursa asked. "As I understand, he was born on a colony world at the very edge of human space, on the boundary with Ancient space?"

"Jackson," Quinn said. "Yes, that's how we met. I like to recruit from people on the edges, whenever I can." Quinn thought for a moment, and then said, "Jackson has ripped a hole in the fabric of reality."

Ursa and Chimera were startled, and there was silence for several moments. Then Chimera said, "He's certainly ripped a hole in the fabric of *my* reality, that's for damned sure! But, there was something spooky that happened while we were at Earth, Anthony. Do you know General Duma, the ESF Security Chief?"

"Well," Quinn said. "Putting 'Duma' and 'spooky' in the same discussion is very perceptive on your part. I have to say though, that he is very effective. As Security Chief, and then his father before him in that position..."

"Wait a minute," Ursa said. "His father was Chief of Security before he was? Is that an inherited position?"

"No, of course not," Quinn said. "Although, if I remember correctly, Duma's grandfather held the position before his father did..."

Ursa had gotten up, and gone to her computer terminal. "I don't think that's right, Anthony. I was looking at some of the ESF historical records, and I could swear the last two Chiefs of Security had different names. Dammit! I'm not used to your records systems yet, and the system is giving me errors. Could you check that for me, Anthony?"

Ursa got up, and Quinn took her place at the desk. "Vorcek was his father's name, as I recall," Quinn said as he started to punch the keys. "They have a tradition of the sons taking the mother's last name in that family, which is actually damned weird in human society." Quinn sat back in obvious frustration, and said "It's not you, Ursa. I can't get the damned thing to work right either. There's a young guy who works for you, head of your engineering section, or at least he was when I left."

"Commander Williams," Ursa nodded with satisfaction. "Of course. He's something of a wizard with computers, that's for sure. Commander Williams," Ursa said to her comm unit. "This is Admiral Ursa. Please join me in my office at your earliest convenience."

Williams arrived in just a couple of minutes, and when he came in the door, Quinn got up to greet him, saying, "Hello, Chris. Are you keeping Admiral Ursa out of trouble?"

Williams silently noted the level of seniority in the room. But, his curiosity got the better of him, and he walked over to Chimera's chair, and put out his hand, saying, "It's an honor to meet you, Admiral Chimera. Commander of the first mission around the galaxy! I've heard some...interesting...things about you."

"Shit!" Chimera said, with a big smile. "I guess I'm in trouble now. A pleasure to meet you, Commander."

Williams looked to Ursa, and said, "Is there something I can do for you, ma'am?" Ursa nodded to Quinn, who said, "We're trying to get some information on General Duma, Chris. Neither Ursa nor I can make the damned thing work right. We thought, that with your magic fingers..." Quinn got up from the terminal, and Williams took his place.

"I'll do what I can, sir," Williams said. "What do you want to know?"

"Parentage, for one," Quinn said. "And whatever he's been doing recently."

"Piece of cake, Admiral," Williams said. "The genealogy databases aren't even classified." Williams started punching the keys, but his look of confidence soon faded, and he stared with increasing concentration, and started punching the keys faster. "This is weird. Duma and his paternal ancestors have been Chief of Security for ESF for at least the last 100 years, all with different names. Dammit!" Williams was frantically typing, trying to keep up with something only he could see. "These records are deleting themselves as soon as I open them! Chimer? Is that a place?"

Ursa stiffened, and said, "The Earth Space Force Chief of Security went to *Chimer*? Is that what you're telling us, Mr Williams? When?"

"I don't know! Dammit! Sorry ma'am..." Williams was getting increasingly frustrated, but when his gazed crossed Chimera, he got a spark in his eye, and said, "Admiral Chimera, can you really move at the speed of light?"

"Sure," Chimera said, and she was instantly standing behind Williams at the terminal, with an enormous grin. She had relaxed considerably after sipping on her drink for a bit.

"Ma'am, would you be willing to watch the screen over my shoulder?" Williams asked. "I can't keep up, but maybe you can..."

"Carry on, Commander," Chimera said. Williams went back to frantically punching the keys, but after just a few minutes, he finally threw up his hands, and said, “That’s it. This system is seriously infested, Admirals. I don’t know how this could have happened. Our security protocols are really quite rigorous. But now, if I ask anything about General Duma, the system locks up. I’m stuck.”

Chimera had been silent for several minutes, and went back to sit in her chair. With a concerned look on her face, she said, “Duma went to Chimer within a week of your visit to Earth last summer, Anthony. Normals going to Chimer unescorted generally turns out badly for the Normals. He seems to have spent a lot of time in the Empire recently. But why?”

“Did you talk to him while you were there, Chimera?” Quinn asked.

“I did,” Chimera answered. “But I did most of the talking. He hardly said anything.”

“He never does,” Quinn said. “What did you talk about?”

“Not much,” Chimera answered. “He was concerned about Ancient pirate attacks on Earth. Can’t say I blame him for that. I left one of the Swarm ships there to protect against that problem, until we can get some modern defensive hardware set up around Earth. I actually felt very comfortable with General Duma. He was just a little...spooky.”

“Now this is strange,” Ursa said. “I was talking to Akido about pirates just this last week. Did you know that there have been no pirate attacks anywhere in the Empire for quite a few months?”

Chimera sat up, and said, “That can’t be right. They were a pretty constant nuisance when we left Valhalla. Good job, I guess! What did you guys do to make that happen?”

“Nothing,” Ursa said solemnly. “Akido’s really pretty spooked about it, actually. He’s afraid they may have found the virus that *Behemoth* planted on the *Frazier*.”

“Virus?” Williams’ ears perked up.

"Sorry," Ursa said. "That's clearance level 25."

"Unless," Chimera replied, "I determine that it's important to the security of my mission, in which case I have full authority to grant level 25 clearances for the issue to everyone in this room. Which I hereby do."

Ursa shook her head, and said "That's a stretch, Chimera. I know you may encounter pirates on the way home, but still..."

"Oh, what the hell," Chimera replied dismissively. "In the context of all the things I'm going to get dinged for already, this is completely in the noise. When was the last time *you* disabled a spacefaring civilization?" Chimera paced for a bit, and said, "Here's the deal. When we captured the three pirate ships at Kotzebue, *Behemoth* came up with the crazy idea to implant one of them with a virus, and send it back to the pirate home base. It would infect them all, and disable their ability to fire their weapons unless they were fired upon first." Another pause, and Chimera said, "Commander, find out when the pirate attacks stopped."

Williams buried himself in the computer again, and finally said, "They started to taper off about a month after your encounter at Kotzebue, ma'am. Two months after your encounter, they stopped entirely."

"Coincidence?" Quinn asked, but he was obviously doubtful of the prospect.

"Not a chance," Chimera said, shaking her head. "Ursa, where is Alexi now?"

"He's with the *Andromeda* at New Valhalla," Ursa said, and smiled. "Every officer who could get leave or an assignment is there to check out that Swarm ship you sent back!"

"That's where we're going anyhow," Chimera replied. "Anthony, I assume you have a good second in command? Come with us! After we meet with Alexi, we can get you back to your squadron in very short order with one of the Swarm ships."

"Wouldn't miss it," Quinn nodded his head. "Captain Ortega will do just fine."

They began to make the final arrangements. From the moment the *Hellions* had arrived, *Sun Tzu* had been in constant communication with Quinn's *Defiant*, and the other ships in his *Schizo Squad*.

May 10th, 2809

Keri had insisted on meeting the *Sun Tzu* and the *Vermin Hellions* a quarter of a light year out from New Valhalla on their initial arrival. The *Vermin Hellion* squadron was, per Keri's instructions, clustered together around a single, small point in space. Keri arrived with a squadron of five heavily modified Grand Imperials, with two superguns each that looked...different, somehow. The guns were tightly focused on the incoming squadron.

Keri boarded a shuttle, which docked with the *Sun Tzu*. He had a platoon of six cantilians with him, and a dozen chimerans, and when he docked, they immediately dispersed around the ship. Amazona stood silently, with her hands in the air. "Forgive me, Admiral," Keri said. "But I require a full security sweep of this vessel before I can allow you to dock."

"Of course, my friend," Chimera said, with all four hands in the air. As soon as the preliminaries were over, Keri vanished, to do a complete, personal, light speed inspection of the ship. Quinn was a bit startled, but Chimera just grinned. "He's a security fanatic, Anthony. After what we've been through, there's no way he'd let us dock at his shipyards without a personal inspection."

"Good man," Quinn said softly.

Keri returned, and with a short command to the cantilian security detail, they stood down. Amazona relaxed. Keri said, "You look OK to me. Welcome home, Chimera!" And with that, Keri grabbed Chimera in a full, four-armed chimeran embrace. "I read all of your reports," Keri said, with obvious concern. "Are you OK, Chimera?"

"I am glad to be home beyond anything you can imagine, Keri," Chimera answered. "I don't believe you've met Admiral Quinn, have you? He was in charge of the *Horatio* station for ESF on the border, and he now commands the Modern Sector Squadron."

Keri turned, and extended his hand to Quinn. As they shook hands, Keri said, "I admire your fortitude, Admiral. As I understand it, you have diplomatic responsibilities that I would have no prayer of carrying out. Welcome to the Empire, sir!"

Quinn shook Keri's hand enthusiastically, and said, "Our responsibilities are complementary, sir. You have a technical regime to manage that I could never fathom! But, as a military man, I have to ask...what have you done to the weaponry on these Grand Imperials? Is there any chance you could actually challenge the shields of a Swarm ship?"

Keri looked at Chimera, and getting a quick nod in return, said, "Probably not. It's mostly just for show. My enhanced squadron could maybe...maybe...take out one Swarm ship. But four Swarm ships? No chance. Still, I had to do it. I have *substantially* enhanced the orbital battle stations around New Valhalla, based on what we're finding out about Swarm technology from Chimera's little gift. If I had to fight your squadron around the home world...it's not clear. I might win! Of course, I'm glad we're not going there. I'll be riding back with you to give the personal 'all clear' for docking. I assume you'll just dock the *Sun Tzu*, and leave the others detached?"

"Yes, that's the plan," Chimera answered.

When they arrived at the shipyards in orbit around New Valhalla, the long range view was stunning. Admiral Keri had established an entire complex to analyze the Swarm ship, and the ship was completely disassembled. And yet, all of the parts were still in their relative assembled position, so the outline of the ship was obvious

The docking went without incident, and as soon as Keri had dispatched crews to all the ships, the members of the *Vermin Hellions* all got shuttled down to the surface for some much needed shore leave. Chimera thought that she might go down to the surface later, but with such a large contingent of chimerans at the shipyards, she decided to stay in orbit with them for a bit.

She very much needed to feel at home.

And, as long as they were at the shipyards, no security detail was required. Chimera had felt somewhat relieved at the *Horatio*, but now, she was *really* home. Keri was leading them to the executive conference room, and the slow pace required in order to allow Quinn to keep up suited Chimera just fine.

Akido was waiting for them in the conference room, and as soon as they entered, he rushed up to embrace Chimera. "You look tired, my old friend," Akido said. "Are you OK?"

"Getting better by the hour, Alexi," Chimera said. "But I understand you have a new pirate issue?"

"Issue!" Akido said. "That's one way to put it. They're *gone*, Chimera. No attacks at all, and we didn't do it. Something damned weird is going on, and I don't like it one little bit."

"You think it's linked to Duma's activity?" Chimera asked.

"Duma's activity?" Akido asked. "What are you talking about?"

"General Boris Duma is head of security for the Earth Space Force," Quinn broke in. "Apparently, he's been doing a lot of roaming around the Empire recently."

"Yes?" Akido said "You think *he's* stopped the pirates?"

"I have no idea, Alexi," Quinn said. "But he's damned good. I wouldn't put it past him. But why keep it quiet, if he did?"

"This is very disturbing..." Akido replied, and shook his head.

"Still," Chimera said. "There *is* some good news. I brought a couple of ships with me that may be useful..." Chimera let the comment hang, with a grin.

“I can see that,” Akido said. “You left with one, you gathered a bunch, and dropped some off. Lost some. Why don’t you give us a summary of your Swarm ship inventory?”

“Uhh, OK,” Chimera said. “As you say, I left with one. At Hades, the Creator site, we gained 12 more, for a total of thirteen. I sent one to Valhalla, and one here to New Valhalla, which Keri is in the process of dissecting. Down to 11. I lost the *Beta* in our battle with The Alliance, and sent one back to Valhalla, to report what had happened there. Down to 9. I left one at our 180⁰ outpost, and lost one at some unknown planet due to a weird metal eating virus. Down to 7. I left one at Trona, down to 6. I left one at Earth. Down to 5. I left one at the *Horatio*. And, I’d like to send one back with Anthony for the Modern Sector squadron, and leave one here at New Valhalla. Down to 2.

“Hey, I’m still ahead by one!” Chimera smiled.

Everyone laughed, and Akido said, “You have succeeded beyond our wildest expectations, Chimera. Well done! We’ll discuss that little issue about you taking out the Alliance home world later. But for now...you’re home! Let’s shut down for the day. Oh, one other thing. I have a request from Councilman Bering to be detached from the expedition, and re-assigned here to work with Admiral Keri on the new warship design. You OK with that, Chimera?”

Chimera thought for a moment, and said, “Sure, that’s the right thing to do. Captain Cygnus will be bummed, but he’ll get over it. Bering has been an enormous asset, but we’ll get along without him for the home stretch.”

“Then that’s the plan,” Akido said. “Admiral Quinn, I don’t believe you’ve been on New Valhalla before. Would you like a tour? I’d be happy to escort you around.”

Quinn nodded in deference, and said, “It would be an honor, sir.”

The meeting ended with idle small talk, and they all eventually drifted off to their own pursuits.

May 11th, 2809

Quinn met Akido at the shuttle bay on the shipyards bright and early the next morning. The security guard melted away, as the two admirals boarded. They detached from the station, and Akido set the autopilot.

Quinn was a bit hesitant, as he said, "Sir, may I take the controls for a bit? I haven't had a chance to personally pilot one of these shuttles yet."

"Of course," Akido said, grinning from ear to ear, and sliding over into the co-pilot seat. "The ship is yours, Admiral! From what I can tell, the control stick is universal. The button in front of the stick is the throttle. The button on top is the comm, but you don't need to worry about that. The airspace is cleared for us."

"Very good," Quinn said. "And the autopilot disconnect?"

"The red button just to the left of the control stick," Akido pointed.

Quinn punched the disconnect, and immediately hauled the shuttle in to a series of radical maneuvers. He did outside loops, he did inside loops. He flipped the shuttle into a series of snap rolls that looked like an electric drill. "So," Quinn asked. "Where's the FTL drive?"

Akido pointed to a blue button on the right side of the control stick, and said, "That's the one. Do *not* engage the FTL drive in the atmosphere, Anthony!"

"Good to know," Quinn said, as he raked the shuttle into a vertical climb attitude, and punched the throttle. As soon as they were outside the atmosphere, he engaged the FTL.

After just a short while, they were outside the orbit of the closest planet out, and Quinn pulled them to a stop.

"Not bad," Quinn said. "A little heavy on the controls for my liking."

"This is a *shuttle*, Anthony. Not a fighter," Akido said, obviously amused. "If you get tired of command, I think you would do very well in our Imperial Fighter Squadron! I'll arrange a fighter demo for you."

"I'll look forward to it," Quinn said with a smile, and set the shuttle back to New Valhalla, and punched the autopilot engage button. "So, where are we going today?'

"First, we've been invited over to the local Guardian HQ for lunch," Akido said. "Councilman Blomstrom has been appointed Deputy Chairman for the Earth-bordering region of the empire."

"Guardians, eh?" Quinn looked a little nervous. "Witches and Warlocks, as I understand it. Of course, all the Guardians I've met personally have been great folks. It's just the concept that gives me the creeps, I guess. I also haven't figured out their role in governing the Empire, either. What do they do, exactly, other than go out and do good deeds?"

"The Guardians have been around longer than the Empire," Akido replied. "In fact, they pretty much established the Empire some 25,000 years ago. Now, their only *official* function is to appoint Emperors. After that, they don't even have the power to recall an Emperor, but they are still very influential. Most Emperors delegate a wide ranging authority for dispute resolution to the Guardians. I certainly did. And, as you say, they always manage to figure out ways to go out and do good things."

"So, what do they want to talk about today?" Quinn asked.

"Earth," Akido replied simply. "Earth history, what humans are like, how your psychology works. Anything. The Guardians see our discovery of Earth to be the most significant opportunity...and risk...to the Empire since the Swarm. In fact, we're arriving now."

The shuttle settled smoothly onto the landing pad carved into the east-facing side of the Guardian pyramid. They were met by two unarmed escorts, and taken to the dining room. Many of the Guardian Council members had made the move back to Valhalla, leaving only a dozen or so in what was now jokingly referred to as "The Periphery." Following standard Guardian custom, the lunch was buffet style.

They were met by a tall, extremely thin, stunning woman, with pale skin that had a bluish tint to it. She smiled as she said, "It's good to see you again, Alexi. It's been a long time!" She then turned to Quinn, and said, "Welcome to New Valhalla, Admiral Quinn. I am Councilman Blomstrom, recently appointed Deputy Chairman of the Guardian Council for the Periphery." Blomstrom smiled, and then let out a soft, soothing laugh, and said, "The 'Periphery' indeed! A year ago, this was the capital of the Empire!"

"Well, you still are, in both a population and a productivity sense," Akido said. "And this will be the cultural center of the Empire for a long time to come. Even with the migration stimulated by Curt's homesteading program, it will be a long time before the *real* center of the Empire returns to Valhalla."

"Indeed," Blomstrom replied. "Why don't you both get some food, and join us." Blomstrom indicated a table with about 10 people, from as many different species. Several others filled their plates along with Quinn and Akido, and when they all got settled in, Quinn said, "Alexi was telling me about the role of the Guardians in governing the Empire. It seems to me that while you folks make an enormous contribution, you don't have any supervision. That you operate mostly autonomously. Is that true?"

"Well, yes, and no," Blomstrom answered. "As Imperial citizens, we're all subject to the authority of the Emperor, just like anyone else. As a practical matter, if a substantial majority of the Council is seriously opposed to something that an Emperor wants to do, the Emperor would be well advised to reconsider. In the very early days, there were a few Emperors who 'decided' on early retirement, based on Guardian encouragement. But that hasn't happened in over 15,000 years.

"And, it depends on the specific Emperor, and the circumstances.

After the Swarm, Emperor Akido here had the fanatic support of the entire military. He was always respectful of Guardian suggestions, but there was never any doubt about who was really in charge. If the military commander who took over after the Swarm had been strong and evil, rather than strong and wise, it could have gotten very ugly."

"What about rogue Guardians?" Quinn asked. "Chimera's report on The Alliance clearly shows that your kind of power is no guarantee against being evil, or being self-interested. How do you deal with that?"

"That happens with some regularity, actually," Blomstrom said. "Usually in some region that's just getting re-integrated into the Empire. As soon as we become aware of it, we deal with it."

"When you say 'deal with it'...?" Quinn asked.

"I mean we *deal* with it," Blomstrom said firmly. "The best result is for the individual to see the error of their ways, and join the Guardians. That's actually the most common outcome, but when it isn't, we deal with it as gently as possible. But, at the end of the day, we *deal* with it, by any means necessary.

"So, your turn Admiral! Tell us about Earth history. We've all read the outlines, of course, but what do you see as some of the critical events? From your personal perspective."

"Well now, that's an interesting question," Quinn replied. "Unlike most worlds in the Empire, life evolved indigenously on Earth. Although, looking at the various life forms in the Empire, it's hard to believe there wasn't some kind of evolutionary connection.

"I haven't been able to study Empire history as much as I'd like, but the re-development paths of civilizations that survived the Swarm are pretty much the same as ours. We developed agriculture, and cities, and governments beyond the tribal level." Quinn chuckled, and said, "Not everyone believes that that last development was a positive one! Technologically, around 1000 years ago, we fully developed the use of steam power, and electricity."

"Wait a moment, Admiral," Blomstrom said. "Are you telling me that humans made the jump from simple electricity to interstellar travel in only 1000 years?"

"A lot less than that, actually," Quinn said. "From the first electric power distribution system on Earth, to our first interstellar voyage, was right around 400 years. But, of course, we had some incentive.

"The United States of America was the technology leader throughout our early years of getting off the planet. Then, in the year 2008, we had an economic collapse on Earth, and the USA starting spinning off onto a degenerate, socialist path. Spreading the wealth became more important than creating it. Innovation was stifled. The USA had been the last bastion against a worldwide socialist trend before the collapse, and once the socialism had spread worldwide, the military got soft. Governments were more likely to invite terrorists over for tea and conversation, than to do the right thing, and just wipe them out.

"This happened in conjunction with the growth of an insane notion that the Earth was somehow fragile, and that humans were destroying it. Pure madness. The productive capacity that wasn't being rotted away from the socialism, was being actively dismantled by the demented 'Greenies'. Both population and standard of living began to decline.

"Fortunately, before the technology base had completely degenerated, some people escaped, and left the planet. Life was hard for them for generations, but at least they were free, and growing. Population and living standards on Earth continued to decline. And then, things changed drastically for the worse. Here's a picture you won't see anywhere else..." Quinn pulled out his PDA, and synchronized with the building network.

A picture appeared on one of the walls, six feet wide, by 4 feet tall. Earth was clearly visible in a corner of the screen, although only part of it. And there was a spaceship in orbit. "Look familiar?" Quinn asked, with a sly smile.

Akido stared intently at the fuzzy image, and finally said, "That looks like a Grand Imperial Starship!"

"It is," Quinn said. "Although no one knew that until recently. As far as I know, I'm the only one who knew it until I told you just now.

Look at the date."

Akido had been studying English intently over the last half year, and he could easily read the imprint at the lower right corner of the image: February 3rd, 2123 AD.

"So that's how you went interstellar so fast!" Blomstrom exclaimed. "You had our technology to use!"

"No, we didn't," Quinn said grimly. "We had to blow that one up before we could get any value from it. But after that, we knew that interstellar travel was possible, and we knew that the stars were full of danger. One of Curt's distant ancestors, Major James D Jackson of the Mariposa Squadron, was instrumental in liberating Earth from the alien invaders...renegade Ancients, we now know...and start the process of rebuilding our devastated world. But, the details of that are a story for another time."

"Wait a minute," Akido said. "Where did you get that picture? Are you saying that humans destroyed a Grand Imperial Starship *before* you had interstellar travel?"

"Yes," Quinn replied. "At the end of the day, you *really* don't want to mess with us. You do what you have to do when your home world is occupied by cruel, hostile aliens. And we did. The picture is from Curt's family archives. He rarely shows it to anyone, but he had shown it to me. When I saw the four Grand Imperials clustered around the *Andromeda* last year, I made the connection.

"After the invading aliens were destroyed, the Great Reckoning began on Earth. All vestiges of socialism were wiped out, and a virulent form of libertarianism took hold. With the off-planet technology of the human rebels intact, and re-introduced on Earth, technological growth was explosive. With the elimination of socialism, economic growth was explosive. And, on the issue of interstellar travel, humans were *completely* obsessed. Our first interstellar voyage was just over 50 years later, in the year 2175.

"Sadly, that crew didn't make it back. Most of the early interstellar explorers died, but we learned, and fixed things, and eventually got it to work. But, to this day, the Earth Space Force and the Human Interplanetary Trade Services organization have a hugely libertarian orientation. I saw the culture clash in sharp relief during my first mission commanding the Modern Sector Squadron, at Sporta. ESF rules of engagement forbade me from intervening. AIS rules of engagement required it. That's how my squadron came to be named the *Schizo Squad*. Our mission is irretrievably contradictory.

"So here we are today, a little over 600 years later, humans and Ancients, enjoying lunch, and discussing history and politics. With me in command of a squadron of ships like the one that devastated my world, so long ago."

Akido stared at Quinn, and then shook his head, and said, "I fear that we have discovered a monster, which will devour us all..."

"Not if you devour us first," Quinn said with a quick smile. "Earth needs to join the Empire. You have things that we lack, and we have things that you lack. It's a natural fit. The Swarm is still out there. We should combine forces."

Blomstrom visibly perked up, and asked, "You think so? It was our understanding that ESF was adamantly opposed to even *considering* joining the Empire."

"ESF in the form of Grand Admiral Arnold is indeed adamantly opposed to it," Quinn said. "Earth sentiment is mixed. There is a deep, abiding fear of being dominated by aliens in human culture. I haven't told anyone else what I figured out about our history with you, the story I just told you. I don't think it would be helpful just now for humans to know that Ancients were responsible for the biggest humiliation and extermination in human history. Many people will not make the fine distinction between the Empire, and renegade Ancients."

"Do you have a plan, Anthony?" Akido asked. "For overcoming the ESF resistance to joining the Empire?"

"Nothing I could dignify with the word 'plan', I'm afraid," Quinn replied. "But I know Yort agrees with me. And he's a much better politico than I am. We'll keep our eyes open for possibilities.

"I realized recently, Alexi, that we have something in common. You and I both gave Jackson a chance, when it wasn't obvious that it was a good idea to do so. I think we both did well. Having a human as Prime Minister of the Empire will go a long way toward making an eventual merger possible."

"In that regard," Akido said slowly, "I also have information it would probably be best to keep quiet for a bit..."

"Oh?" Quinn said. "What's that?"

Akido hesitated only briefly, and said, "Curt is a human/Ancient hybrid. There have been only 13 Modern/Ancient hybrids ever recorded, and most of them have been human/cantilian hybrids. That's mostly what Curt is."

Quinn thought for a moment, and then broke into robust laughter, and pounded the table with his fist. "That completely fits! Curt's mother is a physically large, strong woman. His father was a huge, mysterious figure. Cantilian, I'm sure now. And, even though he hides it, Curt has physical abilities well beyond any normal human." Quinn thought for a moment, and said, "You're right. It's best if this doesn't come out for a bit."

"Well then," Akido said, as he stood up. "Let's get you to your new flagship, and back to your squadron."

"No," Quinn said simply. "I'll welcome the Swarm ship as an *addition* to my squadron. But *Defiant* will remain my flagship."

"As you wish!" Akido said as they left, and headed back to the shuttle.

CHAPTER 15

Kotzebue

May 16th, 2809 —- 130,000 light years out

The *Hellions* rendezvoused with the Grand Imperial Starship *Tolovana* in orbit around Kotzebue. Even at a casual glance, the change since Chimera's last visit was striking.

There were hundreds of ships in orbit, from small indigenous craft, to a dizzying array of modern, Imperial vessels. The one modest station that had been in orbit before had been supplemented by a sprawling array, and it was still under construction. It looked like an explosion in slow motion.

The explosion was mirrored on the edges of the capital city of Nushagak. There was construction around all of the edges, even out into the ocean. Sun Tzu got the message that King Wasilla was looking forward to seeing them, and Chimera, Amazona, and Yappo boarded the shuttle and set course for the palace.

They landed on the same pad they had used on their first visit, which seemed like a lifetime ago. There had been some apprehension the first time, but now, they were met by smiling, unarmed escorts, and ushered into the King's sitting area.

But even to the non-medical members of the team, it was clear that the King's physical condition had deteriorated badly. Still, he stood up to greet them, and haltingly started to walk over to them. Chimera was instantly at his side, and helped him over to the others.

"So good to see friends again," Wasilla said. "Our world has completely changed since you were last here. Some for the good, some for the bad. But mostly for the good. I have read the public commentary about your adventure! I am glad to see you all here, and well."

"Forgive me, Your Highness, but *you* are *not* well," Chimera said with obvious concern. "Please let me take you up to one of our ships, and we'll get you regenerated right away."

"No," Wasilla said. "But I need to talk to you, Admiral. Alone." With a wave of his hand, Wasilla's aides were gone. Amazona was hesitant, but the look she got from Chimera was unmistakable. "We'll be outside if you need us, Admiral," Amazona said.

"Your Highness," Chimera said. "Why won't you let me take you up to the ship to take care of you? I hope you'll forgive me, but I did a complete assessment of your condition. You are very seriously ill, but it's nothing we can't fix. Let me help."

"No," Wasilla said firmly. "Your eternal life technology is completely contrary to our religion. I won't do it."

Chimera thought for a moment, and said, "Very well. But surely, simple treatment for illness is acceptable, yes? With no genetic alteration of any kind, I can simply cure what's currently wrong with you. Surely, you can't object to *that*. Your society has doctors who cure illness, do you not? Meaning no disrespect, but as long as I'm here, I'm the best doctor on the planet. Why should the King not get the best treatment available?"

Wasilla looked at him with somewhat glassy eyes, and said, "Perhaps. Perhaps. But I need your advice first, Admiral. My family has ruled this planet for over 1000 years. There have been mistakes, of course, but we have done well. And for the most part, the people believe we have done well. I am very well liked.

"But, I am dying. And my son, God bless him, is a good man. He is honest, his is kind, but...he's not the sharpest tool in the shed, if you get my meaning. He wants to do well, but it was questionable whether or not he could handle it before, and now, with our new position in the Galactic order...he's just not up to it, Admiral. I don't want to disrespect him, but we need to find a new way to govern this world. We've been the dominant power in this region for a long time, and that position is expanding. I want to pass on my power responsibly.

"What can I do, Admiral?"

Chimera was overwhelmed with emotion. She didn't know what to say. Finally, she asked, "Have you considered moving to a democratic form of government, Your Highness?"

"I have, of course," Wasilla said. "But, just between us, the majority of our citizens are morons. They have no clue about the right path to guide a complex society. How can I, in good conscience, turn the management of our culture over to a mostly clueless mob?"

Chimera thought for several moments, and said, "Your Highness, my officer, Admiral Amazona, is one of the most thoughtful diplomats I've ever worked with. She may be able to help you far more than I could. And she is an absolute master of discretion (Chimera thought back on the incident with Bering and Cygnus). May I invite her to join our discussion?"

Wasilla sighed, and said, "Very well. I don't have much time left. Bring her in."

Chimera made a brief command on the comm unit, and Amazona joined them. Chimera explained the situation. Amazona thought for quite some time, and said, "Your Highness, I assume there are a great many wise, intelligent people in your culture. You could not have been so successful otherwise."

"Yes, of course," Wasilla said. "We have many good people."

"In other societies," Amazona said. "I've seen a successful model of a limited democracy. It spreads the decision making far beyond a monarch, but restricts the voting franchise to competent, educated people, who have a vested interest in the success of the society. Have you considered that?"

"I had not," Wasilla said, but his eyes became a tad bit brighter. "How would that work? How would we decide who was qualified to hold the voting franchise?"

"If I may suggest, Your Highness, our Captain Sun Tzu has access to histories from a wide ranging set of cultures, including some alien beyond belief," Amazona responded. "May I invite him to join our conversation?"

"A *machine*?" Wasilla said, with obvious distaste.

"He is far wiser than most organic beings I have ever met, Your Highness," Chimera said. "He is 50,000 years old, and has seen many, many things. He's subtle, and discreet. I have put him in charge of my mission...in command...on more than one occasion."

Wasilla's eyes widened, and then he looked down, and fidgeted, and finally said, "Very well. I have to have an answer. I *will not* abandon my people to chaos. Bring him in."

Chimera had Sun Tzu join the conversation, and they talked for hours, discussing many options. Finally, Tzu made a specific recommendation, and after some brief thought, Wasilla said, "I like it. It gives my son, and his heirs, ceremonial responsibility, but delegates actual control to people who know what they're doing. I like it. So, how do we make this happen?"

"Meaning no challenge at all to your beliefs, Your Highness," Chimera said. "But your people will be much, much better served if you let me cure you of your current infirmity, so that you can oversee the transition for a few years. I can do this with no alteration of any kind to your genetic make-up, sir."

Wasilla glared at her, but then got thoughtful, and said, "Oh, very well. If I can get the change to the new order done quickly, maybe I can even have a few years of peaceful retirement! What do you propose for the announcement?"

"That's actually pretty easy, Your Highness," Amazona said. "Since you're currently an absolute monarch, you can simply say this is what's going to happen. I'd recommend a huge public ceremony, where you make the announcement. At the ceremony, we'll have one of the Swarm ships hovering overhead. That will unambiguously give the imprimatur of Imperial approval to your decision. There will be details to work out, and conflicts, but no one will seriously question that the change is going to happen, and that the Empire is behind your decision."

Wasilla relaxed, and smiled, and said, "We will make it so."

With that, Chimera said, "Now that we have that worked out, will you accompany me to a proper medical facility, where I can prepare you to do this for your people?"

Wasilla wagged his finger at Chimera, and said, "You are very persuasive, Admiral. You serve your Empress well. I am ready."

Chimera helped the King into the shuttle, and his repairs went without a hitch. Technically, Chimera lived up to her promise to not alter his genetics, but she fixed every blessed thing wrong with him that she could find. He was going to be around far longer than he might have expected.

Two days later, the crowd was a little intimidated by the hovering Swarm ship at first. But when the King made the announcement of the change, it was met with thundering applause, and cheers of "Long live Wasilla! Long live Wasilla!"

CHAPTER 16

Bittersweet Homecoming

May 19th, 2809 —- 135,000 Light Years Out

Chimera was sitting in the Captain's chair, content and happy. The transition on Kotzebue had gone very well, the ships were fine, and the crews were relaxed. It was the home stretch.

Tzu came on the comm, and said, "Chimera, there's a transmission coming in from the *Horatio*. Level 25, your eyes only, ma'am."

"Put it in my office," Chimera said, and moved there immediately. When she opened the message, Commander Williams from the *Horatio* was on the screen.

"Commander Chris Williams from the *Horatio* here, ma'am. Admiral Ursa said I should send this to you. I want to say again, ma'am, that it was an honor to meet you in person!

"After our struggle with the information request you had, I linked together a range of independent data sources from numerous ESF facilities, and with some data cleansing...well, you don't need the technical details. I've gotten additional information on General

Duma, ma'am. It turns out his family has run ESF security for over *250 years*! I think that's really creepy. They've hidden it, until now, and for reasons I can't comprehend, no one has caught on.

"But it's weirder even than that. About 50 years after the first 'Duma' took the reigns, all serious threats against the expansion of human culture vanished. Before that, people resisted the expansion of our hegemony, as you would expect. We had many armed conflicts, and Earth itself was attacked on more than one occasion. But after the Dumas took over security, that just stopped. There was no serious challenge after that. From what I've been able to glean from my limited knowledge of Empire history, that kind of un-resisted expansion is pretty much unheard of.

"On a personal side, there has never, not once, been an instance of corruption or disloyalty on the part of any Duma. They just get the job done. But they've always been spooky. They almost never speak. That's well documented in the record. And yet, they inspire fanatic loyalty and service from those who work for them.

"And, for the last 10 months, Duma has spent more time in the Empire than he's spent in human space. He's been to Chimer many times. He's been to New Valhalla half a dozen times. He's even been to Valhalla! None of this is in the open, ma'am. I hope you'll stand up for me for the numerous violations of regulations I committed to pull this information together.

"This is damned weird, Admiral. This is a huge, important chunk of human history which, for some incomprehensible reason, no one has put together before. I don't know what this means, ma'am. Hopefully you can figure it out. Williams out."

The recording ended, and Chimera thought silently for quite some time. Then, she recorded a response to Williams. "Well done, Commander. I don't know what it means either, but you've done good work. If anyone gives you any static, you tell them they'll be personally answerable to me. Not just professionally. *Personally*. Given my reputation, that should get their attention.

"Chimera out."

Chimera sat back in her chair, and just stared at the ceiling. But almost immediately, Tzu came on the comm, and said, "This is weird, Admiral, but you have another Level 25, your eyes only, communication coming in from Valhalla. I'll pipe it in there."

Moose's image came on the screen, and Chimera jerked forward in her seat. He was disheveled! He looked dirty. Worst of all, he looked *scared*! "Chimera, we've had a big problem here. You need to get here with all deliberate speed. Actually, screw that, get here absolutely as fast as you can. I don't want to put this on the air, even with full encryption. Just get here. Moose out."

Chimera bolted out the door, and sounded battle stations. "Captain Cygnus," she said. "Without Bering, what's the maximum speed you can get out of this tub?"

Startled, Cygnus said, "I can't guide the other ship by myself, without Bering, ma'am. If we go forward alone, I can goose us up to 250 light years/hr, easy. Maybe 275."

"Very well," Chimera replied "Cut 'em loose. Get us to Valhalla at the maximum safe speed you can maintain, Captain. Do it now."

"On it!" Cygnus said. Despite the artificial gravity, they could briefly feel the rapid acceleration.

May 21st, 2809

Approaching Valhalla, Tzu detected several hundred Grand Imperials in the local area. *What the hell?* he thought. The Swarm ships Chimera had sent back were stationary over the Capitol. The battle station Chimera had seen on departure, was in ruins.

Chimera decided to leave her full crew on alert in orbit, and boarded a shuttle alone. She went to the main docking pad for the AIS base, as the controller had suggested.

When she opened the door, there was a small contingent of press waiting for her. Moose was on the landing, and said, "Smile for the cameras, Admiral. Let's get inside as soon as we can."

Chimera was startled, and said, "No offense intended, Moose, but where's Misha? Where's Curt?"

"Misha and Curt are unavailable, ma'am," Moose answered. "Just smile and wave, and let's move on."

Suddenly, a reporter pushed to the front of the crowd, and said, "Admiral Chimera, now that you're the most senior Imperial military official on the Capital, what are you going to do about this vicious attack?"

"The Admiral will have a full statement for you soon," Moose answered. And then at light speed, Moose said to Chimera, "Councilman Cooper will give you a full briefing inside, ma'am."

"Cooper?" Chimera replied. "Where the hell is Merlin?"

"Merlin is not available, ma'am," Moose said urgently. "Just smile and wave, and let's get inside. You'll be heading back out as soon as your briefing is done." A quick pause, and Moose continued. "We've been hit bad, Chimera."

They both shifted back to normal time mode, and smiled and waved to the small crowd, as they walked in to the Ancient Imperial Service HQ.

CPSIA information can be obtained
at www.ICGtesting.com
Printed in the USA
BVOW09s0621061117
499654BV00002B/192/P